PERFECT STORM 2

BOBBY AKART

THANK YOU

Welcome to PERFECT STORM 2, the second installment in the
Perfect Storm survival thriller series by Author Bobby Akart.
Join Bobby Akart's mailing list to learn about upcoming releases,
deals, contests, and appearances. Follow this link to:
BobbyAkart.com

PRAISE FOR BOBBY AKART AND PERFECT STORM

"Author Bobby Akart has done it again. I have read every book and series that he has written. It never ceases to amaze me how he comes up with new and creative ways to introduce characters and concepts that are fresh and engaging."
"How long could you survive a collapse of society? The families in this new series are put to the test in this thrilling, nail biter."

"You will fall in love with the characters immediately!"

"Bobby Akart continues to deliver the top thrillers of the year. Year after year after year!"

"Well written with characters that are so real, you are right there with them urging them on."

"Once again this author has crafted a believable end of days scenario with compelling characters that I can't seem to put down."

"Author Bobby Akart has put together another scorcher of a story in Perfect Storm."

PERFECT STORM 2

by
Bobby Akart

OTHER WORKS BY AMAZON CHARTS TOP 25 AUTHOR BOBBY AKART

The Perfect Storm Series
Perfect Storm 1
Perfect Storm 2
Perfect Storm 3
Perfect Storm 4
Perfect Storm 5

Black Gold (a standalone terrorism thriller)

Nuclear Winter
First Strike
Armageddon
Whiteout
Devil Storm
Desolation

New Madrid (a standalone, disaster thriller)

Odessa (a Gunner Fox trilogy)

Odessa Reborn

Odessa Rising

Odessa Strikes

The Virus Hunters

Virus Hunters I

Virus Hunters II

Virus Hunters III

The Geostorm Series

The Shift

The Pulse

The Collapse

The Flood

The Tempest

The Pioneers

The Asteroid Series (A Gunner Fox trilogy)

Discovery

Diversion

Destruction

The Doomsday Series

Apocalypse

Haven

Anarchy

Minutemen

Civil War

The Yellowstone Series

Hellfire

Inferno

Fallout
Survival

The Lone Star Series
Axis of Evil
Beyond Borders
Lines in the Sand
Texas Strong
Fifth Column
Suicide Six

The Pandemic Series
Beginnings
The Innocents
Level 6
Quietus

The Blackout Series
36 Hours
Zero Hour
Turning Point
Shiloh Ranch
Hornet's Nest
Devil's Homecoming

The Boston Brahmin Series
The Loyal Nine
Cyber Attack
Martial Law
False Flag
The Mechanics
Choose Freedom
Patriot's Farewell (standalone novel)

Black Friday (standalone novel)
Seeds of Liberty (Companion Guide)

The Prepping for Tomorrow Series
Cyber Warfare
EMP: Electromagnetic Pulse
Economic Collapse

Copyright Information

ACKNOWLEDGMENTS

Creating a novel that is both informative and entertaining requires a tremendous team effort. Writing is the easy part.

For their efforts in making the Perfect Storm series a reality, I would like to thank Hristo Argirov Kovatliev for his incredible artistic talents in creating my cover art. He and Dani collaborate (and conspire) to create the most incredible cover art in the publishing business. A huge hug of appreciation goes out to Pauline Nolet, the *Professor*, for her editorial prowess and patience in correcting this writer's brain farts that happen more frequently with age. Thank you, Drew Avera, a United States Navy veteran, who has brought his talented formatting skills from a writer's perspective to create multiple formats for reading my novels. A round of applause for Kevin Pierce, the beloved voice of the apocalypse, who brought my words to life in audio format.

Now, for the serious stuff. While the Perfect Storm series is based on scientifically plausible events, certain parts of the story have been fictionalized for dramatic purposes, and they're not intended to reflect on any actual person or entity.

Accurately portraying the aftermath of a devastating perfect solar storm required countless hours of never-ending research and interviews with some of the brightest minds in the world of planetary science.

Once again, as I immersed myself in the science and history, source material and research flooded my inbox from around the globe. Without the assistance of many individuals and organizations, this story could not be told. Please allow me a moment to acknowledge a few of those institutions that without their tireless efforts and patience, the Perfect Storm series could not have been written.

Many thanks to the preeminent researchers and engineers who provided me assistance, tutelage, and scientific background at the following:

The Space Weather Prediction Center in Boulder, Colorado
The Aerospace Corporation in El Segundo, California
The Haleakala Observatory, home to the Daniel K. Inouye Solar Telescope, in Maui
NASA's Jet Propulsion Laboratory in Pasadena, California
The Geophysical Institute at the University of Alaska, Fairbanks
Of course, a special thank you to the Team, my loyal friends who've always supported my work and provided me valuable insight from a reader's perspective—Denise Keef, Joe Carey, Shirley Nicholson, Bennita Barnett, and Colt Payne.

Thanks, y'all, and Choose Freedom!

ABOUT THE AUTHOR, BOBBY AKART

Author Bobby Akart delivers up-all-night thrillers to readers in 245 countries and territories worldwide. He has been ranked by Amazon as #25 on the Amazon Charts list of most popular, bestselling authors. He has achieved recognition as the #1 bestselling Horror Author, #1 bestselling Science Fiction Author, #5 bestselling Action & Adventure Author, #7 bestselling Historical Fiction Author and #10 on Amazon's bestselling Thriller Author list.

His novel *Yellowstone: Hellfire* reached the Top 25 on the Amazon bestsellers list and earned him multiple Kindle All-Star awards for most pages read in a month and most pages read as an author. The Yellowstone series vaulted him to the #25 bestselling author on Amazon Charts, and the #1 bestselling science fiction author.

Since its release in November 2020, his standalone novel *New Madrid Earthquake* has been ranked #1 on Amazon Charts in multiple countries as a natural disaster thriller.

Mr. Akart is a graduate of the University of Tennessee after pursuing a dual major in economics and political science. He went on to obtain his master's degree in business administration and his doctorate degree in law at Tennessee.

With over a million copies of his novels in print, Bobby Akart has provided his readers a diverse range of topics that are both informative and entertaining. His attention to detail and impeccable research has allowed him to capture the imagination of his readers through his fictional works and bring them valuable knowledge through his nonfiction books.

SIGN UP for Bobby Akart's mailing list to learn of special offers, view bonus content, and be the first to receive news about new releases.

Visit www.BobbyAkart.com for details.

DEDICATIONS

With the love and support of my wife, Dani, together with the unconditional love of Bullie and Boom, the princesses of the palace, I'm able to tell you these stories. It would be impossible for me to write without them in my heart.

This story was written during a difficult time in our lives. For my longtime readers, you know that our English bulldogs, Bullie and Boom, affectionately known in my stories as the princesses of the palace, are the center of our universe. At Christmas in 2021, Boom Chukka suffered a significant tear in her gastrointestinal tract caused by chewing a pressed rawhide bone.

Because of Dani's watchful eye, she noticed Boom-Boom's gums turn more and more pale. I also noticed that her poop became black and tarry. Both of these were symptoms of internal bleeding. I relay this to you because, one day, you might experience this with your beloved pups.

Internal bleeding is nothing to be trifled with. Without urgent care, your fur babies can die within days, if not sooner.

We rushed Boom Chukka to our vets in Georgia. The entire team, led by Drs. Rambo and McNair, came to her rescue. By the early evening of New Year's Eve, her packed cell volume (PCV) and hematocrit (HCT) fell below twenty percent, where thirty-five percent is normal. Thanks to a dog-to-dog blood transfusion from Dr. McNair's dog, Liza, Boom-Boom was able to survive long enough to transport her to the University of Georgia Veterinary Hospital in Athens.

With the help of God watching over our entire family during this difficult time, Boom Chukka fought to live another day. As of this writing, Bullie and Boom are the ripe age of twelve years and eight months. However, they firmly believe they're one-year-old pups.

I urge you to love those who are closest to you, including your four-legged, bestest pals.

AUTHOR'S NOTE

March 2022

For years, I've tackled the disaster thriller genre. As an author, the hardest part might be choosing how to destroy the Earth, therefore imperiling all of mankind. Look at all the options I've written about asteroids, nuclear electromagnetic pulse attacks, pandemics, earthquakes, volcanoes, bioterrorism, cyber warfare, pole shifts, etc.

However, in a class by itself is severe space weather. If its ominous name didn't clue you in, severe space weather can cause some serious complications to life on our planet. Much like Earth-based weather, it's uncontrollable. It also has the potential for massive destruction and disruption of modern technology. Imagine the collapse of power grids, radio blackouts, satellite interference or even destruction, and airline operations ceasing, all in less than a minute. Without electricity, how would you communicate with your family, call 9-1-1, get clean water, or keep food from spoiling? With a radio blackout, how would airplanes land safely? Massive solar flares have the potential to change life as we know it.

Now, if I haven't gotten your attention, let's take a look at the science and a little history, shall we?

Severe space weather is the result of large-scale eruptions of plasma and magnetic fields from the Sun's corona. Known as coronal mass ejections (CMEs), these eruptions can create magnetic storms in the magnetosphere and Earth's upper atmosphere, which can damage power lines, cause blackouts, and even dislocate Earth's radiation belts, damaging satellites.

Thankfully, such magnetic storms are classified as low frequency, but high impact. To be an impactful magnetic storm, CMEs from the solar disk must be fast and massive, launched from near the center of the Sun, and directed toward Earth's magnetic field. CMEs also need to have a strong magnetic field with the opposite orientation of Earth's own magnetic field. Although classified as low frequency, when these conditions are met, CMEs are high-consequence occurrences. Here are some examples.

In recent history, the collapse of the Hydro-Quebec grid occurred in March 1989, leaving the province of Quebec without electricity for nine hours. The outage closed schools, businesses, public transportation and grounded flights at Dorval Airport. Citizens found themselves stuck in traffic on darkened roads without street signals, and many workers were stranded in office buildings, elevators and stairwells. The storm was felt in other parts of North America as well, with approximately two hundred solar-storm-related events reported, including the failure of a transformer at a New Jersey nuclear power plant.

Amazingly, the 1989 magnetic storm that struck Quebec pales in comparison to other magnetic storms in our history.

The strongest storm in recorded history to directly impact our planet came in September of 1859. The CME behind the Carrington Event, as it became known, was first seen by Richard Carrington, a British amateur astronomer. Nearly eighteen hours after it was observed, the powerful CME impacted the Earth's magnetosphere, triggering a severe geomagnetic storm that disrupted telegraph networks around the world. The rare, fast-moving (CMEs normally impact Earth around thirty-six hours after being observed) CME hit the planet, and highly charged particles enveloped the Northern Hemisphere. Telegraph operators were electrocuted, and fires were ignited as flames traveled along the telegraph lines.

The 1921 Geomagnetic Storm, also known as the New York Railway Storm, included geomagnetically induced currents that would have been ten times more intense than those responsible for the 1989 Quebec solar storm. Taking place over several days in May 1921, the New York Railway Storm is widely considered the largest recorded in the twentieth century. It is this perfect solar storm event that forms the scientific basis for my book series.

WHAT IF FICTION BECOMES REALITY?

A word of caution when thinking about history and the timeline of events. It's easy to dismiss any discussion of past catastrophes when one considers events like supervolcano eruptions taking place every seven hundred thousand years, as in the case of Yellowstone. Massive solar storms occur far more frequently. Let's look at a recent event from just ten years ago.

On July 23, 2012, two CMEs erupted from an active patch of sunspots on the far side of the Sun, which is monitored by the Parker Solar Probe that circles the sun ahead of Earth in the same orbit. Emerging about fifteen minutes apart, the CMEs quickly merged into one massive shock wave of charged particles that washed over the probe's sensors.

Behind the shock wave, this energy raced along at about 2,250 kilometers per second—five times their normal speed at Earth's distance from the Sun—and the magnetic field strength there was more than ten times that normally seen at Earth's orbit.

If pointed in our direction, such a combination would have produced the strongest geomagnetic storm to have struck Earth in history. It could have knocked out satellites and earthbound power grids, researchers say. Fortunately, the event, a prime example of a *Perfect Storm*, was directed into a region of space where the solar wind and the magnetic field had been weakened by a solar flare four days earlier.

While the flare occurred in Earth's orbital plane, the solar matter missed us by the equivalent of nine days. Similar to the Carrington Event, the particles traveled from the Sun to the Earth in just seventeen hours. Had Earth been in the way at the time, the global damage toll would have crested the $10 trillion mark: the first fourteen-figure natural disaster in history. It was only luck that caused this perfect storm to miss us.

I add this example as a word of caution to us all. These severe solar storms happen with regular frequency. We dodged a powerful catastrophic solar flare in 2012. Next time, we might not be so lucky.

REAL-WORLD NEWS EXCERPTS

SOLAR STORM COULD SUPERCHARGE NORTHERN LIGHTS
AS FAR SOUTH AS NEW YORK

~ Space.com, April 14, 2022

It came from a dead sunspot.

After a dead sunspot hurled a ball of plasma, or superheated gas, toward Earth earlier this week, medium-sized auroras may stretch farther south than usual as Earth's atmosphere absorbs the material.

The genesis of the event was a "dead" sunspot called AR2987. More scientifically speaking, the sunspot had entered a quiescent period, and then unexpectedly erupted.

"Occasionally," according to NOAA, "sunspots can 'restart,' with more magnetism appearing later at the same region, as if a weakness was made in the convection zone, or as if there is an unstable region under the surface that is particularly good at generating magnetic fields beneath. These particular solar events are disconcerting as they are wholly unpredictable and are emitted without warning."

Auroras are associated with coronal mass ejections, which are sets of charged particles that jolt from sunspots, often after solar flares. If a CME is aimed toward Earth, often the particles can generate auroras in upper latitudes while causing disruptions to power grids.

MASSIVE GEOMAGNETIC STORM: CORONAL MASS EJECTION FROM THE SUN COULD KNOCK OUT THE POWER GRID AND INTERNET

~ *SciTechDaily, April 2022*

Just a matter of time ...

Telegraph networks all throughout the globe failed catastrophically on September 1 and 2, 1859. The telegraph operators reported feeling electrical shocks, telegraph paper catching fire, and being able to operate equipment without batteries. The aurora borealis, sometimes known as the northern lights, could be seen as far south as Colombia in the evenings. This phenomenon is typically only seen at higher latitudes, such as in northern Canada, Scandinavia, and Siberia.

The planet was hit by a tremendous geomagnetic storm on that day, which is now known as the Carrington Event. When a massive bubble of superheated gas called plasma is blasted from the sun's surface and collides with the Earth, it causes these storms. This bubble is called a coronal mass ejection.

The Carrington Event of 1859 is the largest recorded account of a geomagnetic storm, but it is not an isolated event.

Geomagnetic storms have been recorded since the early 19th century, and scientific data from Antarctic ice core samples has shown evidence of an even more massive geomagnetic storm that occurred around A.D. 774, now known as the *Miyake Event*. That solar flare produced the largest and fastest rise in carbon-14 ever recorded.

It gets even scarier when you compare the Carrington Event with the Miyake Event. Scientist were able to estimate the strength of the Carrington Event based on the fluctuations of Earth's magnetic field as recorded by observatories at the time. There was no way to measure the magnetic fluctuation of the Miyake event. Instead, scientists measured the increase in carbon-14 in tree rings from that time period. The Miyake Event produced a 12% increase in carbon-14. By comparison, the Carrington Event produced less than 1% increase in Carbon-14, so the Miyake Event likely dwarfed the G5 Carrington Event.

Today, a geomagnetic storm of the same intensity as the Carrington Event would affect far more than telegraph wires and could be catastrophic. With the ever-growing dependency on electricity and emerging technology, any disruption could lead to trillions of dollars of monetary loss and risk to life dependent on the systems. The storm would affect a majority of the electrical systems that people use every day.

It is only a matter of time before the Earth is hit by another geomagnetic storm. A Carrington Event-size storm would be extremely damaging to the electrical and communication systems worldwide with outages lasting into the weeks. If the storm is the size of the Miyake Event, the results would be catastrophic for the world with potential outages lasting years if not longer. Even with space weather warnings from NOAA's Space Weather Prediction Center, the world would have only a few minutes to a few hours' notice.

SUNSPOT SENDS OFF DOUBLE FLARE AS SOLAR ACTIVITY RAMPS UP

~ *Live Science, April 28, 2022*

So far, the restless sunspot is only disrupting radio communications.

The recently discovered sunspot designated AR2993 erupted with two solar flares in quick succession, according to the Space Weather Prediction Center. Solar flares are eruptions of electromagnetic radiation that can disrupt some radio frequencies and result in significant complications for power suppliers.

Sunspot AR2993 is hundreds of millions of square miles in area. Earth would sit in the active region as comfortably as an egg in a nest. Sunspots are regions of the sun where the magnetic field is temporarily much stronger than the surrounding areas. These magnetic forces block the flow of hot gas from the sun's interior, making sunspots much cooler than their surroundings. Solar flares happen when the magnetic field lines near sunspots reorganize explosively. Sometimes, these eruptions of radiation also trigger coronal mass ejections (CMEs), which are explosions of the sun's plasma.

It's been a busy few weeks for the sun, with multiple active sunspots sending off flares. Solar activity occurs in regular 11-year cycles, which have been recorded since 1775. The sun is currently in Solar Cycle 25 and is in a period of ramping up its activity. Solar Cycle 25 is expected to peak in late 2024 or early 2025, meaning that the frequency of sunspots, solar flares and CMEs are expected to increase.

EPIGRAPH

Appear weak when you are strong, and strong when you are weak.
~ Sun Tzu, Chinese philosopher, author of the Art of War

---

*It is not the strongest of the species that survive, nor the most
intelligent, but the one most responsive to change.*
~ Charles Darwin, English, naturalist and biologist

A journey of a thousand miles begins with one step.
~ Laozi, Chinese philosopher

Never give in, never give in, never, never, never, never—in nothing.
~ Winston Churchill, British statesman

Your compassion is a weakness your enemies will not share.
~ Henri Ducard, Bruce Wayne's tutor, *Batman Begins*

PROLOGUE

Two Days Prior
Friday, the Day the Sun Brought Darkness
The Lincoln Tunnel
New York City, New York, USA

The Lincoln Tunnel was an accomplished creator of calamities. Every day there's something. Vehicles break down and crash into one another. Homeless pedestrians wander along the catwalks and find their way onto the road, which never ends well. Drivers flick still burning cigarette butts out of their cars, sometimes igniting the thousands of pieces of debris that fly through the tunnel like confetti on New Year's Eve.

Occasionally, a driver will catch a glimpse of something strange in the inbound lanes of the tunnel. It causes them to blink and take a second glance. For those visiting the city, wispy vapors rising from a steam pipe, canisters of nitrogen on the sidewalks, or, within the Lincoln Tunnel, a grinning face might cause consternation.

For regular commuters, however, the sight of the smiling face of Juanita Suarez was not all that unusual. The uniformed Port

Authority worker who spends her nights inside a tiny, lighted security booth within the depths of the Lincoln Tunnel has seen it all during her thirteen years on the job. Until that fateful night when the power grid collapsed.

Her booth, located at the maximum depth of ninety-seven feet beneath the Hudson River, was strategically located so she could react quickly to the dopes who ran out of gas or to the poor driver who succumbed to a panic attack as claustrophobia overcame them.

She'd begun her shift that Friday night at eight o'clock, just like always. She'd grown accustomed to working in cramped spaces since she began her career as a toll booth operator for the New York City Transit Authority. The day before, she'd worked with emergency personnel to extract a driver from a Kia who'd rear-ended a jacked-up pickup truck. The man survived the wreck, with the bulk of his injuries coming from the airbag that blew up in his face. The Kia, however, had been squished like a bug.

Suarez thumbed through her copy of the *New York Post*, riveted by the story of a woman who'd been murdered and carried off from her home in a suitcase. The city had grown increasingly dangerous over the last several years. That said, Suarez considered some homicides to be more interesting than others. This one had all the markings of a crime novel, her favorites.

Bored and breathing in gas fumes from the passing vehicles, she was mindlessly munching on a bag of Cheetos, reading all about it, as they say, when the lights in her booth flickered and flamed out. Suarez was puzzled at first. A system of backup generators powered the lighting within the tunnel, instantly triggering emergency lighting along the catwalk and above the roadway.

This was different. Not only was the power out, but the headlights on the vehicles passing by had been extinguished as well. Not all at once, but sporadically over a matter of a minute. Within her line of sight, one or two vehicles seemed to be running. The others, however, were dead.

Suarez fumbled through her bag in search of her cell phone.

Years ago, ATT had wired the tunnel for cell phone service. It was actually one of the best places in the city to make a call because of users' proximity to the tower, which ran the length of the tunnel.

Tonight, the cell phones couldn't connect. In fact, they couldn't power on. Like the cars, they were dead.

She slipped off her chair and dropped to her knees in the cramped space. From memory, she knew where her emergency backpack was crammed under the desk. She groped through the bag and located the ChemLight emergency evacuation sticks she used to manage accidents. She snapped one, and an eerie green glow, not unlike the one that painted the sky that night, filled her booth.

She reached for the phone and tried to connect to the Port Authority's central switchboard. Nothing.

She smacked her video feeds and her desktop computer, urging the devices to do their job. Nothing.

Suarez stood there for a moment, staring up and down the tunnel as people began to emerge from their vehicles, dumbfounded. Some had flashlights. Others recalled their concert days in front of a stage and whipped out their BIC lighters. Light was their friend. Darkness was the enemy.

Curious, and suddenly overwhelmed by the heat in her stuffy booth, Suarez wandered out into the tunnel. What struck her first was the volume of gas fumes filling the air. With the power out, the massive exhaust fans built into the tunnel's superstructure had ceased to function. As the vehicles rolled to a stop, crashing into one another, the remnants of their combustion engines continued to pour out of their pipes.

Suarez, like many others, began to cough as she choked on the poisonous carbon monoxide. She'd been taught at her annual safety training meetings that overexposure to the colorless gas can cause death.

She began to feel dizzy and nauseated. A headache quickly began to pound both of her temples. She felt the urge to lie down.

Take a little nap. Wait for the power to be restored so she could go back to reading about the murdered woman, God rest her soul.

However, she'd never napped on the job and wasn't going to on this night either. She managed to get her wits about her. Somewhat revived, she squared her shoulders after retrieving her battered Stanley lunch box and tote bag. She glanced at her booth one final time and muttered the words, "Sorry, but I quit."

Juanita Suarez wanted no part of the mayhem that was about to overtake the Lincoln Tunnel. She hustled along the catwalk in search of fresh air.

.

PART 1

Sunday

Due to unforeseen circumstances,
the light at the end of the tunnel has been turned off.

CHAPTER ONE

Sunday
The Lincoln Tunnel
New York

Everyone has a plan until they get punched in the face. Literally.

Less than thirty minutes ago, Asher had been leading his wife and new friends out of New York City in the ultimate bug-out vehicle—a used Humvee. Then, out of nowhere, a fist tore open his cheek and rearranged the cartilage in his nose. The next thing he knew, he was lying on the pavement with blood gushing onto the porous asphalt.

The pain in his face was still throbbing, and a trickle of blood continued to drip from his nose. But none of that mattered. The carjackers had absconded with their truck and young Catherine Cubbison, who'd stowed away in the rear compartment. He had to save Cat even if it meant leaving his wife alone in the city until they could reunite.

Darkness was setting in as Asher stopped to catch his breath and assess the scene in front of him. The two lanes entering the tunnel leading under the Hudson River to New Jersey were mostly blocked with stalled vehicles. Over the last forty-eight hours since the Perfect Storm had created a massive power outage, city workers had managed to push the cars to the outer edges of the two-lane road, leaving the white, flexible lane delineators in place.

Asher turned around in search of the Humvee. Could the advice he'd been given by the onlookers been inaccurate? The truck had no other option but to enter the darkened tunnel. Was it even possible to travel the mile and a half to the New Jersey entrance?

Asher gathered himself and rushed into the pitch-black void, using the delineators as his guide. His eyes searched ahead for any sign of light. He shoved his way past refugees, who carried their worldly belongings in rolling luggage or grocery carts. *Everyone's homeless now*, he thought to himself as he forced his way past a family.

As he ran, he asked anyone he encountered about the Humvee. Many didn't understand him, as they were not fluent in English. Or his words sounded garbled due to his heavy breathing. Others, too weary to offer a verbal response, simply pointed ahead.

He pushed ahead, using the gentle slope toward the lowest point of the tunnel to gain speed and the flashlights of the refugees to guide him. He stopped asking them for assistance. The Humvee and Cat were in the tunnel, or they weren't.

Then he saw it. Like glowing beacons in the fog, the red taillights were still illuminated. As he got closer, he could see the bottom of the tunnel illuminated by the truck's headlights. However, it was silent. The engine had stalled, or the truck had been abandoned. Not that it mattered. He was close.

"Cat! Are you there!" Asher shouted as loud as his tired, burning lungs would allow. "Cat? Can you hear me?"

Asher began to cough as he inhaled the remains of the diesel exhaust from the Humvee. The Lincoln Tunnel once breathed. Exhaling as vehicles roar through it. Inhaling when the ventilation system sucked in fresh air from outside. Now the air remained stagnant, devoid of movement as all life came to a halt. Except for the struggling refugees streaming out of New York.

Cautiously, Asher approached the Humvee, which had crashed into a pileup of vehicles too mangled to be moved. This was the end of the line for any operating cars to depart through the tunnel.

Using the lights as a guide, the refugees were assisting one another atop the wreckage to traverse the hoods and trunks until they reached the other side. The catwalks were filled with debris and dead bodies—the unlucky few who'd died in the wrecks or succumbed to the fumes. The two-day stench of the decomposing corpses was at its worse in the middle of the tunnel.

Asher tried again. "Cat! Can you hear me?" His shouts went unanswered. He reached the Humvee and frantically searched its interior. It was completely empty. All of their duffel bags and belongings were gone.

And so was Cat.

Had he missed her as he raced through the tunnel? He'd called her name every hundred yards or so. Had he even seen anyone walking against the human exodus from New York? Maybe she was hiding in a vehicle, and he didn't know it.

Asher began breathing heavily, the stale air filled with the smell of death causing him to panic. He looked in all directions. He grabbed people as they walked by, interrogating them. Begging them.

"Did you see a young girl alone? Or one who had been kidnapped? Anything?"

Those who looked in his direction simply provided a blank stare in response.

CHAPTER TWO

Sunday
Entrance to the Lincoln Tunnel
Weehawken, New Jersey

The shadows of the skyscrapers grew longer as John Cubbison led his son Matthew down the embankment to a ten-foot-tall retaining wall above the street. Together, they assisted each other as they dropped down, landing hard on the concrete. John tumbled and skinned his hands and left knee. Not a good start. The stinging pain shot through his body; however, he quickly shook it off.

Matthew helped his father up while he glanced around to surveil their surroundings. He was in awe at the masses of people pouring out of the tunnels. A granite and concrete surround adorned the three tubes that made up the Lincoln Tunnel. Each was two lanes wide. The center allowed for traffic in both directions, and the others were one-way in or out.

"Are you okay?" he asked his father.

John brushed off his jeans and winced as his hand came in contact with his bleeding knee. "I'm too old for jumping off walls."

Matthew shrugged. He was not talkative by nature, especially with his parents. Since he'd reactively shot and killed an attacker earlier, he'd become less withdrawn. It was an odd reaction that puzzled his dad.

"Dad, I gotta feeling we'll be doing a lot of stuff we've never done before."

"Like shooting people?" John asked nonchalantly. He observed his son's physical reaction to his comment. Once again, Matthew shrugged.

"No big deal. I didn't have a choice."

John had thought about the circumstances since they'd fled the scene. Matthew was right. He really didn't have a choice although John supposed a nonlethal shot might have done the trick. Then again, why chance it? He might've been dead if Matthew hadn't instinctively reacted to their attacker.

He changed the subject. He took a few steps toward the tunnel entrance and glanced up at three billboards. He pointed as he spoke.

"Home of the free," he muttered aloud as he read the billboards sponsored by Washington Mutual. "Yeah, right."

"They could've used any of these three," said Matthew as he joined his father's side. "The one in the center has the most people coming through it. I guess it's used more." He contorted his face as if he wasn't sure his logic was sound.

"What's your gut tell ya?" John asked.

Matthew pointed toward the center. "They're all full of stalled cars. I think the one with the most people will be harder to walk through. So it depends on whether we expect to come across them in the tunnel or at the hotel."

John wandered toward the center tube and began quizzing people. "Where does this tunnel come out in New York? Is it near Times Square?" Those few who bothered to answer seemed to have a consensus. The center tunnel was the way to go.

"They weren't exactly helpful," observed Matthew as John led the way toward the tunnel's entrance. They wound their way through the stalled vehicles, curiously peering inside the windows, which were oftentimes broken out by looters.

"No, but it doesn't matter. We'll be fine as long as they don't cause us any trouble."

John and Matthew walked single file along the inbound lane, using a concrete ledge to pass to the side of the oncoming masses. Every inch of concrete was filled with refugees walking in a mostly orderly fashion past the inoperable vehicles. The catwalk on the opposite side of the tunnel was filled with people who only had enough room to walk single file.

It was smooth but slow going as they descended into the tunnel. The slope was so gentle it was difficult to determine when they reached the bottom. Until all at once, the dynamic changed. For some unknown reason, the herd of humanity got spooked, and people began running toward them at full speed, knocking the children and the elderly to the pavement.

John and Matthew pressed themselves against the wall, inching their way against the rush. They tried to use the chaos as an opportunity to move closer to the city. Ignoring the panicked refugees, they pushed forward. Deeper into the darkness that had become suddenly damp.

The sound of feet sloshing through water could be heard, and then the shouts of the refugees told the story.

The tunnel was flooding.

CHAPTER THREE

Sunday
Lincoln Tunnel
New York

Asher needed a different perspective, and a flashlight would be nice. He ran his fingers through his hair and picked up some crusty blood, which he dropped onto the pavement. The setting sun had taken away any ambient light that earlier had found its way into the tunnel. To find his way, he walked along the narrow catwalk, stepping over the occasional dead body and car parts tossed from the wrecks. Undoubtedly, he'd need to light up the lanes below him in order to search for Cat. He turned to the approaching refugees for assistance.

"Help!" he shouted. Then he lied to garner sympathy. "Um, my daughter was kidnapped by the men driving this Humvee. I need a flashlight! Can anyone please help me?"

People shoved past him to begin their climb over the multivehicle pileup. They refused to make eye contact with Asher as they helped one another over the vehicles.

"Please! Anyone! My daughter was kidnapped. Can't you let me have a flashlight to find her?"

"Whadya got to trade?" A man's voice came from behind him. Asher swung around to address the man.

"Seriously? Trade?" He was incredulous. Granted, he was embellishing the truth, but what kind of heartless bastard negotiates with a grieving father over a flashlight?

"Yeah, man. Ain't nothin' free anymore. Whadya got to trade?" He repeated the question.

Without thinking of the consequences, Asher grabbed the man by the arm and twisted it until he could slam it against the sharp edge of a busted fender. The man groaned in pain as he dropped his flashlight.

Asher didn't hesitate. He retrieved the flashlight, and with catlike quickness, he leapt onto the hood of a crashed car, ran over its roof, and pushed off the trunk lid. His midsection crashed hard into the steel railing separating the catwalk from the road, although he managed to keep his breath. He never looked back at the injured man, who groaned in pain and cursed Asher six ways to Sunday.

Despite the obstacles and the gore he was trudging through, Asher moved quickly now toward New Jersey. He was only a few feet above the street level, but the rising exhaust fumes and stench seemed to double in intensity. He pulled his shirt over his nose and mouth and continued at a quicker pace. Using the flashlight, he shined it on every face making their way through the tunnel and into every vehicle that had stalled. Periodically, he'd stop and ask if anyone had seen Cat or the men. He'd shout out her name, begging anyone within his voice's reach to help.

Nobody offered. The Lincoln Tunnel, once one of the most traveled stretches of road in America, was now full of humanity. Moaning, crying, and trying to escape to New Jersey. They had their own problems, and Cat was not one of them.

Asher picked up the pace. He had to find her before he exited the tunnel into New Jersey. The thugs who'd abducted the child could disappear into the streets. Pick any building. Do unthinkable things.

Jogging, he rushed forward, alternating between shouting her name and asking for information. The flashlight worked overtime scanning the refugees' faces and the stalled cars. He hoped he didn't miss her. Then he suddenly lost his balance.

Asher's body crashed hard against the tiled wall of the tunnel and then rebounded against the railing. He tripped until his rib cage smashed hard onto the concrete, followed by his already damaged nose hitting the rail. Blood immediately began pouring out onto his face. He tried in vain to stem the bleeding with his hands.

Stunned, Asher lay there for a moment, trying to make sense of what had happened. Incredibly, he'd maintained a death grip on the flashlight. After wiping the blood off his chin, he sat there to get himself together, shining the light ahead of him. That was when he saw it.

Their neighbor's child had given Cat a backpack together with a journal and some pens. The pack lay open on the catwalk, and the contents had spilled out onto the concrete. He allowed the light to illuminate the backpack as he crawled on his hands and knees toward it, disregarding the pain in his ribs as well as the blood dripping from his nose.

When Asher reached the backpack, he rose onto his knees and directed the light forward down the catwalk in search of Cat. That was when he discovered a steel door that had been left open just ahead. Somehow, he felt he was close.

CHAPTER FOUR

Sunday
Lincoln Tunnel
New York

John stopped to assess the situation. The water was rising below them but very slowly. People were pushing and shoving their way past the parked vehicles. John and Matthew were above them slightly, trying to hold onto the moist tiles covering the walls.

"Dad? What should we do? Turn around?"

John wasn't sure how to answer his son. So he didn't.

A panicked couple rushed just below them. The woman dropped her flashlight as she wildly swung her arms to keep up with her husband. She abruptly turned to pick it up, but the man grabbed her by the arm and pulled her along without it. John stepped down from the curb, retrieved the flashlight, and rejoined his son.

"We've got to get to New York, and this is the quickest way. I can't believe the tunnel is collapsing. Electricity has nothing to do with the structure. It has to be something else."

He shined the light on the street where he saw the water

puddling under the refugees' feet. Then he pointed it upward and around the walls. There were pipes running just above the catwalk along the entire length of the tunnel. John furrowed his brow as he illuminated the set of pipes.

"Electrical or water?" he muttered.

"Dad? We need to decide." Matthew had to raise his voice to be heard over the shouts and screams of the panicked masses.

"Let's keep going. Try to stay on this curb. If it gets too slippery, we'll use the cars like stepping-stones."

John picked up the pace and occasionally glanced back at Matthew, who was close behind. "Are you sure, Dad? I bet there's a movie like this where everybody dies."

John managed a laugh at his son's unexpected humor. *He's changed since the shooting. For the better, actually. But why?*

"It'll be fine," he said without conviction.

Within minutes, the water was deep enough to cover the curb they'd been using to avoid the foot traffic in the street. With people still pushing and shoving, their advance was going to be more difficult.

"I'm having trouble keeping my footing," Matthew said loudly. "You wanna try the cars?"

The water was deeper. It seemed the number of people running toward them had thinned out. "Let's try it. Just watch your step, and don't try any crazy jumps."

"No prob," said Matthew calmly.

The guys made good time, and soon the amount of water in the streets was dissipating. So was the number of people coming their way until, unnervingly, there was no one else.

John slid off the hood of a car and assisted Matthew to a safe landing by his side. He shined the light back where they'd come from and then ahead toward the New York entrance.

"What the hell?" he said under his breath.

The sound of heavy footsteps running their way was accompanied by the beams of flashlights dancing all around the tiled walls.

Men were shouting to one another, but the echoes within the tunnel distorted their voices.

"Hey, look," began Matthew. "The water's not as deep. We must be heading up and out."

John agreed. "Let's get out of here!" They began running unimpeded through the cars now devoid of evacuees. They squeezed past a transit bus that had turned across both lanes before coming to a stop. That was when John saw the orange sparks created by a powerful, handheld saw.

A crew of workers was standing along the catwalk, cutting into one of the pipes John had observed. Water was flowing out of the end closest to the city, dousing the workers before splashing onto the pavement.

John slowed his pace to a walk as he and Matthew casually walked past the men without being noticed. The tunnel wasn't collapsing. It was a water main break. However, the prospect of rising water in the Lincoln Tunnel had frightened the refugees, who trampled one another on the way out.

Fifteen minutes later, the guys emerged from the tunnel, where police barricades had been set up to prevent people from entering the tunnel. It was still hot, humid, and muggy although the sun was setting to the west. Those who were trying desperately to escape New York City cursed law enforcement and the Port Authority workers for stopping their progress.

As John studied the faces of the downtrodden, desperately hoping to catch a glimpse of Cat and Grandpa Sam, he wondered if they'd embarked on a fool's errand. He took a deep breath and nodded to Matthew. It was time to find their family.

CHAPTER FIVE

Sunday
Hell's Kitchen
New York

Sam Cubbison had been in a fistfight once. As a kid. It was a rite of passage. At some point in time as young boys longed to be young men, they found a reason to fight. The fisticuffs were usually for stupid reasons, and the fight generally didn't last long. Blood was rarely drawn, so the exchange of blows was certainly not the brutal beatdown he'd just experienced.

Moments ago, the pressure in Sam's head had become unbearable. He tried to keep up with the Doyles as they raced to find his granddaughter. But the more his pulse raced, the more his head pounded. His chest heaved, begging for air to fill his lungs. He suddenly found himself dazed and confused, unsure of whether he was running in the right direction. Then nausea overtook him.

Sam fell to his knees in the middle of Twelfth Avenue. The onetime busy thoroughfare that ran parallel to the Hudson River in

Midtown Manhattan was now littered with disabled vehicles and dozens of people aimlessly walking in all directions.

He tried to get his bearings. To his left was a bowling alley. To his right was a sign that seemed to read Pier 81. Or was it Pier 31? Partially blinded by the setting sun, Sam tried to focus on the marker that, in the scheme of things, meant nothing. The strain on his eyes from looking into the bright light caused him to become more nauseated. Until, all at once, he emptied the contents of his stomach on top of a manhole cover.

He could vaguely hear the passersby commenting on his vomiting. Many misconstrued Sam's plight as that of a drunk. They didn't want to assist a man who was covered in his own blood and who'd soiled his clothes during the beating he'd taken at the hands of the carjackers. Most steered clear of him as they made their way south toward the Lincoln Tunnel or even the Holland Tunnel in Lower Manhattan.

After he'd emptied the contents of his stomach, he tried to stand. It was a fruitless exercise. The concussion he'd sustained from the beating caused him to lose his balance. The dizziness coupled with blurry vision sent him in a sideways walk that could easily resemble the drunkard the refugees around him accused him of being. He stumbled into a raised median and fell sideways onto the grass, where his bruised ribs smacked into the traffic signal pole.

Sam moaned in agony. His health was deteriorating. His mind remained confused. Yet some things were now coming back to him with remarkable clarity. If he could only lie down for a little while to take a catnap, maybe he could create a movie-like dream, of sorts, portraying the happy times in his life. Sam's semiconscious brain had it all figured out.

His eyes fluttered, reacting to the sun peeking through the tree limbs near the entrance of Pier 81. The final light of day sent bolts of energy through his head, exacerbating the headache. He chose to shut them and focus on his beloved wife, Charlotte, who'd died of cancer ten years prior.

Charlotte had been a vibrant, life-loving wife and grandmother. She had always been healthy and rarely went to the doctor. That summer, she occasionally complained of shortness of breath, especially when working outside in the garden. She and Emma were constant companions. Best friends, really. Gardening was their passion, and they shared a love of her grandbabies.

It was Emma who first broached the subject of Charlotte seeing a doctor. Charlotte brushed it off using a variety of explanations ranging from allergies to needing to lose a few pounds. The fact of the matter, as Sam had noticed, was that Charlotte had been steadily losing weight despite continuing her normal eating habits. Nothing had changed in her way of life except for the consistent weight loss and the shortness of breath.

Finally, Sam insisted. No, actually, he demanded his wife go see the doctor. They traveled into Susquehanna to see the family doctor. Dr. Franks had been the family's physician for over forty years. He was a community fixture and considered a family friend. After a brief visit, during which time he conducted a cursory examination, Dr. Franks prescribed montelukast for her allergies and the onset of asthma.

For the remainder of that summer until the leaves fell in October, Charlotte claimed the drug was helping. The family disagreed. Her weight loss was noticeable, and her labored breathing was becoming more prevalent. This time her son, John, took control of her health. He and Sam loaded Charlotte into the truck and drove to see a doctor in Scranton. He started with full blood work, and chest X-rays were ordered. The results devastated the family.

She was diagnosed as having a rare, soft-tissue sarcoma that had attached to her descending aorta and wrapped itself across her esophagus to her left lung. It was a death sentence.

At first, the family grieved. Then they rallied. *We won't let this thing beat us. We're Cubbisons. We'll do whatever it takes. Wherever it leads us.*

The gradual transition from shock to grief to willingness to fight was not unusual. Unfortunately, it was too late. After months of treatments, including a stay at the Cleveland Clinic, Charlotte died in Sam's arms one night in bed. He clutched her frail, lifeless body until Emma had to lovingly pry his arms away.

The discovery of Charlotte's sarcoma and the long path to her death was just the beginning of Sam's grief. After her death, he became paralyzed over the loss. He withdrew from social activities outside of Cubbison's Farm. He gradually avoided family gatherings, choosing instead to remain in his bedroom or walk the pastures amongst the cattle alone.

In his mind, he was being disrespectful to let anyone else into his consciousness except the memory of his beloved Charlotte. His grief was overwhelming. The family tried to bring him out of it, and they even called upon their church to help. However, nothing could bring Sam back to his old self.

Unbeknownst to Sam, Emma contacted a psychiatry professor at Columbia University who specialized in prolonged grief disorder. She told her that for most people, symptoms of grief peaked in the six months after the loss of their loved one. Only a small percentage remained stuck and miserable for a longer time. Sam, she determined, would continue to struggle with moodiness, inability to function, and sleep deprivation for an indeterminate period until one day, it would pass.

For Sam, it took a little over two years. He'd finally agreed to seek professional help and began taking mild antidepressants. None of that seemed to work. He began to accept that he'd remain in a never-ending loop of grief for the rest of his life. He had no expectation that his despair would pass unless Charlotte returned to him.

Then, one Sunday morning, Sam emerged from his room at breakfast time. The sun had begun to rise as the family gathered in the kitchen. The smell of ham and red-eye gravy permeated the Cubbisons' home.

Sam announced that he'd like to attend church with everyone.

Then he whispered to Emma, "Would you mind helping me pack Charlotte's things? I know now she isn't coming back."

Sam lay in the warm sun in the center of Twelfth Avenue in a strange place. His mind was slipping away. He was ready to join the love of his life. Reunited once again. In his subconscious state, a slight smile came across his bloodied mouth as she called out his name.

"Sam. Sam."

CHAPTER SIX

Sunday
Hell's Kitchen
New York

Lauren Doyle's feet were set in concrete; however, her mind ran like the wind. It had only been half a minute, but it seemed like hours before she was able to make a decision. She feared for her husband's safety. Asher was wholly capable of writing chase scenes for *Blue Bloods* although he had no experience in hunting down brutal kidnappers. Even if he was able to find Cat, how would he be able to deal with the men who took her? He'd already been badly beaten trying to reason with the thugs.

Yet she trusted his judgment, and she didn't disagree with his efforts to save the young girl. She wanted desperately to help him. Should she disregard his instructions and chase after him? Or should she find Sam, who'd experienced serious injuries from their attackers, as Asher had instructed?

"Dammit!" she shouted as she spun around twice and raced off toward the Hudson River. *I'm wasting time.*

Lauren pushed her way through the crowds of people slowly following one another down Fortieth Street toward the tunnel. She'd regained her strength and her stamina as she moved steadily against the oncoming foot traffic. On a couple of occasions, she ran head-on into a refugee. After accepting a barrage of criticism and curse words from the New Yorkers, she continued toward the waterfront.

As the day wore on, the number of people wandering the streets had increased considerably. Twelfth Avenue was filled with refugees traveling north and south along the river, using all modes of transportation in addition to their feet. Bicycles. Skateboards. Moms pulling kids in wagons. Dads pushing belongings in shopping carts. Even one man was riding a garden tractor that had been commandeered from a maintenance shed.

Lauren slowed her pace to study every human being within her field of vision. In her panicked state, she'd forgotten what Sam was wearing and struggled to remember his physical features. She cursed herself for not being more attentive. While they'd only known each other for a couple of days, how could she be so remiss to not remember what the man looked like?

She cursed herself under her breath and continued toward the point where they'd been attacked. She scanned the people's faces and regularly called out his name.

"Sam! Sam!"

She pushed her way through a large group of people at the entrance to Pier 81. They angrily shoved her as she attempted to make her way past. Lauren knew better than to engage the hostile group. She was alone and unarmed. She profusely apologized but pressed through, nonetheless.

"Sam! Sam!" she shouted again as she reached the Circle Line Sightseeing Cruises dock. The boats that took tourists around Manhattan to get a unique view of the city were parked at Pier 83. They were being looted. Food was being taken out of the reception facility, and dozens of people were scampering around the decks of the boats with armloads of supplies.

Finally, she found her way to the point where they'd been attacked. Dried blood where Asher and Sam had been beaten covered the pavement. Lauren shed a tear as she thought about her poor husband, whose face had been struck so hard that his cheek was torn open. And Sam, the elderly man who tried to hold his own against the carjackers, had been mercilessly kicked. She could only imagine the internal damage he'd sustained.

Lauren pushed the traumatic event out of her mind and spun around again. Where had they left Sam when she and Asher had chased after the Humvee? How far down the street had they gone?

She tried to remember the details that she so desperately wanted to shove into the deep recesses of her mind. She started back toward the Lincoln Tunnel. This time she jogged along the northbound lanes of Twelfth Avenue.

"Sam! Sam!" She shouted his name more often as she became concerned that she'd missed him. Had he turned off a side street? Had he sought refuge in one of the many buildings that had been looted? As she slowed to a fast walk, she studied the pavement for evidence of blood.

Her eyes scanned back and forth. Her ability to see both sides of the street was better now that she wasn't running against the flow of pedestrians because she no longer had to worry about bumping into people.

Then she saw a body. A man curled up under a tree in the tall grasses of the median. His face was pointed toward the sun. Lifeless. Without expression. Or was it a slight smile?

"Sam! Sam!"

CHAPTER SEVEN

Sunday
Hell's Kitchen
New York

Lauren climbed over the short concrete retaining wall and crawled through the grass to Sam's side. He was unconscious, but alive. Her eyes roved over his body, looking for signs of additional trauma. A small amount of foamy drool had trickled out of the side of his mouth and mixed with the crusty blood on his chin.

"Sam! Wake up!" she begged as she tried to hoist his body upright to lean him against the traffic post. She turned around, looking for anyone to assist her.

"Hey! Can somebody help me? He needs water. Please!"

One by one, people walked past the median. They looked in any direction at all manner of interesting sights. Anything was worth seeing except Lauren's pleading eyes.

"Come on! Anyone? Can't you give us some water? He's dying!" Her voice was desperate. She tried to get someone's attention, but after more than a minute, over a dozen people had passed with no assistance.

Lauren carefully tilted his head back to keep his airway open. She had a firm grip on his wrist to feel his pulse as she gently slapped Sam's face in an effort to revive him. Sam seemed like he was just sleeping because his breathing was regular. However, even though she touched or shook him, he didn't wake up.

"Help!" she yelled. Lauren was panicking now. If Sam had been unconscious this entire time, she was concerned he might suffer some type of brain damage. "I need water! Please!"

Then she heard a quiet, innocent voice of a child. "Mommy, can't we help the man?"

"Come here, child. Stay away."

"But, Mommy." The young boy pulled away from his mother and walked directly toward Lauren with his arm outstretched. A half-full bottle of water was being offered to save Sam's life. "He can have mine."

Tears came to Lauren's eyes as she mouthed the words *thank you*. She took the water from the youngster and slowly poured some into Sam's mouth in an attempt to revive him. She quickly wiped any that trickled out on Sam's neck. Seconds later, Sam coughed, and his body jerked awake.

"What? Charlotte?" He became slightly agitated.

"Calm down, Sam. It's me. Lauren. Please drink some more water but very slowly."

Sam reached up to touch Lauren's hand as she slowly poured a couple of ounces into this mouth. He eagerly gulped it down. He nodded his head as he blinked several times. Sam Cubbison was going to live.

Now that she'd fought back the tears and regained her voice, Lauren turned to thank the young boy; however, his mother had already whisked him away. The people walking past them never gave them a second glance. Apparently, those trapped in New York City had become desensitized to the suffering of the injured and the dead.

Sam reached for the water and drank a little more this time. The bottle was covered with beads of moisture from the humidity. Sam rolled it across his face and neck, enjoying the cooling effect it had on him. He was beginning to regain his strength as he drank the last of the water.

"Cat?" he asked. Sam closed his eyes and rubbed his temples, causing him to wince. The water might have revived him; however, it did little to ease the excruciating headache.

"We chased the Humvee down the street. Some people saw it turn toward the Lincoln Tunnel," Lauren replied as she helped Sam to his feet. She didn't want to reveal to Sam they weren't certain that was the case.

Still weak in the knees, he leaned against the traffic signal pole until he could steady himself. "We have to go after them."

Lauren kept a firm grip on his shoulders with both of her hands. She wanted Sam to remain upright and, more importantly, still. She feared he'd abruptly run toward the tunnel, not realizing the median where they stood was a couple of feet above the street. He could ill afford a face-plant on the pavement.

"Okay, but slowly. Asher was told they went against the stalled traffic in the eastbound tunnel."

"That doesn't make sense," muttered Sam as he wiggled away from Lauren's grip. He slowly made his way to the retaining wall. He crouched and eased one foot down, followed by the other.

"I agree. We were—" Lauren cut herself off. She hesitated to tell Sam that Asher had based his decision on the suggestions of a few stragglers along Fortieth Street.

"What, Lauren?" Sam's question was firm. He suspected there was a problem.

"It was hard to get any cooperation. Based upon what people said, we believe they went down that way. We didn't actually see the Humvee go into the tunnel."

Sam rolled his head around his shoulders to relieve some tension and to will away the pain throbbing in his head. "Lauren, what is the other possibility?"

"Well, they might've headed into Midtown, although nobody indicated that. I believe we're on the right track."

Sam looked ahead and walked slowly toward the tunnel. "It's all we've got. Let's go." He gestured for her to join him, and the two began walking briskly down the street, joining the stream of humanity looking for a better option than the city.

CHAPTER EIGHT

Sunday
Midtown Manhattan
New York

The last vestiges of daylight greeted John and Matthew as they emerged from the tunnel in Midtown Manhattan. After getting past the scrum of refugees demanding to enter the tunnel, John began to ask for directions.

"Can you tell me where the Marriott Marquis is?"

At first nobody responded, and then, as the crowd thinned, he was given shrugs or *I don't knows* in reply. He decided to broaden his request.

John tried again. "How about Times Square? Which way is Times Square?"

A young woman replied, "No parties in Times Square, mister. You don't even want to go there right now."

"Yeah. They're tearing it up," added her friend.

"Whadya mean?" asked Matthew.

"C'mon, bro. Where you from? They're partyin' like it's 1999 tonight." Making reference to the song by Prince.

"Last night, too."

"You should've seen them running out of the Hard Rock with all those guitars."

"Lunacy, right?"

"1999, baby!"

Suddenly, John and Matthew were bombarded with unsolicited advice and anecdotes about the state of affairs in Times Square. Everything from people having sex in the streets to businesses being looted. None of it was encouraging.

They kept walking, and despite the barrage of bad news, John continued to ask questions. Finally, a woman pointed them in the right direction.

"If I were you, I'd go another block over to Seventh. Take a left and you'll be in the heart of Times Square. Where exactly are you trying to go?"

"The Marriott Marquis hotel. Do you know where that is?" asked John in response.

"Okay. Okay. That's different. Forget Seventh Avenue." She pointed behind them. "Go back to Eighth. Walk up to Forty-Sixth and hang a right. You can't miss it."

"Perfect, thanks!" said John cheerily.

"Sure thing. Oh, and watch your back. Seriously."

The woman began her trek toward the Lincoln Tunnel as darkness overtook the city. The lights that were once the hallmark of New York were nonexistent. Only the pulsating glow of structure fires in the distance brought any kind of illumination.

"Stay close, Matthew. It appears Times Square has become a magnet for the crazies."

"How far is their hotel from Times Square?" asked Matthew as he focused his attention on a group of young men marching down the other side of Eighth Avenue. They glanced toward him but continued on as if they were on a mission.

"I think it's right in the middle of that whole area. You know, where the ball drops on New Year's Eve."

The guys walked shoulder to shoulder, so close that they occasionally bumped into one another. Each of them kept their hands near their pistol grips in case they had to defend themselves with little warning. All around them, people were shouting. Some were arguing. Others, as John put it, were simply howling at the moon. Many words rattled around in his brain as they approached West Forty-Sixth Street. Mayhem was the one that seemed to describe their surroundings the best.

The closer they got to the entrance of the hotel, the louder the noise became. It was almost as if the New Year's Eve ball drop were underway. Thousands of people had descended upon the famed intersection of Broadway, Forty-Second Street, and Seventh Avenue in Midtown Manhattan. Only, there was no police protection or barricades corralling the revelers. They were completely unrestrained.

"Where's the entrance, Dad?"

The guys had made their way through the throngs of people to Broadway only to find themselves in front of several businesses that had been hit by swarms of looters. The guys pushed their way through the people milling about, many of whom were drunk or high.

Matthew was shoved hard by accident, but he reacted, nonetheless. He swung around and appeared ready to pull his weapon when John quickly restrained him.

"Relax, son. In this madness, you'll squeeze off a shot or two before we'd be pummeled by these people. Stay with me. I see the entrance up ahead."

He pointed toward an awning that jutted out from the tall building. It was hard to read although the white background made the red-lettered Marriott logo readily apparent. They pushed their way past a group leaning against the concrete pillars marking the entrance to the hotel. They had been built after 9/11 to deter a terrorist attack using a vehicle full of explosives. Beyond the pillars, several men dressed in all-black clothing stood in front of the doors, cradling AR-15s in their arms.

John moved through the few stragglers who'd ducked under the awning to watch the chaos. Suddenly, a flashlight was illuminated and shined in his eyes, causing him to be temporarily blinded. He covered his face with his arm and squinted to recover from the bright light.

A gruff voice bellowed at them, "That's close enough, pal. You two can turn around and leave now."

John lowered his arm and squinted to address the men. "We're looking for my dad and my daughter. They were staying at the hotel when, well, all this happened. May I speak to a manager or—"

"No," the man replied brusquely. "There are no guests at the hotel. They've all been removed."

"You kicked them out into the streets?" Matthew asked. He was incredulous. "You threw my little sister to the wolves? Assholes!"

"Take it easy, buddy!" shouted one of the men. "Everyone had to get out. There was no ventilation or food. They were a legal liability not to mention the hotel management didn't want to deal with a bunch of dead bodies."

John balled up his fists. He wanted to lash out at the crass guards but managed to restrain himself. "Fine. Can we at least see their room? I'd like to know if they gathered their things or not. That'll at least give me an idea if they headed home."

"Sorry. The answer is no. The power outage prevents the room doors from opening easily with the key card system. They can be opened but are damaged in the process. Management is trying to minimize the loss."

"Screw them!" shouted Matthew, startling John. "You're gonna let us in!"

The three men raised their weapons and began pointing them at John and Matthew. Red dot lasers began to dance around on their chests, indicating they couldn't advance another step without getting killed.

"Okay! Okay," said John. "We got the message. Can you at least give me directions to Rockefeller Center? They were watching the aurora from the top of 30 Rock."

The men lowered their weapons slightly and exchanged glances. The first man, ostensibly the leader, replied to John.

"Sir, 30 Rock caught on fire. I heard it was completely gutted by the time it finished burning this morning. I'm sorry."

John gasped for air. His chest tightened as his knees began to buckle. He leaned toward the wall of the entryway until he could close his eyes and catch his breath. Matthew helped his father remain standing.

"When did the fire start?" Matthew asked.

"Listen. This is all hearsay," the man responded.

Matthew pressed him for an answer. "What have you heard? When did it start?"

The man took a deep breath and replied, "Right after the power grid went down."

CHAPTER NINE

Sunday
Midtown Manhattan
New York

"Dad, we'll find them." Matthew tried to offer words of encouragement to his father. He'd never been empathetic toward his family. For years, he'd lived with a chip on his shoulder, whether imagined or deserved.

During his formative years, Matthew had perceived his brother, Luke, was the favorite twin in the family. He could never put his finger on a single event or series of circumstances that changed the family dynamic, but in his mind, it had. As a result, he'd drifted farther and farther away from the Cubbison way of life.

By the time the boys entered the sixth grade, his friends were completely different from Luke's. They experimented with smoking cigarettes. They engaged in pranks and petty theft. Their world revolved around the latest video games. Luke was a country boy through and through. Hunting, fishing, and outdoor activities made up his day. While Luke looked forward to doing his chores around the farm, Matthew rebelled against them.

However, despite being exposed to the kinds of things parents lose sleep over at night, Matthew had never crossed the line. He rejected experimenting with drugs when his friends pressured him. In high school, he cut class from time to time. Then again, so did Luke. The difference was that Luke went to the lake with his friends. Matthew hung out playing video games in the game room basement of his friend.

Someone well-versed in psychobabble might look at Matthew as the bad twin simply because his interests were different from his brother's. Matthew was less Cubbison than his more Cubbison brother. However, that didn't mean he wasn't a good kid. He was just different. And it was that difference that would enable him to contribute to the survival of his family.

John stopped in the middle of Sixth Avenue and turned toward Matthew. "I know in my heart they're out here somewhere. Son, your mom and I talked about the most likely scenario. You know, that we wouldn't find them."

"We had to try," interjected Matthew.

John took a deep breath. "I'm not gonna let those guards cause me to lose hope. We have to search everywhere we can. And we have to ask questions. Somebody might remember seeing them. Anything we learn will be helpful."

A fight broke out across the street from them as the entrance to a sandwich shop had been breached. A dozen or more people slugged it out as they tried to enter the small hole in the wall. Hunger was a powerful motivator.

John steadied himself and led the way. Although Rockefeller Plaza was only a block and a half away, they were at the base of a canyon of skyscrapers, which, coupled with the complete darkness, obscured their view.

The closer they got to Forty-Ninth Street, the stronger the stench of the fire became. By the time they turned the corner, Rockefeller

Plaza came into view, and the moon reflected off the façade of the massive structure. The lower windows reflected the moonlight. However, halfway up the skyscraper, panes of broken glass provided them a better picture of the damage caused by the fire.

John reacted by breaking out into a run, shoving his way past people milling about. Matthew tried desperately to catch up to his father without drawing the ire of the displaced New Yorkers. He eventually caught up and urged his father to be careful.

"Dad, you're crashing through these people. Can you slow down?"

"I have to know," he mumbled through his heavy breathing as he bounded up the granite steps toward the entrance. He was immediately met by yellow police tape and pylons designed to cordon off the entrance.

Two uniformed NYPD officers stood guard near the revolving doors entering the building. They seemed uninterested in the people who'd gathered around the entrance, including those who were pulling down the one hundred ninety-three national flags of the United Nations' member states. All things considered, people trying to survive should have more important things to focus on. The cops certainly did.

John stopped in his tracks, his chest heaving from his fight through the crowded street. He stared up to the top of the building and began shaking his head. In the darkness, his tears weren't easily noticed. It was his sniffles that gave him away. Matthew joined his side and put his arm around his dad's shoulders.

"Dad, this doesn't mean anything. Remember?"

John didn't immediately respond. His imagination ran wild: They were at the top of the building. The elevators didn't work. The emergency stairwells were packed. The fire consumed the building and everyone in it.

He unconsciously shuddered, trying to expel the negative thoughts from his mind. He struggled to regain his composure. After wiping the tears away, he took a deep breath and exhaled. The moment had passed.

"Let's see if they'll tell us anything," he said with a nod toward the police officers.

Matthew patted his dad on the back and carefully adjusted his shirt to hide the two pistols strapped to his waistband. He checked his father's clothing to make sure his weapons were secured as well. He imagined the cops were on edge under the circumstances. Even the sight of a pistol might cause them to panic in response.

They slowly approached the caution tape. Matthew raised his hands so the officers could see them, and John followed suit. They leaned into the yellow tape, and the officers immediately reacted.

"Stay back!"

John had regained a sense of calm. "Okay. Okay. We understand. Friday night, my dad and young daughter were at the top of the building, watching the aurora. We're from Pennsylvania and came to find them. Can you please tell us something about what happened? Anything will help."

The older officer stepped forward after glancing around the front of the building. He removed his hat and wiped the sweat from his brow. Then he lit up the guys' faces before washing their bodies with the light to determine if they were a threat. Satisfied, he shined the light toward the ground to provide some illumination.

"All I know is that soon after the power went out, a fire broke out somewhere around the fiftieth floor. That's about twenty stories from the top."

"Was there emergency power?" asked Matthew.

"No. Everything was fried. I do know that people escaped the building from the lower floors by using the stairwells." The officer hesitated to continue.

"There's more, isn't there?" asked John.

The now retired desk sergeant, who'd donned his old uniform and volunteered to help the city through the catastrophe, nodded. "Yes, sir. There were several hundred deaths. The bodies were recovered yesterday and this morning. Those who could be identified were removed and taken to the closest cemetery. The others, um, were left behind."

John shut his eyes and slumped, his shoulders drooping as he sighed.

Matthew addressed the officer. "Is there a list of, you know, the ones they could identify?"

The officer pointed past Matthew. "That night, emergency personnel set up a triage to treat the injured. Because of the unrest, the mayor ordered it to be dismantled. They're in the process of doing it now. If you hurry, you might be able to find someone who can answer your questions. They also have a list of the deceased."

John had already turned toward the faint glow of the white infirmary tents. Matthew thanked the officers and once again found himself chasing after his dad, who was hell-bent on getting there before they moved out of Rockefeller Plaza.

They crossed the open space where the ice rink was set up in the wintertime and made their way down the steps leading to the Channel Gardens. The landscaped gardens and water features were filled with hundreds of people splashing in the remaining water, hoping to gain some respite from the excessive heat that continued to beset the region.

While John was focused on the workers breaking down the temporary infirmary, Matthew glanced right and left at the high-end shops that once graced the plaza. All the windows were broken, and their contents spilled out onto the sidewalk. The thought of looting hadn't crossed Matthew's mind as he'd remained focused on finding Cat and Grandpa Sam. However, in that moment, he realized it was a reality. That said, if he was going to join the ranks of the looters, it would be for food. Not shoes, handbags, and Tiffany jewelry.

They reached the end of the Channel Gardens where the infirmary had once stood. This time, they were met by the city's special operations unit wielding automatic weapons. John skidded to a stop before running headlong into the barrel of a rifle.

CHAPTER TEN

Sunday
Midtown Manhattan
New York

Lauren and Sam were careful to avoid confrontation as they made their way to the Lincoln Tunnel's entrance where she'd last seen her husband. Despite being anxious to reunite with Asher, she had to tend to Sam's injuries, or he'd be unable to travel far. She recalled her surroundings near the point where she and Asher had parted ways. There was a bodega nearby that had already been looted. She hoped she could find a minimal amount of medical supplies to stop Sam's bleeding and start the healing process of his open wounds.

She also needed a flashlight. The lack of light in the city was disconcerting. She'd always associated darkness with danger. Living in Manhattan in the last several years was no longer safe. Crime was rampant. Prosecutions were less prevalent. Cops were hamstrung by policies that prevented them from doing their jobs. As a result, petty criminals had been emboldened as they began to realize there were little or no consequences for their actions. After the grid collapsed, Lauren could only imagine what lengths these people would go to.

Once they entered the small store, the first thing she did was rummage around behind the counter in search of a cigarette lighter. Not surprisingly, all of the cigarettes and cigars had been stolen. However, in the thieves' haste, they'd ransacked the shelves around the smoking options. She didn't locate a pocket lighter but did come across a BIC stick lighter that had been kicked under the checkout counter. Her smiling face was revealed as she rolled the ignitor and a flame appeared.

"It's not much, Sam. It'll do for now."

"You wanna make a torch? You know, like the old days?"

Lauren laughed. "Not a bad idea."

She dropped down to her knees and lit the lighter again. She searched for a can of lighter fluid. "Yes!" she exclaimed under her breath when she located two yellow bottles of Ronsonol lighter fuel shoved to the back of the bottom shelf. She stood and handed them over to Sam.

She held the stick lighter high overhead to maximize the small amount of light the flame provided.

Sam had a suggestion. "Let's find the utility closet. A mop handle will do. Then a tee shirt or some kind of clothing ..."

His voice trailed off, as Lauren had already retrieved two *I heart NYC* shirts from a small rack in the center of the store.

Sam smiled. "I think one will do."

"Yeah, I know. The other one is for Cat. A souvenir in case she still loves New York City."

Sam let out a hearty laugh, followed by a coughing fit. The congestion in his lungs from the smoke inhalation coupled with the beating made the humorous statement painful, but well worth the chuckle.

"Grab me a large," he said with a grin.

The two found their way to the back of the store, shuffling their feet through the destroyed merchandise and broken display shelves.

Once they located a broom, they focused on locating gauze, tape, bandages, and antibiotic ointment. They were successful on all counts although the bandages and gauze were not necessarily sterile, as their original packaging had been torn open. Sam insisted Lauren patch him up anyway. He reminded her that his wounds being exposed to the grime of the city was far worse.

It took them less than fifteen minutes to gather up what they needed. The flashlights and batteries were gone, but the torch would be more than sufficient to illuminate the tunnel and ward off any potential attackers.

As they made their way to the tunnel, Lauren relayed her last conversation with Asher before he'd disappeared from view.

"Sam, he said no matter what, we'd wait for one another on the other end. He understood that you and I may have difficulty catching up. Plus, he had no idea what happened to Cat."

"That's what worries me," said Sam. "What if they didn't drive into the tunnel?"

Lauren refrained from responding for a moment. There were some NYPD officers milling about the entrance, and she wanted to listen in on their conversation. When they didn't say anything of substance, she leaned in to Sam and whispered in his ear, "Let's light our torch after we're out of their sight. They might freak out if they see us taking a flaming broomstick into the tunnel."

Sam nodded in agreement and allowed Lauren to lead the way. For a while, they followed a group of half a dozen refugees, taking advantage of the light provided by their flashlights. However, Sam's injuries prevented him from keeping up with their pace. He frequently became out of breath, forcing them to stop to rest. This was concerning to Lauren, but she didn't want to address it until she reunited with Asher.

Fewer people were entering the tunnel, although it would still be slow going as they shuffled their feet to avoid debris from the car wrecks. Sam suggested they create their torch. Rather than use their tee shirts, they soaked the corn-husk broom with the lighter fuel.

Once the straw was fully engulfed in flames, it not only put out a significant amount of heat, but it lit up the tunnel around them as if it were daytime. For the first time, Lauren and Sam were able to get a clear picture of the carnage.

The large number of vehicles pushed to the side surprised them. However, it was the number of dead bodies scattered about that nauseated them both.

"Why haven't the police moved them out of the tunnel?" asked Lauren.

"I'm surprised the smell isn't worse," added Sam. "Plus, they'll become diseased. On the farm, it's a big deal when we lose one of our livestock. We don't waste any time moving the carcass away from the herd and burning it before covering it with dirt. We make sure every-one's face is covered up as we do it."

Lauren pulled her shirt over her nose and mouth, not because of the stench, but now she was concerned about the potential for diseases. She turned to Sam. "Are you okay to pick up the pace?"

He nodded. "After seeing this, you bet. You lead, and I'll be right behind you."

Lauren walked faster, glancing over her shoulder from time to time to check on Sam. From recollection, she thought the tunnel was less than two miles from one end to the other. With the road cleared in the center and minimal foot traffic, she calculated they could make it through in about forty-five minutes.

Then she saw the Humvee.

Without regard for Sam, she began jogging down the slope to the point where the truck had been abandoned. Sam shouted after her, encouraging her to hurry. She did, running faster until she reached the vehicle. Like Asher before her, she discovered it was empty. Frantically, she swung the torch around her, searching for any evidence of Cat and Asher. To her relief, there were no bodies and no blood.

His chest heaving, Sam finally caught up. He was too out of breath to ask his questions; however, Lauren could easily discern them.

"Sam, I don't see anything that would indicate they were injured. No blood. No torn clothing. No evidence of a struggle. Listen, Asher was here long before we were. He's got this."

He waved his arm back toward the tunnel entrance. His voice was full of trepidation. "We saw blood and bodies back there."

Sam bent over and rested his hands on his knees. He nodded up and down as he tried desperately to catch his breath. Since the fire, that had become increasingly difficult. The thugs repeatedly kicking him in the ribs hadn't helped.

She didn't want to agree with his conclusions. Cat was not one of the bodies they'd encountered. Now, however, the Humvee's progress had come to an end. *What lies ahead?*

Lauren wandered toward the front of the Humvee. The relatively open walkway provided by the cars being moved to the side was closed up beyond the Humvee. Her mind visualized all the possibilities. She closed her eyes to focus until something snatched her back into the present.

Sam's difficulty breathing would be less of an issue now. However, the broom's husk falling to the pavement, leaving only a burning handle, would be.

CHAPTER ELEVEN

Sunday
Lincoln Tunnel
New York

Fearing getting burnt, Lauren tossed the flaming broom handle onto the pavement. She narrowly missed leaking fluids from the engine of a wrecked sedan. The steady drip of oil mixed with gas was trickling its way down the tunnel toward the bottom.

"We need light," said Sam as he grasped Lauren by the arm and pulled her past the wrecked Humvee. When she was clear of the smoldering torch, he opened the driver's side door of the Humvee and began to search under the seat with his outstretched arm. With a grunt, he loosened the fire extinguisher that was affixed to a bracket. "Here. Put out the fire."

Lauren felt for the safety pin and pulled it free. Seconds later she'd doused the broom parts with fire retardant. Several people walked past her as she returned to the Humvee. She found Sam lying prone across the two seats.

"Hey, are you okay?"

"Yeah," he replied with a muffled voice. His legs swung up until they were suspended in air. Then he shouted, "Got it!" Following a click, the passenger's side floorboard was illuminated, revealing Sam's grinning face.

Lauren tugged on his legs and assisted him in crawling backwards out of the behemoth of a truck. "Good job, Sam. We'll be able to move faster now. Let's go find them."

With Sam leading the way, they moved deeper into the tunnel, scanning the abandoned vehicles for signs of life and shaking their heads in dismay as they came across the dead. At times, groups of people were huddled against the walls of the tunnel, sobbing out of grief or frustration. Others they encountered were the opportunists. Those scavengers who searched through the vehicles, looking for anything of use or value. Sam and Lauren steered clear of them to avoid conflict.

"I don't know how they can do that," lamented Lauren. "I mean, do they have to take advantage of other people's loss?"

Sam didn't answer immediately. He hadn't thought about the social and moral ramifications of living in a world without power. Was it every man for himself? Well, not necessarily. Asher and Lauren had left their home in order to help two strangers. Maybe it was the nature of the individual. Was that person a looter or a survivor?

He continued to guide her through the tunnel until they could feel the change in their pace. They were walking a steady incline now. "Lauren, I think it's a matter of perspective. I'd imagine there are a lot of people in the city, the homeless, namely, who learned to forage for their survival."

"That's true," she said as she pointed toward a man trying to force a shopping cart between two cars without success. "We used to call them dumpster divers until Asher reminded me they were mostly people down on their luck or afflicted with some kind of mental illness."

"Think about it," added Sam. "We're in their world now. These are people who know the value of every personal item in their possession. From a fresh pair of socks to a cigarette lighter. If this outage is prolonged, the economy as we know it will be over. Those who gather and accumulate the most necessities should have the best chance of surviving this catastrophe."

Lauren suddenly stopped and gasped. She pointed toward the catwalk. "Sam, did you see that? Shine your light to the left along the wall."

"Oh, God. Is that ...?" His voice trailed off.

Lauren raced through the cars, using the bumper of one to catapult her onto the catwalk. She picked up the backpack her neighbor had given Cat. Tears immediately came to her eyes. The straps were sticky with fresh blood.

CHAPTER TWELVE

Sunday
The Lincoln Tunnel
New York

Nobody just disappears, right? Thirteen-year-old Catherine Cubbison curled into a ball, drawing her knees as close to her chest as possible. Closing her eyes in an effort to wish away what was happening to her. Her mind raced as she considered her plight.

This was not a movie or television show. She wasn't there one moment and gone the next, never to be seen or heard from again. She remembered watching a documentary with her mother about Jaycee Dugard, the eleven-year-old girl abducted while walking to the school bus stop. She was gone for eighteen years, and the man who took her made her do unspeakable things.

She didn't want to watch the documentary. However, her mother made her. To remind her that the world was full of bad people. To be aware of her surroundings. To avoid strangers. To fight like hell to survive so it wouldn't happen to her.

Yet here she was, hiding in the back of the truck. Placed there by the well-intentioned Lauren, who thought she'd be safe. She wasn't safe. She needed help.

Despite her efforts to comfort herself by recalling that even Jaycee Dugard wasn't gone forever, Cat wasn't convinced she'd see her family again. People can up and vanish. There were no all-powerful sorcerers or magicians or fairy godmothers standing over her, prepared to wave their wands in order to deliver her to safety. Nobody had the power to make her appear in the arms of her parents with one simple flick of the wrist.

However, in an instant, she'd been whisked away. Stolen from Grandpa Sam and their new friends. A stowaway in a truck that was careening off the fenders of other vehicles while its driver and the men inside got a good laugh.

With each brush of steel on steel, Cat was thrown about. However, she never made a sound. She'd tried to conceal herself under the tote bags and clothing that surrounded her. Once, one of the men in the backseat looked over the Humvee's bench seat. Cat was barely visible, but her eyes were able to peer through the bags to see the man's tattooed-covered arm reaching around to touch the bags. Then he turned his attention forward as the driver laughed uproariously when he ran over one of the refugees. The men applauded and exchanged high fives.

They were savages. Car thieves. Kidnappers. And killers.

Cat realized fear had overtaken her. She'd forced herself to stop breathing to remain silent. When the Humvee crashed in the dark recesses of the tunnel, her eyes grew wide. The men cursed the end of their ride. They exited the truck and made their way to the rear door.

Cat's racing heart was thumping in her ears. She prayed this was a dream. The metallic clicking sound of the door's hinge being opened caused her blood to go cold. With the removal of the first pieces of luggage, she was fully exposed. In the dim light, Cat could see their astonished, hungry eyes staring at her.

I think they're going to kill me.
Eventually.

CHAPTER THIRTEEN

Sunday
Lincoln Tunnel
New York

"What the hell do we have here?" asked one of the thugs. His tone of voice was more than curiosity. It was sarcastic and snide. He intended to torment the child hiding away in the back of the Humvee.

One of the men lit a cigarette, allowing the cherry to brighten, which in turn cast an eerie light on Cat's frightened face. Her eyes darted from the face of one man to another. Looking for a glimmer of humanity in them. She was disappointed. Their eyes were black. Dark. Hiding thoughts that would make her emit a primal scream if she could hear them.

She mouthed the words *leave me alone*. Only a slight whisper that couldn't be heard came out.

One of the men reached for her arm and jerked her upright. His grip hurt Cat, causing her to yelp. She reacted by screaming for help before the man's powerful hand covered her mouth.

Cat began to fight her kidnappers. She swung wildly with her fists, trying to reach the face of the man who had a firm grip on her. She kicked at the bags around her in an attempt to get some leverage in order to break free. Her squirming did nothing but draw laughter from the other three men who surrounded her.

"*Una luchadora!*" shouted one of the men with an *M* and an *S* tattooed across his forehead. He was the only one of the four who was a member of the brutal El Salvadoran MS-13 gang who'd taken over parts of New York. He'd remained mostly quiet, never breaking eye contact with Cat.

He was not the leader of the group, Cat discerned. That was the driver. The man who'd attacked her grandfather. The large, muscular man who could barely squeeze behind the steering wheel of the Humvee. The man who held her in a death grip.

In Spanish, he issued his orders to the others. *Take everything. Leave the girl to me.*

Cat didn't understand what they were saying, but she knew they intended to take her with them. She fought again, harder this time. As the monster dragged her out of the truck, her feet hit the pavement. She tried to run but lost the chance when the man lifted her off her feet with his arm around her neck and his hand pressed against the back of her head.

Cat tried to scream but couldn't. She gasped for air. She tried to wiggle her way out of the chokehold, which only caused him to press harder against her throat.

He was killing her. Just as she predicted. She was about to die.

And then, seconds later, she lost consciousness.

CHAPTER FOURTEEN

Sunday
Rockefeller Plaza
New York

"Not another step, pal!" the Emergency Services Unit officer shouted. He was wearing body armor and wielding a powerful Colt M4 Commando. He waved its barrel menacingly between John and Matthew, both of whom quickly raised their hands.

"Sorry. We're trying to get some information on my father and daughter before the medical people leave," John offered as an apologetic excuse.

"They're a little busy," the man growled in response. "There are temporary bulletin boards set up outside 1PP for those looking for lost loved ones." 1PP was an abbreviation for One Police Plaza, the NYPD headquarters located near city hall.

"But listen. The other officers said the people here had a list specific to the building's fire," John countered, pointing over his shoulder toward 30 Rock. "Um, a list of those who died. If I could just—"

"1PP. Go there. Now move along."

John pulled a photograph out of his jean's hip pocket. "Please, Officer. Let me ask the nurses if they've seen my daughter and father. They were on the top of the building, watching the aurora, when the lights went out."

The apathetic officer rudely responded to John's pleas. "Most of those people didn't make it. 1PP has a list of the bodies that weren't charred beyond recognition."

"Screw you, asshole!" Matthew couldn't restrain himself. "You might be talking about my sister."

The brutish officer took a step toward Matthew and snarled.

"What the hell is going on over here?" a man shouted from the center of the activity. He pushed his way past the police and revealed himself. He was wearing light green scrubs covered in dried blood.

The officer's tone of voice changed as he replied, "Nothing, Doc. These people don't understand our protocols."

John saw an opening. "We're looking for information on my missing daughter and my father, who were in the building when the fire took place. I have their picture." He thrust it into the doctor's face, much to the chagrin of the rude officer, who scowled at John. The doctor took the photograph of Sam standing by a tractor with Cat perched in the seat. He studied it in the dim light.

"Where are you from? Not many tractors and fields in the city."

"Northeastern Pennsylvania. Susquehanna area."

"My brother lives in Binghamton," the doctor replied. He raised his hand to indicate he'd be right back. "Wait here." He turned toward the officer, whispered something to him, and rejoined the group of medical personnel supervising the breakdown of the temporary infirmary.

Five minutes later, he returned with a nurse who was also in blood-covered scrubs. She was carrying a yellow legal pad under her arm along with the photo of Sam and Cat. The doctor gently nudged the officers out of the way to make room for her to address the Cubbisons.

"Gentlemen, I think I've found someone who can help. I want to wish you both luck, and it goes without saying, please be careful."

"Yes, sir, Doctor," said John, appreciative of someone being helpful. He turned to the triage nurse with trepidation. "Um, would you mind looking on your list to see if my father and daughter are on it?"

Without responding directly to his question, she extended her hand and introduced herself. "That won't be necessary."

"What do you mean?" asked Matthew.

"I'm Edna Bailey, the head nurse overseeing triage. I remember your daughter. I treated her after she'd been rescued from the fire."

John gasped and fell to his knees. He immediately teared up and buried his face in his hands. He looked up to her. "Is she okay? Where is she? What about my father? His name is Sam."

"Grandpa Sam, if I remember correctly?"

Now Matthew became emotional, too. "Yes. He's my grandpa. Cat's my sister. Are they both okay?" He reached down to help John to his feet. Now both of the guys stood shoulder to shoulder, inwardly begging for good news.

"Okay, first of all, to ease your concern, both of them were treated and released. Cat was badly battered and possibly had some internal injuries. However, I didn't consider them to be life-threatening as long as she was properly monitored. Grandpa Sam was brought in some time later. He'd been trapped on a different floor but rescued by one of our heroic firefighters. He was suffering from smoke inhalation and minor burns. Not unusual, considering."

"Do you have any idea where they are?" asked John.

"Well, no. However, I do know the people they're with."

"Oh, my god!" shouted John. His body swelled with hope and anticipation. Their search was almost over. They'd done the impossible.

"Hold on, sir. This is where the level of my good news may come to an end."

"Why?" asked Matthew.

"The two of them were accompanied by a couple who live here

in New York. The man, Asher Doyle, is the son of the former communications director to the NYPD commissioner. That, however, is the extent of what I know about him. I didn't even catch his wife's name. All I know is that Asher comes from a good family. A highly respected family within the rank and file." She glanced at the officers to her left and right. She'd heard about the verbal altercation and rude behavior from earlier.

"Asher Doyle. Does anybody know him? Or where he might live?"

None of the officers responded. The triage nurse shrugged as well. "Your only option is to find a phone book. I have to say, though, nobody uses them anymore."

"What about a phone booth?" asked Matthew innocently.

"Fuggedaboutit," replied one of the officers in a heavy New York accent. "The homeless steal them as soon as they come out. They use the pages as clothes insulation during the winter."

The nurse pointed toward the looted storefronts on both sides of the plaza. "You might try in there. The thieving locusts cleaned out everything of value. I seriously doubt they took the phone books."

John nodded and then studied the faces of the NYPD officers as if he was looking for permission. They were clearly indifferent. They didn't stop the looting. They certainly weren't gonna arrest a phone book thief.

He repeated his task. "Okay. Asher Doyle. Probably local. Phone book."

He reached out to shake the nurse's hand again. He desperately wanted to hug her to express his gratitude; however, the yellow tape and automatic weapons deterred him. Instead, he thanked her for taking care of his family and for the information. He retrieved the picture, looked at them once again while he still had some ambient light, and led Matthew toward the first store entrance with a renewed sense of purpose. Cat and Sam were alive.

CHAPTER FIFTEEN

Sunday
Lincoln Tunnel
New York

Cat was awakened by the cold that had swept over her body. She was shivering. Not just from fear, but from being wet. Despite the heat she'd experienced above ground, in the dark bowels of the Lincoln Tunnel, she found herself unable to control the convulsions caused by the lowering of her body temperatures.

Her mind struggled to find clarity. She'd been sleeping, yet she didn't know why. She strained to listen. *Am I alone? Are my kidnappers nearby? Am I dead?*

Oddly, she hoped to hear the heavy accents of her kidnappers. She wanted to know they were near. If they were, she was alive. Otherwise, she thought, she'd been sent to some form of purgatory between the hell on Earth and the hereafter in Heaven.

She sensed a trickle of water around her. Slowly, deliberately, Cat unclenched her fist and reached for the concrete where she had been dumped. The floor was moist as if it had been sweating.

However, there wasn't enough water to account for her drenched clothing.

As she woke up from the sleeper hold the man had deployed against her, Cat recalled the events that had led to her abduction. She tried in vain to determine how long she'd been knocked out. She had nothing to go on.

Remaining completely still, she began to flex the muscles and joints in her limbs. She curled her toes slightly. She squeezed her thigh muscles. She twisted her upper body ever so slightly. Other than the dull aches and pains associated with being manhandled by the brute who'd dragged her out of the Humvee, her body seemed to be intact.

Cat took a deep breath and concentrated. She focused her thoughts on other parts of her body. She recalled the warnings her mother had given her about boys using drugs or alcohol to take advantage of her. She didn't know what a sexual assault would feel like, but based on her self-assessment, she was comfortable that hadn't happened to her yet.

Voices. Muffled. Foreign. They were still with her. Somewhere close yet far enough away for her to contemplate her escape. Cat risked raising her head to get a look at her surroundings. The only glimpse of light came from beneath a door several feet away. It was orangish in color, flickering like a candle.

She inhaled through her nose, trying to assess her surroundings by smell. She took in the damp, musty air and almost coughed. Cat clamped her hand over her mouth and closed her eyes to suppress the urge. She needed her kidnappers to leave her alone while she devised a plan of escape.

However, she had no idea where she was. She rolled over and raised her body onto her hands and knees. She crawled toward the door, easing her face along the concrete floor to get a look through the sizable crack under it. The men were sitting on the floor, backs against the wall of a long corridor. Their duffel bags had been opened, and their clothing had been strewn about. Empty bags of snacks and power bar wrappers lay on the floor at their feet.

Suddenly, one of the men stood. He kicked at the debris and began walking toward the door. Frightened, Cat rolled on to her backside and began to push herself away from the door with her feet. She didn't stop until her back crashed into a large drainpipe, and her head struck the steel wheel that opened and closed the valve.

She closed her eyes and violently shook her head to relieve the pain from the blow. With both hands, she rubbed the back of her head to overcome the unexpected collision of steel and skull.

I'm not gonna die, and he's not gonna take me.

Cat jumped to her feet and set her jaw. She was penned in and had only one option in her mind—fight.

She moved quickly to the side of the door and pressed her back against the moist wall. As soon as the door started moving, Cat's body tensed. She balled her fists so tight that they turned white, if one could see them.

The door swung open and crashed hard against the wall. Cat refused to let the noise startle her. The man eased into the room, perhaps surprised that Cat was not in view. It was all the hesitation she needed to strike.

With a grunt, she reared back and threw a hard punch that landed on the bridge of her kidnapper's nose. She followed the first strike with her left hand clawing down his face, her nails ripping open his skin.

Stunned, he dropped to his knees, and Cat pounced on him. She scratched his eyes, gouged at the torn skin on his cheekbone, and continuously clawed at his bleeding nose.

Left, right, left, right. Each blow was followed by another. A straight punch to the nose again with the right. The left ripped at his bloodied cheek. The right landed hard with a roundhouse to the man's temple.

Fierce. Confident. Cat didn't hesitate to bolt out of the room and run past the shocked men. She rushed down the corridor, having no idea where it led. It could've been the wrong way. It could've led to a locked door. It could've led to being trapped once again only to face men who were now angry. Grandpa Sam had always warned her if she was gonna poke a hornet's nest, she'd better be prepared to get bit.

Well, Cat had sure enough kicked the hornet's nest, and she had zero regrets. With her heart racing and hands swelling from the beating she'd administered, she pushed through an emergency exit into the next hallway, where she ran head-on into a shadowy figure lurking in the dark.

CHAPTER SIXTEEN

Sunday
Lincoln Tunnel
New York

Asher gathered himself and picked up Cat's backpack with his bloodied hands. When he saw that it had been emptied, he tossed it on the catwalk. Without fear, he willed his battered body through the steel doorway into a utility room full of steel pipes and control panels. None of the gauges registered any readings, the result of the power outage. If the mechanical room controlled ventilation or flood mitigation, it was disabled now.

Another partially opened door led to a long hallway that ran parallel with the tunnel. Asher walked down it with purpose, knowing that either the sound of his heavy footsteps or the flashlight's beam could give him away. He was mentally prepared to fight for his life in order to save Cat.

As he surreptitiously tried every door handle, he wondered what Cat's parents were going through. If John and Emma were anything like Grandpa Sam, they were kindhearted, salt-of-the-earth people who were probably worried sick about their daughter's safety. Asher tried to put himself in John Cubbison's shoes. If his daughter had gone missing under these circumstances, he'd be out of his mind with worry. In that moment, he made a silent promise to the man, the father he'd never met, to keep his head on straight to save Cat.

Suddenly, Asher forced himself to stop. He turned off the flashlight and closed his eyes, straining to focus his senses on the sounds that were emanating from a door at the end of the corridor.

Men laughing. The occasional thumping sound. Muffled voices and shuffling footsteps. Asher had no confirmation that Cat was in the dark labyrinth of hallways and mechanical rooms that made up the bottom of the Lincoln Tunnel. He might have found a group of teens screwing around. Or a group of displaced refugees living off a successful looting expedition.

He moved forward, using the moisture-covered walls as his guide. He dared not turn on the flashlight for fear of discovery. He finally reached the end of the hallway, where it ran perpendicular into another corridor. To his right, it ended at a doorway. To his left, he could see a light emanating from the bottom of the door frame. Asher inched into the center of the intersection of the two corridors.

Then he stopped to listen. He held the tragus of his right ear down so that it covered the external part of his ear canal. The thick flap of skin on his outer ear blocked out any sounds from his right. The voices became more discernible. They were Spanish, and they were emanating from the dimly lit room at the end of the hallway.

Asher moved closer, using his shoulder to wipe the blood off his right ear. Just a few more feet.

Suddenly, the men's voices became excited, and the sounds of them shuffling could be easily heard. Asher was prepared to use his flashlight like a club, bludgeoning the first person who came through the door. Without regard to his safety, he'd slug his way through the men who'd beaten the adults and kidnapped Cat. He would save her.

Asher stopped breathing as he tensed his body. With his left hand, he reached for the door handle. With his right, he clutched the flashlight and held it over his head like a hammer ready to strike a sixteen-penny nail.

The door flung open, and Asher was ready. He turned his body square toward his assailant and prepared to swing with all his strength. The first blow needed to crack a skull, he thought to himself. Send a decisive message to the other attackers that he meant business. They needed to fear him.

The first body came rushing through but with so much speed he had no time to bring the flashlight down upon their head. Their bodies crashed together, almost knocking Asher backwards onto the floor. Instead, they ended up in a welcome embrace.

CHAPTER SEVENTEEN

Sunday
Rockefeller Plaza
New York

Matthew was becoming discouraged. "Dad, are we sure they still make phone books? That cop may have been messin' with us." They'd entered one storefront after another, fumbling in the dark in search of the elusive phone directory.

"We've gotta try, son," replied John as he moved out of a fancy chocolate store into the adjacent retailer. Finally, behind the sales counter in Mulberry, a United Kingdom-based designer store featuring leather handbags, they came across the Verizon Yellow Pages. However, no residential listings were included.

"This is a waste of time," said Matthew, who was disgruntled and tired. It was approaching midnight. Both of them were physically and emotionally exhausted.

John didn't disagree, but he was compelled to search for any possible lead to where Asher Doyle lived. In the chocolate store, he found a tote bag in their storeroom that included a flashlight. He used it to peruse the listing in the yellow pages. After a moment, he found what he was looking for.

"Look at this," he said, waving Matthew over to the counter. He turned the open phone book so Matthew could get a better look.

Without warning, two young men burst into the store. John turned off the flashlight and drew his weapon. Matthew had already pulled both of his guns out of their holsters. They were pointing at the silhouettes of the two men, who rushed into the center of the store before stopping. They seemed oblivious to the presence of the Cubbison men.

"Aw, man," complained one of the intruders. "Freakin' purses and crap like that."

"No jewelry?" asked the other.

"Nah. This is a bust. Come on."

And in less than a minute, the would-be looters moved on to better options.

John exhaled and replaced his gun in the paddle holster. Matthew was a little slower to put his weapons away. Since the shooting in New Jersey, he seemed more comfortable with the guns. In John's mind, a little too comfortable. He seemed eager to pull the firearms if even a remotely dangerous situation presented itself.

John returned their attention to the phone book. "I know this is a long shot, but I think we have to give it a try. New York City Hall and the police headquarters are near one another. I think we should be there at first light to study those bulletin boards. Sam and Cat may have gone there to post a note to us. Also, maybe somebody at either police headquarters or city hall could help us find an address for Asher Doyle. Whadya think?"

Matthew shrugged. "It's all we've got to go on. We'll probably get ourselves in trouble going in and out of these stores. How far is it?"

John studied the map. "It's hard to tell from this. I do know that it's practically straight down Broadway. If we walk along Fifth Avenue and pick up Broadway, we should be able to do it in an hour or so."

"Okay. I'm pretty tired. Do you think we should walk there now?"

John patted his son on the back. "I know you're exhausted. So am I. I think it would be safer in the morning, don't you?"

Matthew was glad to hear his father's suggestion. "I was hopin' you'd say that. Plus, there are a lot of cops around here. Maybe we could find a store or something closer to where they're loading up the medical stuff."

"Great idea. They could have our backs, at least for a few hours."

"How about that smelly perfume store with the French name?" asked Matthew. "Lock-a-tane, or something like that." Matthew destroyed the pronunciation of L'Occitane, the women's beauty product retailer that was pronounced *lox-e-tan*.

John laughed for the first time since they'd arrived in the city. "Yeah. All of those strong-smelling perfumes ran off the looters. That store was still half-full."

The guys backtracked toward the illuminated tents where the infirmary was being dismantled. The armed police officers were still protecting the medical personnel, and it appeared they would be there for some time.

John and Matthew rummaged through the store, looking for anything resembling bedding. All they could do was break down store displays and remove anything soft to lay their heads on. Not that it mattered. The exhausted men were asleep in the storeroom within minutes.

CHAPTER EIGHTEEN

Sunday
Lincoln Tunnel
New York

"Run!" said Cat in a loud whisper after she regained her balance.

Asher responded quickly. He illuminated his flashlight and led the way. He and Cat had a full head of steam as they approached the T-intersection of the corridors. His light shined on the door immediately in front of them. It would be a logical exit to the tunnel's utility hallways.

He glanced behind them and saw that several men had emerged from where they'd held Cat captive. One man was hollering instructions in Spanish but expletives in English, combining the two languages in his fit of rage.

Asher noticed they did not have flashlights, so he used it to his advantage. What they were about to do was a risk, but it might divert the men in the wrong direction. He turned to Cat as they approached the corridor that led to their right.

"Go that way," he whispered. "The door's at the end of the hallway on the right. It's open. Trust me."

Cat didn't argue. She fled down the dark hall, holding her arms wide at her sides to use the walls for guidance.

Asher continued forward and burst through the push-bar handle of the emergency exit. He forced the door open until it slammed into the concrete wall behind it. Then he raced along the catwalk toward New York, his light shining along the route to see Cat as she emerged from the open door.

There she was. He picked up the pace and shined his light down to keep his footing. When he reached Cat, he was nearly out of breath. He turned off the flashlight.

"Listen to me," he began his instructions. "Go to the other side of the road and hug the wall. Quietly make your way toward New Jersey. I'm going to lead them away from us."

"But—" interrupted Cat, but Asher cut her off.

"Hurry. I'll catch up with you. Go!" He gently pushed her on the back to urge her off the catwalk. She slipped through the rail and landed on the street with both feet.

Asher illuminated the flashlight and began running toward New York just as the men emerged from the utility corridor's emergency exit.

"*Este camino! Ahora!*" This way! Hurry!

Asher took a deep breath and took off. He hurdled bodies and shoved his way past refugees. He purposefully shined his light upward so it would dance off the tiled wall. He wanted the men to follow.

Then, when there were no other refugees to witness his actions, he set the flashlight on the catwalk with its light shining toward the city. He wanted it to point his pursuers in the direction he wanted them to go.

The wrong way.

Asher slid through the railing and dropped to a low crouch. He could hear the heavy footsteps and shouts of the men as they rushed along the catwalk toward his position. As they moved east, he headed west.

He ducked between two stalled cars as they ran past. Pushing and shoving their way past the refugees he'd just encountered. Their shouting and rambunctious pursuit gave him much-needed cover.

Now he was moving at a quick pace, dodging refugees and hurdling cars' fenders to catch up with Cat. The farther he traveled toward New Jersey, the fainter the voices of the kidnappers became. Soon, the flashlight they discovered could no longer be seen, and their voices were off in the distance.

Asher slowed somewhat, perplexed as to why he hadn't caught up to Cat. Was she that much faster?

Then he was startled by her voice.

"Asher?"

Asher swung around. "Where are you?"

"Over here. I was trying to stay out of sight in case, um, you know. They caught you."

Asher moved through the dark until he reached her position. The two hugged one another, and the tears flowed.

Asher regained his composure. "Are you okay? Did they hurt you?"

"No. I mean, um, not like you think. One of the men choked me until I passed out. That's all."

Asher didn't say it aloud; however, he screamed it in his head —*what a relief*. He hugged her again and led her toward the tunnel's exit with his arm wrapped around her shoulders. Occasionally, he glanced backwards to confirm his ruse had worked.

He allowed his body to relax for the first time as a breeze of fresh air washed over them.

CHAPTER NINETEEN

Sunday
Outside the Lincoln Tunnel
Weehawken, New Jersey

"Cat! Asher!" Lauren's voice echoed through the concrete entrance to the Lincoln Tunnel in New Jersey. Sam, despite his propensity to cough, joined in the chorus.

"Cat! Asher! Are you here?" He stopped walking, pausing to listen for a response. He turned to Lauren. "How could we have passed them in the tunnel? We looked in every car."

"Should we have tried all those doors?" asked Lauren.

"I thought about it," replied Sam. "Surely, once Asher found her, he would've gotten out of the tunnel quickly. Right?"

"Yeah. Listen, let's not panic. Remember, we didn't come across them in the tunnel, which means ..." Her voice trailed off.

Sam frowned. They weren't dead or injured as far as they knew. "I know what it means. Let's find a truck or something to stand on so we can see better. It's dark, but at least we'll be more noticeable."

Lauren looked around using the ambient light from the aurora to assess their options. She pointed to a couple of SUVs that had stopped on the two outside lines entering the tunnel. "You take the one on the right, and I'll take this one. We can cover everything in the middle together."

The two split up and found perches atop the roofs of the SUVs with their legs dangling on the windshields. It was fairly quiet, as the refugees exiting the tunnel were starting to thin out, and their exhaustion took away their desire to make small talk.

Trying to remain positive, Lauren turned her attention to the next step on their journey. "Sam, are you certain you can navigate your way back to the farm? Maybe we should look for a map?"

Sam did have his concerns. After what they'd experienced in the city, it was possible his preferred route would be blocked or too unsafe to travel on. He also had hopes that his son would come looking for them. He firmly believed John would take the same route into New York City that Sam would take home.

"I know the way. I've also learned that you never know what you'll encounter on the road. We may have to find a different route if, you know, people get in the way."

Lauren contemplated his statement and didn't respond. She remained quiet, studying the groups of people who emerged from the tunnel. Then she caught a glimpse of two shadows, people walking side by side. One was taller than the other. A man and a child. A girl?

Lauren hastily slid off the roof of the SUV down the hood until her feet hit the pavement. Full of hope, she rushed through the stalled vehicles, forgetting Sam was unaware of where she was going.

"Asher! Asher! Is that you?" She shoved her way through a small group of refugees until she reached the man and girl. "Asher?" Her voice was hopeful, but uncertain.

They moved closer to her. It was if the air had been sucked out of her lungs, and the blood drained from her body. The man and his much shorter wife held each other closer as they steered clear of Lauren.

Tears flowed down her cheeks as she began to sob.

Seconds later, Sam reached her side and gently hugged her. He spoke to her reassuringly. "I'm sorry, Lauren. Please don't give up. They'll be along. I can feel it."

Lauren cried for a moment, and then the wave of emotion subsided. Her body relaxed as she allowed Sam to comfort her. She closed her eyes and visualized the husband who worshiped and adored her. The man she longed to be with her every moment of every day. She recalled the last glimpse of him as he raced into the tunnel to rescue Cat. A stranger. Not that it mattered. That was who Asher was. A hero to all. Especially to Lauren.

"Hi, guys." His loving voice reached into her mind as if he was standing by her side. Then she felt the touch of his hand on her shoulder. It awakened all her senses. Asher?

Before she could respond, Cat rushed into them with her arms held wide. The four of them hugged each other, thanking God for keeping each other safe. As the tears flowed, the Cubbisons thanked Asher for saving Cat. Lauren thanked her husband for returning to her. And the group promised to never be separated again.

Sometimes, you can't keep your promises.

PART 2

Monday
There's No Place Like Home

CHAPTER TWENTY

Monday
Weehawken, New Jersey

Their joyous reality was looked upon with scorn by the poor and downtrodden refugees exiting the Lincoln Tunnel into New Jersey. Gathered in the middle of the pathway between stalled vehicles, the foursome blocked people pushing carts and strollers or pulling wagons and luggage. Asher was the first to notice the grumbles and subtle insults being hurled their way. None of the people around them had a reason to be hopeful, much less exuberant.

Cat tried to examine her grandfather in the dark. She patted his arms and chest before gently touching his face. "Grandpa, are you okay? I was worried."

Sam laughed despite the fact that a man brusquely forced his way past the group. "You were worried about me? Bruises and scars heal. I'm the one who should be asking about you."

Cat gulped before she answered. During the entire ordeal, she'd tried to block out any thoughts of what might happen to her. She'd focused on the love of her family to get her through the abduction.

"I'm fine. I promise. I'm very thirsty, though."

Another group of people pushed their way past. At well after midnight, the toddlers they were dragging along by the hand were barely able to stand. Asher and Lauren broke their embrace when two men began arguing near the entrance to the tunnel.

"Let's get going, everyone. We need to find a place where—" His sentence was cut off by screams.

"He's got a gun!"

"Please don't shoot us!"

"Run!"

The tired and weary refugees escaping New York found the strength of a herd of stampeding buffalo. Their heavy feet and panicked shouts echoed in the darkness as they raced up the hill away from the tunnel.

"Come on, guys," Asher frantically urged the group. "Follow me."

The aurora provided Asher, who stood six feet two inches, sufficient illumination to carve out a path away from the tunnel. He avoided families and large groups in their path who were moving slowly. Unencumbered adults created a conga line like speeding motorists in the left lane of the freeway. Within seconds after the first shot rang out, they'd made their way along the rock retaining wall into a short tunnel leading into Weehawken.

By the time they'd run the quarter mile up the hill to Park Avenue, all four of them were gasping for air, with Sam having the most difficulty. He'd inhaled more smoke than the others during the fire at 30 Rock. He'd likely feel the effects for many months.

They walked briskly past a residential apartment building built on the cliff overlooking the street. The complex's trash cans had been strewn about it, and the single-bay garage had been broken into, revealing knocked-over shelves and gardening tools on the floor.

Twenty yards later, Sam insisted they stop. He leaned against a three-foot-tall retaining wall made of stacked stone. The structure had held back a towering hill covered with overgrown vegetation for a hundred years. His breathing became fast and labored. Almost panicked. Asher helped Sam to calm down.

"Sam, we can't have you hyperventilating," said Asher. "This will be difficult at first, but we need to limit your airflow. Close your lips like you're gonna whistle. Focus on breathing through your nose, even pinching down one nostril if that's what it takes."

Sam nodded. He even slowed his breathing to once every five seconds or so. Then, without warning, he had a coughing fit. His throat and lungs were still irritated from the damaging effects of the chemicals in the smoke. It took a moment for him to recover. In addition to clearing his lungs of phlegm, his sudden coughing served another purpose. Sam was no longer on the verge of hyperventilating.

He used his arm to wipe the gray mucus from his mouth. Like the others, he was parched and desperately needed to drink some water.

Asher turned to Lauren. "Stay with them. I'm going to try to pop this hydrant."

"What?" asked Lauren, confused as to what Asher intended.

"There were quite a few tools in that garage," he explained. "We had a scene years ago that involved kids opening up a fire hydrant. Jamie and Eddie were called to the scene."

"You remember this?" she asked.

"Yeah, sort of. Naturally, we had the FDNY on hand to control everything. The firefighters referred to it as *popping the hydrant*. They had a special tool for it, but a big pipe wrench will work."

Asher rushed off as Lauren asked, "Isn't that dangerous? I mean, all the pressure could blast out of there."

"I'll be careful!" he replied loudly as he disappeared into the garage.

Lauren took a few steps toward the hydrant before returning to Sam and Cat. "We'd better stay over here."

Asher rummaged through the garage, feeling his way around in the dark in search of a pipe wrench. He couldn't locate one; however, he did find a large monkey wrench. He slapped the adjustable tool against the palm of his hand and grinned as he marched toward the hydrant. There, he laughed at himself for not thinking of this sooner.

Inner-city kids in New York and across the Hudson in New Jersey were notorious for opening fire hydrants on hot summer days. This can be very dangerous, as the hydrant's pressure pours a thousand gallons of water through the opening per minute.

Fire departments began installing a fitted cap with a few holes in it to allow a minimal amount of cool water to escape to help the mischievous kids cool off. The water came out of the hydrant in a gentle sprinkle of twenty-five gallons per minute rather than the powerful gush necessary to fight a structure fire. The spray caps were being installed throughout the five boroughs and in New Jersey.

Asher fumbled with the spray cap, manipulating the cotter pin and twisting it slowly until water began to seep out as a slow trickle. He looked around as a steady stream of refugees passed by, seemingly uninterested in what he was doing, for now. He abruptly stopped and called for the others.

"Hey, guys. Over here."

"Did you have any luck?" asked Lauren, who was the first to arrive.

When the group was together again, he revealed the plan. "Yeah, but there's something we need to do first," he began. He looked around again. "Listen, I know this sounds gross. We need to go through the trash over there and find containers to store the water. Plastic bottles, cups, jugs, etcetera. Try to avoid milk and orange juice containers. They're probably full of bacteria from sitting out in the heat the last several days."

"Other people's water bottles? Eww," said Cat.

Asher agreed. "I know. Like I said, sounds gross. Here's the thing. As soon as I open the cap on the hydrant, water is gonna come out like a water hose spraying through a nozzle. We'll be able to drink, wash off and fill our containers. However, as you can see, we're not alone. There will be people pushing and shoving their way to the hydrant. I want us to get what we need and then clear out. Make sense?"

Sam had a thought. "Um, Asher, we have farm hydrants at our place that pull from our wells. I don't know if this will be the case here, but I think we should let some of the water clear through first. There's a lot of minerals and gunk that can settle in the pipes if they're not used often."

"Good point, Sam. We'll let it flow out as long as we can before we draw a crowd. Let's find our containers and get ready."

CHAPTER TWENTY-ONE

Monday
Weehawken, New Jersey

It had been recycling day, and the residents of the building were diligent about separating their trash from the clear bags full of plastics and stacks of cardboard. The dark brown trash cans were toppled over, and their contents covered the sidewalk and part of the street. The bags full of recyclables were untouched. One resident had an affinity for 7 Up and Mountain Dew in sixteen-ounce plastic bottles. When Sam tore open the bag, more than a dozen empty bottles and their caps fell to the pavement.

While Lauren and Cat matched caps to bottles, Asher prepared to open the proverbial floodgates. Sam reassembled an Amazon shipping box by folding the bottom. It held sixteen of the soda bottles standing upright.

"We're ready," Lauren announced as they rejoined Asher.

"Okay," he said after taking a deep breath and exhaling. "I have no idea what this will look like. Remember, I'm gonna allow it to empty out a bit, then taste it. If I don't turn green and puke, we're good to go."

Cat, without a hint of humor, said, "I'm so thirsty, it won't matter. I'll drink it."

"Here we go," warned Asher. He carefully manipulated the spray cap until more water found its way out of the hydrant. He nervously turned around to observe the passersby, none of whom seemed to notice. He glanced toward the throughway leading to the Lincoln Tunnel entrances below. There was a break in the wave of refugees entering New Jersey.

He opened the spray cap until it was fully flowing. The average flow rate of a kitchen faucet was just over two gallons per minute. The spray emitted by the hydrant was ten times that. And it had the coverage of a lawn sprinkler.

"It stings!" said Cat loudly before catching herself. "But it feels good."

Asher cupped his hands to capture some of the escaping water. He hesitated at first, then allowed himself a sip. Like a drunk pretending to be a wine connoisseur, he swished the moisture around in his mouth. He raised his eyebrows and allowed a slight smile.

"Not bad. Fill 'em up, and then we'll wash the street grime off our bodies as much as possible before we draw a crowd."

They'd barely finished rinsing and filling the soda bottles when it seemed the entire population of metro New York discovered the water source. The crowd became so belligerent and pushy that Cat became frightened as humanity crushed her into the fire hydrant.

With Sam and Lauren hugging the Amazon box full of filled soda bottles, Asher wrapped his right arm around Cat, who hunched down and pressed her face into his chest. With his left, he pushed people out of the way until they were all clear of the scrum that was beginning to turn violent.

The four of them hustled away down Park Avenue. They reached two billboards side by side. One of them urged motorists to hire Laundry Pal, a dry-cleaning service. *Don't stress the mess* was the company's motto. As the group regained their composure in front of the sign, Asher thought about the stresses of daily life that caused so many people angst. Laundry was one of them, he supposed. At least it was a stressor as far as Laundry Pal was concerned.

He shook his head in dismay. Other than lying on one's death bed, he couldn't imagine any stresses of their prior life that compared to what they were going through now. Every step of the way, they'd had to scratch and claw their way forward to safety. He performed some mental calculations and realized they were barely ten miles from his home.

In rapid succession, he recalled the events since that moment the lights had gone out on Friday night. Surely, it'd get easier. Right? He wasn't so sure. He also realized every single choice they made might result in them facing a life-or-death scenario.

"What's the plan?" asked Lauren, snapping Asher back into the present.

Asher closed his eyes for a moment and tried to visualize a street map of this side of the Hudson. He'd crossed the river once when they'd first moved into their condo. The Home Depot was located at the intersection of Interstate 95 and the 495. He opened his eyes and looked back toward the tunnel entrance. Then he turned toward the billboard and looked up the hill. Vagrants had carved a trail through the trees and underbrush next to the sign that led up to the road above them.

"We need to get up there first. Then we can head west. I really think we have some things to consider, though."

Lauren turned to Cat and Sam. "Can you make it up the hill?"

Sam gave her a thumbs-up. "Let's do it. And I agree with Asher. Before we run off half-cocked, let's think about our options."

Asher took possession of the Amazon box while Lauren led the way. They pulled their way through the trees and saplings until they arrived on the high ground. Unlike Park Avenue below them, the two-lane street above them was devoid of pedestrian traffic. Even the number of stalled vehicles was minimal compared to the other streets they'd traveled upon.

It was Cat who noticed a perfect place to rest and talk. "Hey! I've never been in a limo before," she said excitedly as she pointed up the street. A white Lincoln stretch limousine had pulled against the guardrail after its engine stopped working. The driver's door and the left passenger door stood open.

Cat impetuously ran away from the group toward the limo. Lauren gave chase, urging her to slow down.

"Cat! Wait!" Lauren exclaimed. Then she noticed what appeared to be bits and pieces of blue, green, and purple sea glass on the recently paved asphalt. "Watch out for the glass!"

Cat slowed her approach and waited for Lauren. Broken glasses and decanters littered the street at the side and back of the limousine. Lauren placed her arm between Cat and the open door to gaze inside. She fully expected it to be inhabited by a newly homeless refugee or a dead person.

While the interior was dark, she could see that it was empty. Asher and Sam arrived at the driver's door and inspected the interior.

The sleek Lincoln body was elegant on the outside and once stunning in the interior. Since the perfect storm, multiple people had rifled through its interior in search of anything of value, especially the liquor served to those riding in the back.

Lauren was leaning in the passenger door, and Sam was kneeling on the front bench seat, looking toward her via the privacy window, which had been lowered.

"I think we're good," Sam determined as he backed out onto the street.

Asher handed him the box filled with water. "Let me try something," he began as he turned his attention to Lauren. "Honey, shut the door and push the door lock down."

Lauren did as he requested, slowly pushing the chrome door pin in the panel of the older model Lincoln before closing the door. Asher slid into the front seat and pulled the door closed before locking it. Because all the windows were still intact, he yelled his request to Lauren.

"Try to open it!"

He heard her attempt to pull the handle, but the lock held. They had a safe place. He forced his lanky frame through the privacy window until he landed headfirst onto the leather seat facing the rear. Ducking to avoid hitting his head on the ceiling, he felt his way to the rear, wary of any broken drinking glasses. The rear compartment, capable of seating ten, had a bar that ran the length of one side of the limo. Its contents had been removed. Any liquor had been consumed, and then vandals had chosen to break the leaded crystal glassware on the pavement.

Asher opened the rear door and stepped outside. He surveilled his surroundings. No one had approached them as of yet, so he motioned the group to get into the car. With a final glance, he eased into his seat and gently pulled the door closed. He depressed the door pin and let out a noticeable exhale.

While their surroundings were mostly quiet other than the constant sound of shuffling feet and muted conversations, inside the limousine, it was if they'd put on headphones. It was a dull, hollow sound in the enclosed space. Only their nervous breathing was detectable.

Cat, the first into the limo and the shortest of the four, took up a position behind the driver's seat. Sam leaned against the side across from the bar while Lauren and Asher sat in the spacious front-facing seats usually reserved for the VIPs of the limo-worthy events that employed the vehicle. For several minutes, they all forced themselves to wind down, soaking in their surroundings and contemplating what they'd been through. They deserved the respite.

It was Sam who broke the silence. "Water, anyone?"

"No, thanks," whispered Asher.

Lauren waved off the offer with her left hand before speaking. She correctly presumed her inner thoughts at the moment matched everyone else's. "I vote we forget about everything we've been through so far. It's almost a new day, and we're setting our sights on getting Sam and Cat home."

"It'll be your new home, too," interjected Sam. "And I agree. What's done is done. We're alive, and for the moment, we're safe." His qualifier was a grim reminder they had a difficult journey ahead of them.

Asher nodded. "I don't know that much about this side of the river. I know that Home Depot is a couple of miles from here. Once we reach the interstate, we'll have some options."

Lauren eased up to the front of her seat. She could only observe Sam's silhouette against the ambient light entering the limo from the front windshield. All of the rear windows had been darkened for privacy.

"Sam, can you recall the way you drove into the city?"

Sam sighed. "Sort of. I realize it's been less than a week since we drove here. A lot has happened since then to clutter my old brain. I do know that I avoided the interstate. I like back roads, so we took Route 6 most of the way until Interstate 80. From there, I just remember driving through one nonstop big city using the phone's routing suggestions to the hotel."

"That'll be past the Garden State, right, honey?" said Lauren inquisitively. She was referring to the Garden State Parkway that runs north-south across New Jersey from Cape May near Delaware until it reached the New York state line.

"Yes," he replied before pausing to gather his thoughts. "Well, that helps somewhat. It's quite a walk through some heavily populated areas. A map would be nice."

"We'll make that a priority as we make our way toward the interstate," suggested Lauren. "I suppose we can ask for directions." Her tone of voice changed, reflecting her doubtfulness.

"Yeah, because our fellow man has been so helpful so far," added Asher.

"We'll just follow the sun," suggested Sam.

Lauren laughed. "Spoken like a true country boy, Grandpa Sam."

Asher joined his wife on the edge of the limousine's rear seat. He grew pensive. "Let's talk about that for a moment. Considering what we've been through, you know, experiencing the depravity of man, are we better off traveling during the day or at night?"

Lauren shrugged. "I know I said we should leave it all behind us, but consider this. We were carjacked in broad daylight and beaten down. Nobody stopped to help us."

"We didn't even see them coming, and it was daytime," added Sam.

"That's my fault," said Asher apologetically. "I was showing you guys the sights rather than being aware of our surroundings. I won't let my guard down again. I promise you that."

"Me too," added Lauren. "We've got to be on our toes at all times."

Sam weighed in. "I look at it two ways. What is safest, and what is practical. The heat index has to be over a hundred degrees during the daytime. Trying to walk any length of time will exhaust us and maybe even make us sick if we can't find more water." He rapped the side of the box with his knuckles.

"However, from a safety standpoint, we can observe our surroundings better during the day," added Lauren. "In other words, we can see them coming, unlike at night when we could be surprised."

Asher had been thinking about this. "It's almost as if we have two trips to take. The first is from here to the suburbs outside the greater Newark area." He turned in his seat to face Lauren. "You know, past Clifton, Parsippany, and Troy Hills."

"I don't think we've ever been that far west from the city. I do know that some of the Random House executives have homes there, but they stay in apartments during the workweek. Those are much nicer areas than where we are now, or even Secaucus or East Rutherford."

"That's what I mean," continued Asher. "Once we get into those suburbs and then the countryside, like this Route 6 Sam mentioned, we could safely walk at night when it's a little cooler."

"During the daytime, we'll stick to the major highways until we're out of this densely populated area," added Lauren. "Tempting as it might be to take a shortcut, I believe we're more likely to run into trouble on a side street."

"Plus, there's strength in numbers," Sam added. "I imagine most people will be fleeing the city on major streets and highways. We can follow the herd, as they say on the farm."

"Agreed," said Asher. "So in the morning, at first light, we'll hit the road."

"Okay," said Lauren.

Sam turned toward the front of the limousine, where Cat had stretched out. "Whadya think, Cat?" She didn't respond. He repeated her name. "Cat?" Concerned, he reached out to touch her leg, when they heard the gentle snore of the young teen who'd been through so much.

"There's your answer," said Lauren with a chuckle. "First light it is."

CHAPTER TWENTY-TWO

Monday
Rockefeller Plaza
New York

"Dad, Dad, wake up. Somebody's inside the store." Matthew gently shook his father, hoping to ease him awake without drawing attention to themselves. He'd slept lightly, and in his half-sleepy state, he mistook the commotion for a dream. When a woman's voice began to plead to be left alone, Matthew forced himself to sit up and focus his senses on the activity inside the retail store.

"What is it?" asked John as he forced his weary body to sit upright. The aches and pains were unlike any he'd experienced in recent memory. Working around their farm generated muscle sore-ness at times. The encounters of the last couple of days had left him feeling as if he'd been hit by a bus.

"Dad, I think there's a girl out there who needs our help," replied Matthew as he leapt to his feet.

John listened. He heard shuffling sounds and a man's voice. It was muffled, so he was unable to discern what was being said. He cleared the fog of sleep out of his brain and tried to recall the layout of the store. It was a fairly open space, especially after looters had been through it looking for anything of value, not to mention he and Matthew had taken apart displays to make their bedding.

"We don't need the drama, son," John said, but his words fell on deaf ears. Matthew had drawn his pistols and flung open the storage room door, rushing into the space without hesitation.

"Get your hands off her! Both of you!" he shouted. When a gunshot exploded inside the store, John sprang into action. He, too, pulled his weapons and charged out of the storeroom to provide his son backup.

"Hold on, man! We're just playin'!" one of the men shouted with hands held high and his pants around his ankles.

"Yeah! Um, he's my boyfriend," the girl added.

"What about that guy?" Matthew asked, his guns waving back and forth between the two young men.

"He's my buddy. We're just messin' around."

John joined his son's side and made a quick assessment. These twenty-somethings were just partying. Not his kind of party. But certainly not the kind of attack Matthew or any other person might assume. He whispered to his son, "Lower your guns. I've got this."

During the pause, the young men dressed themselves, and the woman slid off the counter and adjusted her clothing.

"You can't just shoot at people, you know." The girl's voice had a hint of incredulity.

"I thought ..." Matthew tried to explain, but his words didn't come out.

"He was trying to help." John attempted an explanation. "We've been on the road, and we've seen a lot of bad things happening to good people."

"He could have killed us!" said one of the men, who took a step toward John with his fists balled up. The first light of dawn had begun to find its way into Midtown Manhattan.

"That was a warning shot," countered John insincerely. "If he wanted you dead, you would be. Why don't we all go about our business?"

"Not in the mood, dude," said the woman dryly. She grabbed her boyfriend by the hand and dragged him toward the entrance, where a small crowd of sleepy-eyed homeless people had gathered to witness the activity.

"Yeah. Whatevs," the boyfriend said. As he and his friends left the store, he stuck his arm in the air and flipped the Cubbison men the bird.

Matthew holstered his weapons and flipped them off in return, with both hands. He shouted after them, "I was just trying to help!"

John also secured his gun and took a deep breath. After the shooting in Weehawken when he and Matthew had been jumped by men attempting to steal their bicycles, John had been concerned about the impact taking someone's life would have on Matthew. On the one hand, John was appreciative that his son was able to act decisively to save his life. However, the ease with which his son killed the young man and the apparent lack of psychological impact had concerned him.

Now it appeared his son had adopted a shoot first, ask questions later mentality. Granted, John was beginning to recognize that a powerless world was also a lawless world; however, pulling your weapon at the first sign of trouble could result in an unnecessary gunfight.

He gently placed his hand on his son's shoulder and asked, "Are you okay?"

Matthew nodded without responding at first. Then after a brief pause, he mumbled, "I was trying to help. I mean, I thought they were raping her."

"Listen, that assumption was warranted considering everything going on around us. Next time, let's ease into the situation." John made sure he had Matthew's full attention. "Together. Okay?"

He frowned and nodded. Then he pointed toward the door, where the crowd had grown larger. "Um, we'd better go."

John was concerned by the number of people blocking the door. What did they want? Their guns? He whispered to Matthew, "Step behind me and slip into the storeroom. Find the emergency exit."

"I don't remember seeing one," said Matthew.

"It has to be there. It wasn't important to locate it last night. Go on. I'll be right behind you."

As instructed, Matthew placed his dad between him and the growing mob of people. He hunched down and walked quickly into the storeroom. John stood his ground, staring down the people outside, who were becoming more vocal. He kept his right hand on the pistol's grip, ready to draw.

"Found it," said Matthew in a loud whisper as he stuck his head through the storeroom door.

John didn't hesitate. He walked backwards until he reached the opening. Then he turned and quickly followed Matthew to the emergency exit. They pushed the panic bar on the large steel door and burst into an alleyway behind the shops. The stench of garbage and city sewers immediately hit their nostrils. It just served to remind them they were in unfamiliar territory.

"This way!" Matthew exclaimed as he spotted a corridor under the parking garage leading toward West Forty-Ninth Street.

Seconds later, they were standing in the middle of disabled taxis and vehicles that had been busily transporting people around Manhattan last Friday night. Doors and trunk lids were flung open. The windows of locked vehicles had been smashed. Debris was everywhere. As were the dead and the injured. It was a grim reminder to John of the challenges his father and daughter faced when the grid collapsed.

With a sigh, he closed his eyes for a moment. He shook his head in dismay as he realized a few hours of sleep did nothing to quell the apocalyptic nightmare wrought by the perfect storm.

CHAPTER TWENTY-THREE

Monday
Weehawken, New Jersey

Asher was the first to awaken that morning, his body sore from the physical activity of the day before. Not unexpectedly after consuming as much water as possible out of the fire hydrant, he found himself desperately needing to relieve himself. However, he didn't want to wake up the others by opening the door, as they were most definitely sound asleep. So he sat there and tried to visualize their day to take his mind off his need to pee.

Because of their close proximity to Central Park, he and Lauren took frequent walks on the weekends when weather permitted. There were marked trails throughout the vast park that provided distances. Also, their Apple watches had a built-in application that measured their distance. The app also provided them data on their walk, like miles per hour and heart rate.

A casual pace of twenty minutes per mile would yield three miles per hour. A brisk walk, a fifteen-minute mile, equated to four miles per hour. While he and Lauren were certainly capable of that pace even in their weakened condition, he doubted Sam and Cat could maintain a brisk walk for more than an hour before dropping off the pace precipitously. He felt an average of three miles an hour was doable. The question was how far would their stamina take them?

Approximately thirteen hours of daylight would certainly provide them the ability to travel nearly forty miles in a day. However, the heat index, their lack of stamina, and extraneous circumstances, such as Humvee-stealing-thugs getting in the way, all played a factor.

Asher squirmed in his seat, trying to talk himself out of bolting through the door to whip it out in the middle of the road. To make matters worse, his mouth was dry from sleeping in an upright position. It was not unlike the airline flights he'd taken during which he fell asleep. His head would roll from side to side, mouth opening and closing depending upon where it stopped. The enclosed confines of the aircraft sucked the moisture out of him, oftentimes leaving him dehydrated. The limousine was having a similar effect. He resisted the urge to gulp down half a bottle of water. He'd surely pee his pants then, he thought to himself.

His mind wandered again. If they could make their way to the Westbrook Mall that day, the trip would become less risky. Going from memory, he thought Wayne, New Jersey, where the mall was located, was about twenty miles from New York City.

"Eight hours, max," he muttered to himself. They could slow their pace and take frequent breaks and make it to there by day's end. From Interstate 80, he presumed Sam could lead them to the Cubbisons' farm.

He leaned back in the seat and began to sway back and forth, gently tapping his head against the headrest in an effort to clear the clutter out of his brain. He repeatedly studied the other members of the group, watching and hoping for signs of them stirring awake. Soon, he'd have to just go for it.

He closed his eyes for a moment and then opened them, looking past the limo's bar toward Cat. At first, he scowled, lowering his eyebrows as he focused on movement in front of the car. Then his eyes grew wide out of concern, as there was a group of people walking toward them. Despite his need to pee, he had a bigger problem. They were about to have company.

He started with Lauren. "Honey, wake up. Somebody's coming."

She struggled to become coherent, looking around the limo as if she was unsure how she got there. New book launch parties with too many cocktails came to mind. Those were her rare opportunities to land in the back of a limousine.

"Sam," said Asher as he leaned forward and gently shook his leg, "somebody's coming. You need to wake up. You too, Cat."

Within seconds, everyone was fully awake and turning in their seat to observe the approaching men and women walking toward the driver's door. They appeared to be empty-handed, mostly looking at the limo out of curiosity.

"What do we do?" asked Cat. They were picking up the pace as they walked down a slight slope.

"Stay still," replied Sam.

"What if they try to get in?" she asked nervously. She was squirming in her seat, her eyes darting between the approaching group and her companions.

"The doors are locked," replied Lauren reassuringly. "I think they'll move on."

"I see a crowbar!" said Sam loudly.

Asher saw it at the same time. One of the men took the lead as the group approached. He'd been holding the crowbar in his right hand next to his leg, so it was easily missed. If he tried the driver's door and found it locked, he'd bludgeon the car windows until he gained entry. He had to think fast.

Asher flung the passenger door open and quickly stepped out. His sudden appearance startled the group, who stopped in their tracks before moving backwards a few paces.

"Hey! Good morning!" said Asher nonchalantly. He held his hands to the sides to show he wasn't a threat.

"Whatcha got in there?" the man with the crowbar said after he found his voice.

"Just my wife and a couple of friends. We thought it would be a good place to sleep for the night."

"Got any liquor?" asked one of the women.

Asher laughed. "Nah. Somebody beat us to it. They broke all the glasses on the way out." He pointed around his feet to show the newcomers that the limousine had already been pillaged. Then he added, "We're about to leave if you guys want it. It's a little stuffy in there, but it's not a bad place to sleep."

The crowbar spoke for the group. "Nah, man. We don't need sleep. We're hunting booze. Got any?"

"No, sorry. We're not drinkers."

As he finished his response, Lauren, Sam and Cat began to pour out of the limo. Sam turned to retrieve the box of water. However, Asher imperceptibly shook his head just enough for Sam to turn back toward the group staring them down.

The man holding the crowbar gave them a long stare and then nodded his head to the others in the group, who followed him down the street past the limo. All of them studied Asher and the others as they passed, leery of the people who'd slept in the limousine.

As soon as they'd passed, Asher gently pushed the others in the back, urging them to go in the opposite direction. He grabbed the box of water and kept it close to his body.

"I have to go to the bathroom," announced Cat as she looked around.

"We all do, trust me," replied Asher. He'd just realized it had been twenty-four hours since he had.

"There's a building up ahead under construction," Sam observed. He began walking briskly in front of the group and then picked up the pace considerably. "A porta-potty! No, two of them. In the parking lot."

They broke out in a jog with Cat leading the way, easily passing her grandfather. Lauren breezed past him as well, arguing that ladies were first in all things, including using the portable toilets.

Sam and Asher didn't care about who had first dibs at the port-a-potty. They did just fine taking care of business between the disabled cars in the parking lot.

"It stinks in here!" complained Cat.

"I know. I'm hovering, too," added Lauren with a little too much information for the guys.

After a long minute, everyone finished their business and gathered on the sidewalk across from a row of houses. Several people had emerged from their homes to watch the group's antics.

"What time do you think it is?" asked Cat.

Sam instinctively patted the left side of his pants in search of his pocket watch. He remembered he'd left it at home. At least he remembered the wind-up timepiece would work, unlike the fancy new computer watches. He shrugged.

"Probably after seven," Lauren replied. Then as if she anticipated the next question, she added, "It gets dark around seven thirty."

"Guys, I've given this some thought," began Asher as he pointed up the street. He wanted to keep moving, especially with the curious onlookers staring at them. "If we can keep a steady pace of walking a mile every twenty minutes, we can take breaks and still manage to get to the less populated areas by nightfall."

"That's ambitious, young man," said Sam.

"I know. I'm not even sure I'm capable of walking forty miles in a day. I do know, however, the farther west we travel, the less danger we should be in. Even by noon, we could be past the worst neighborhoods."

Lauren didn't want to frighten anyone although she knew fear was a great motivator. Asher was right. The sooner they got past Secaucus and East Rutherford, the less likely they'd run into trouble.

Cat couldn't grasp the calculations. She hated math, once arguing with her mother that there was no practical use for stupid things like algebra and geometry. Besides, if she needed to perform any complicated equations, they had calculators and Google for that. She could, however, remember the trauma she'd experienced, and didn't want to deal with something like that again.

She found a new spring in her step. "Come on, Grandpa Sam. We can keep up, can't we?"

"I'll follow until I fall down. Lead the way!"

CHAPTER TWENTY-FOUR

Monday
Midtown Manhattan
New York

John knew their trek to New York's city hall and One Police Plaza might not yield any results. It was certainly a long shot, but they had to try. All he knew was that they were alive and possibly with a couple led by a man named Asher Doyle. His father had worked for the NYPD commissioner at one time. Perhaps, with some name-dropping, someone would go the extra mile to help them.

They headed down Fifth Avenue toward the Empire State Building. The iconic structure rose over twelve hundred feet into the air, standing proud amongst the other skyscrapers of the city. As they walked down Fifth Avenue, he couldn't help but notice the retailers' signage. Virtually all the names were recognizable.

John wasn't much of a shopper. Really, no member of his family was. He chuckled to himself as he recalled taking Grandpa Sam to Binghamton, New York, so he could be properly dressed to accompany Cat to the museums. At the end of the day, Sam was comfortable in the types of clothes he always wore. He simply purchased newer versions.

He marveled at the fact every single storefront had been breached and the merchandise looted. Even the Starbucks had partially opened bags of coffee strewn about the sidewalk near its entrance. Plastic drinking cups were seen in use by the displaced residents occupying the city.

Farther down the street, the mayhem that had occurred since Friday night was evident outside the Adidas flagship store and especially at the multilevel NBA merchandise store. Even the famed logo featuring the silhouette of a player dribbling the basketball against a red, white, and blue background had been partially torn off its bracket.

The adjacent Best Buy store had been emptied of its contents. Even Matthew found it comical that looters would find any value in electronics under the circumstances. It was simply another example of opportunists ransacking the retailers because they could without fear of law enforcement intervening.

Armed guards flanked the main entrance to the New York Public Library. John imagined that was the case at the museums in the city as well. He wasn't knowledgeable about the scientific aspects of solar flares and power grids collapsing. However, he assumed that at some point, the nation would get back on its feet. He quietly applauded the NYPD for stepping in to preserve historical artifacts from the looters. Flat-screen televisions could be rebuilt. Antiquities could not.

"Do you have any idea how far we have to go?" asked Matthew as he dutifully kept pace with his dad. His curiosity about the broken storefronts led him to stop at times, wondering if there might be something he'd be interested in taking for himself.

"I think it's a few miles," John replied. "An hour, maybe, unless we pick up the pace."

"Too hungry," Matthew muttered.

John understood. It was going to become an issue soon. Fresh water, too. Every eatery they came across had been emptied. He even considered the break rooms of offices as an option. Many of their entrances, closed to the public after business hours, had steel doors or cages blocking access. To enter, he and Matthew would have to get creative and take risks. It was too early for that.

As they reached the intersection of Broadway and Fifth Avenue, they got confused as to which street to take to city hall. At first, people were uncooperative or simply didn't know where city hall was located. When he changed the question to ask about One Police Plaza, the answers came quickly.

They walked in silence for several minutes, taking in the sights while being hyperaware of their surroundings. Both of them were diligent about keeping their guns hidden from view. Their goal was to blend in with the crowd. John told his son to avoid eye contact with others and not to appear threatening. Walk confidently and with purpose, he suggested.

They remained in the center of the street, using the cars as a buffer between the hundreds of people who were waking up from whatever nook and cranny had been available to them the night before. The Converse store, like Adidas, was hugely popular that morning. John couldn't imagine that there was anything left to acquire, yet people were still walking out with boxes of shoes.

He suddenly stopped. "Hey, I've got an idea. Look." He pointed to the plate-glass windows to the right of Converse.

"Wrong kid, Dad," said Matthew sarcastically. "Cat's the museum type."

John slowly walked toward the Museum of Ice Cream, one of the few businesses or organizations along Fifth Avenue that hadn't been broken into. Probably, he thought at first, because any ice cream inside would've melted long ago.

"You wanna break in there with me?" asked John.

"And slurp up melted ice cream off the floor? Um, no thanks."

John laughed at his son's sense of humor, sarcastic as it was, despite what they'd faced thus far. "No ice cream. But what if they have cones and toppings? You know, nuts, candies, and stuff like that."

Matthew looked around the street as if he was concerned they might be arrested. Naturally, there were no cops to be found, as defending storefronts would've been futile.

"Sure. Why not? I could go for a waffle cone full of M&Ms for breakfast."

So that was exactly what he got. John eased in front of the plate glass that turned at a forty-five-degree angle to the front façade. He faced away from the store and then slammed the base of his pistol's grip into the glass. It cracked, slowly at first. Then, with a little help from the heel of his boot, it shattered and crashed into the store.

"That was easy," he commented to Matthew as he kicked a few remaining shards out of the aluminum frame.

Matthew laughed. "Look. Nobody even noticed."

"Come on," John said as he led the way. The interior was well lit from the sun shining through the ceiling-to-floor plate-glass windows. They moved quickly along the wall to avoid detection by any pedestrians. John wanted first dibs on anything edible.

After rushing through the gift shop, they entered another open space that was designed to be a tasting room of sorts. The smell of spoiled milk filled the room, but it didn't deter the guys from having their way with the toppings.

A variety of nuts, including pecans, walnuts, almonds and peanuts, were stored in plastic containers. In Ziploc-type bags were dried fruits and raisins. A variety of granola and cereals were also available.

The guys spent almost an hour filling the baggies with their personalized, handpicked form of trail mix. Not unexpectedly, Matthew focused on the sweets like chocolate chips and sugary cereals. John forced him to add some balance, as he called it, in the form of dried fruit and nuts. Matthew absolutely objected to eating raisins. He said they made him feel shriveled, whatever that meant.

After filling their bellies and stuffing two shopping totes with their personalized trail mix, the guys found the restroom and freshened up using the last water they discovered in the gravity-filled faucets.

Refreshed and in high spirits, they marched down Broadway at a quick pace toward the area around City Hall Park, where both the police headquarters and the main city administration buildings were located. They were still several blocks away, near the Jacob Javits Federal Building, when they began to see the thousands of people filling the streets and sidewalks leading to the city complex.

It appeared they were not the only ones searching for loved ones in the most densely populated area in America.

CHAPTER TWENTY-FIVE

Monday
Cubbison's Farm
Harford, Pennsylvania

Emma Cubbison didn't know why she bothered any fitful attempt to sleep. Luke, her oldest son by all of a hot minute after a painful twenty-one-hour labor produced her twin boys, was too hyped up to sleep following the confrontation with the four men the evening before. He insisted on taking the night shift as he patrolled the farm nearest to the main house.

At least three times during the night, Emma lay awake, tossing and turning before checking on Luke. She offered to stay with him; however, he insisted she sleep. She tried and couldn't. Her level of anxiety had grown exponentially since the men had demanded food out of their market plus a cow for good measure.

She'd found a wind-up alarm clock in a guest bedroom drawer. It was the old-school kind with the twin bells on top that would rattle the tooth fillings out of anyone who deployed the device. After John and Matthew had left for New York, she'd set the alarm for four thirty, her normal wakeup time, in order to maintain some sense of normality. She was already dressed and pacing the floor when the mechanical device startled the bejesus out of her.

As part of her routine, Emma ran the diesel generators at regular intervals throughout the day. One was designed to provide temporary power to the main house, including its refrigeration units. The other was shared between the barn and Cubbison's Market.

Her goal was to maintain the temperatures in the coolers and freezers to keep their food fresh. She also used it as an opportunity to charge batteries for everything from power tools to flashlights to her handheld mixer. After an hour's run time, she'd shut the gennies off for four hours during the daytime and eight hours after sunset.

She exited through the back door with the flashlight to start up the CAT diesel generator. Sam and John had carefully selected the used unit more than a decade ago because of its near-silent operation and its protection against power surges. With the success of the market and the large amount of inventory stored inside, they'd purchased a newer model to preserve their investment.

Each of the units held forty gallons of diesel. They were kept full, as they were rarely used. The day before, Emma had Luke provide her an estimate of how many gallons of farm diesel they had stored. She performed some calculations and determined they could follow her run schedule for nearly six months.

The question was whether the power would be restored in that time frame and, if not, where they would replenish their supply. Grandpa Sam had always bragged he could make his own farm diesel if push came to shove, although Emma had never witnessed him do it. Well, in the history of modern mankind, if push had ever come to shove, now was the time. "We'll see," she'd mumbled to herself.

Once the generator started, several lights came on in the house, which immediately grabbed Luke's attention. He came hustling toward the kitchen door to greet his mother. She hugged him like any mom would embrace a long-lost son. Despite her confidence in him, she still remained concerned for his safety while he wandered the farm alone.

"Did you see or hear anything?" she asked.

"Just a couple of screech owls. The chickens got fired up for a minute or two, then calmed down. There might have been a fox roaming around. Otherwise, no bad guys."

"Let me make you some breakfast," she said with a smile reflecting her relief. She patted her son on the cheek and mussed his hair. "You're getting shaggy like your brother. I know I'm not as cute as your friend at Sport Clips, but I do cut your father's hair, you know."

Luke laughed. "Yeah, I know. We all do. Maybe I'll give it a try first?"

She gave him a playful shove. "Come on. Let's gather some eggs and check on the rambunctious chickens. Then we need to talk about how we're gonna get ready for tonight's visit from those moochers."

After turning on the generator at the market and gathering the eggs, they fixed breakfast together and talked. First, they speculated on how the search for Cat and Grandpa Sam was going. Luke was more optimistic than his mother. She'd mentally prepared herself for a week or two before they returned. Mainly, she didn't want to get her hopes up only to be disappointed at the end of every day.

While they ate, Luke relayed his thoughts on securing the farm and protecting themselves. "I've given this a lot of thought based on what Dad told us and common sense, really."

"I'm listening," interrupted Emma, proud to see her son blossoming into a man determined to protect his family.

"Okay. Well, first of all, we can slow them down. They came on foot yesterday. Think about it. How much food could they have taken? Sure, they could sling their rifles over their shoulders, but at best, they could carry one box of canned goods each."

"Those Mason jars are heavy," added Emma.

"Right. And if they were in those heavy wood crates Grandpa Sam has stacked in the shed, the weight goes up."

"So what are you suggesting?" she asked.

"Let's give them something, with conditions, of course."

"Really?"

Luke finished his breakfast and slid his plate to the side so the table was cleared in front of him. He drew on it with his finger as he spoke. "I'm going to assume they come again on foot. I've never seen these guys before. They were all heavy, you know. Fat, almost. If they had horses or an old vehicle that still ran, they would've been riding."

"Makes sense," Emma interjected and then added, "That also means they must be staying nearby. Even if we'd given them food last night, they would have to carry it back to where they're hiding out."

"One guy said they had babies to feed," added Luke. "He might've been lying."

Emma leaned back in her chair. Her face became serious. "Or if he's not, it could be a figure of speech meaning children. You know, not literally babies. I think it's logical to assume they are holed up in somebody's house."

"Exactly," said Luke. "So my idea is this. We need to buy some time until Dad and the others get home. What if we give them four crates of throwaway food?"

"Throwaway food?" asked Emma.

"Yeah. You know, stuff that doesn't have great nutritional value. Canned cobblers, for example. Or foods in the market that don't have a long shelf life."

"They'll come back," Emma asserted.

"Okay, maybe they will. If they have to walk more than a few miles, it'll take them an hour or more to get to where they're hiding. If they come back, it might be tomorrow. We can either do it again or be better prepared."

"Or John will be home."

"Yes."

Emma thought for a moment and nodded her head in agreement. "I'll also write them a note. Tell them this is it. They can go elsewhere for their next meal. They'll probably ignore it, but if they respond, we might be able to figure out who they are or where they're located."

"And in the note, tell them no cow," added Luke and then shook his head. "Idiots."

Emma cleared their plates and left them in the sink. Then she checked Sam's pocket watch. "You need to get some sleep."

"Um, about that," began Luke as he stood from the table. "Mom, there's no way I could sleep right now. It would be a wasted effort."

Emma sighed and closed her eyes to make them stop twitching, a sign of sleep deprivation. She knew where Luke was coming from.

"Okay. So what's next?"

"I'd like to ride to the adjacent farms on a little scouting mission. I'll take my rifle and the binoculars. I wanna find out where these jerks are living."

"That's too dangerous, son."

"Mom, I'll be careful. Besides, we know everyone for miles on all sides of us. None of them are dangerous. Some of them might even be willing to help."

Emma was hesitant. "I don't know, Luke."

Luke continued to make his case. "Plus, if we can locate them, it opens up our options."

"What kind of options?" she asked.

He took a deep breath and exhaled. He subconsciously dropped his hand to the pistol holstered on his hip.

"Well, that'll be up to them and how they react to our generosity. If they wanna fight, then I believe we should take the fight to them."

CHAPTER TWENTY-SIX

Monday
Secaucus, New Jersey

Every November, Asher took a moment to watch the start of the New York City Marathon. The twenty-six-mile race began on Staten Island and wound its way through all five boroughs before finishing in Central Park near their condo. Well over fifty thousand men and women participated in the annual event. The first two miles were confined to Staten Island before the tens of thousands of runners crossed the Verrazzano Bridge into Brooklyn.

Even at this early hour, it appeared a marathon, of sorts, was making its way west through Secaucus, New Jersey. The participants weren't wearing skimpy athletic wear with numbered signs affixed to their shirts. Today, the masses wore all the clothes they could, in layers, despite the anticipated heat that hovered over the city like the Black Death.

They moved slowly. Deliberately. Packed together with little room to maneuver. They kept their conversations to a minimum. Frankly, there was nothing to talk about. NFL exhibition games had ceased to exist. Baseball was cancelled. Politics was of no interest to anyone. At this moment, everyone hated any government or elected official for failing to anticipate the catastrophe.

Most of the conversations centered around how long the crisis would last and what people planned on doing to survive until then. The near universal answer was they didn't know about how prolonged the outage would be. In the meantime, they were going to find a farm that would take them in until the world righted itself.

Asher and Sam were walking together, directly behind Lauren and Cat, who seemed to have more energy than the guys. They were adept at finding holes and gaps in the crowd to shoot through to gain a slight advantage. The challenge for Asher and Sam was to keep up with them.

"Sam, if I've heard it once, I've heard it a dozen times. These people think they're gonna knock on farmers' doors, like yours, and be invited in with welcome arms."

Sam laughed and looked around to see if anyone was eavesdropping on their conversation. "Not gonna happen. There aren't that many family-run farming operations like ours. You know, that's capable of wholesaling to grocery stores or who have retail markets like ours. These farmers they plan on moving in with only have crops for their immediate family and nearby loved ones. They're in for a rude awakening."

"It's gonna be hard to turn them away," said Asher. "I mean, look at them. I thought we were in dire straits. These people are at the end of their ropes."

Sam agreed. "They're never gonna make it to the farms. To be honest, it's gonna be difficult for us to get home, and we know where we're going. Sort of."

The two continued pushing through groups of people who separated them from Lauren and Cat from time to time. Asher expressed his frustration at the pace they were traveling. It had been several hours since they started on the freeway, and they were just now crossing the Hackensack River.

"We're going too slow to get tired," he commented. "How do you feel, Sam?"

"Fine. By the way, this all looks familiar to me. I remember seeing the MetLife stadium on the way into New York."

"That's good because we haven't exactly gone searching for a map. Every car or truck we come upon seems to have been ransacked."

Sam pointed toward an off-ramp that led to several hotels. "People are trying to find a place to rest or are searching for food. I'm glad we came across these empty backpacks along the way. Nobody needs to see our water supply, even though it's not much."

Lauren looked back toward Asher. They were thirty feet ahead of him. "It's thinning a little!"

He gave her a thumbs-up and a much-needed smile. "Well, if you're comfortable this is the road you took in, we'll keep moving west. It eventually runs into Interstate 80 near the Willowbrook Mall. If we still feel like we need a map at that point, I'm sure there will be places to look."

Sam stretched his arms over his head to work out the kinks in his shoulders. "It'll be dark by the time we get there, don't you think?"

"Yeah, considering the slow crawl. We'll just keep pluggin' along."

"Food is gonna become an issue." Sam was stating the obvious although it was intended to remind Asher that they had a thirteen-year-old with them. Adults could mentally prepare themselves to skip a day's worth of meals. Teens were different.

"I've thought about this," said Asher. "This area we just passed through is known for its gang activity. Bloods. Crips. Latin Kings. Elements of these gangs are all over Secaucus. Really, anywhere between the Hackensack River and the Hudson. Territories are big deals for these people."

"It gets better this way, I assume," said Sam, pointing ahead of them.

"Yeah, so I've heard. When I'm on set, there are a lot of law enforcement personnel around. Some are retired, acting as consul-tants. Others are VIP guests of the show because *Blue Bloods* is one of the most popular in New York history. Crossing the Passaic River up ahead makes a difference in crime activity. It's almost as if politi-cians and cops drew a line in the sand using the river as the boundary."

"That still seems like a pretty wide swath of real estate for the gangbangers to do their thing," opined Sam.

Asher laughed. "Yeah. Well, when I was growing up and my dad was on the force, the Hackensack was the so-called line in the sand. I guess the gangs erased it at some point."

Lauren and Cat found their way to an on-ramp that widened the road to ten lanes. The number of cars traveling westbound on the night of the perfect storm became fewer. Refugees were able to spread out more, which allowed their group to walk faster.

"What do you think about searching for food in these neighbor-hoods?" Lauren asked when the men caught up to them. "Cat's hungry."

Asher sighed and looked up the sixteen-foot-tall sound-barrier walls that lined both sides of State Road Three. The neighborhoods were old but certainly not subjected to gang activity. Nonetheless, it would require them to take risks by breaking and entering. Asher didn't want to come face-to-face with a frightened homeowner's loaded weapon.

"I understand. It's still a long way to the interstate. More than half a day if I'm correct. Here's the thing. It's going to take some time to find a retail business to search or a willing resident to give us some-thing. It's gonna delay us is all I'm saying."

Cat crossed her arms in front of her. Dejected, she said, "I under-stand. I'd rather get to where we're going. I'm not gonna die of starva-tion." She reached into her backpack and drank some of her allocation of water. Like their stamina, Asher hoped the water could last them the rest of the day.

After the brief respite, they continued on. Talking very little, they ticked off the miles without incident. However, they fell far short of their day-one goal of reaching the Willowbrook Mall. They were able to cross the line in the sand, breathing a sigh of relief as they entered the town of Clifton, where an abundance of food opportunities was laid out in front of them.

To fill their bellies, they'd have to employ some ingenuity. They weren't the first hungry travelers to arrive on the west side of the Passaic River.

CHAPTER TWENTY-SEVEN

Monday
Cubbison's Farm
Harford, Pennsylvania

Emma and Luke talked about a few things she could do while he was away. First, they identified the farms closest to theirs. Luke chose to head toward the interstate, the same direction the men seemed to come from. Stranded travelers would naturally migrate toward the countryside in search of refuge and food. While they agreed the logical direction for refugees would be into town on the west side of the interstate, a few might venture toward the east where the Cubbisons' farm was located. Especially, as Emma pointed out, if they saw the billboard along Interstate 81.

Luke resisted the urge to ride his father's horse, which was much faster than his. If there was trouble, he knew how to calm his mare down, whereas John's stallion was still high-spirited. Although the family had no plans for breeding him in the past, they hadn't made the decision to have him castrated either. The county's veterinarian, Dr. Caitlin Quinn, had urged John to castrate the stallion if he didn't plan to breed it. Now, with the world changing, Luke was glad they still had breeding as an option.

He avoided riding along County Road 547. Although it was a more direct route to the adjacent farms, even hot, softer asphalt can cause problems if a horse has sensitive hooves. Besides, he thought, nothing tells a neighbor *here I come* like the clomping sound of hooves on pavement. Luke felt he could use the trails he'd ridden a hundred times over the years to approach the rear of the farm properties without being detected by the men.

He made his way through the adjacent woods and found the slightly overgrown trail that led through the state's property. The rolling hills obscured his view of the open farmland behind until he reached the clearing on the other side of the woods. That was when he saw smoke twisting into the sky from Stanley's barn.

Gene Stanley, a widower, had refused to sell his property years ago to Grandpa Sam. Although the property wasn't immediately adjacent to Cubbison's, it would serve a useful purpose to separate the breeds of cattle the Cubbisons owned. Also, Stanley's barn was designed to move cattle into haulers to take to auction, something the Cubbisons didn't have at the time.

Luke urged his horse to pick up the pace as he took a roundabout way toward the Stanley home. He wanted to ride along the tree line in case he was noticed by the occupants. The closer he got to the farmhouse and adjacent barns, the more concerned he became for Mr. Stanley's safety. Two of his outbuildings had been burned to the ground. The barn was still smoldering. The small farmhouse, however, was still intact.

He had to make a decision. He assumed the four men who'd threatened them could be occupying Stanley's home. Mr. Stanley was in poor health, having been diagnosed with multiple myeloma a couple of years ago. The rare form of cancer was a death sentence, as there was no cure. He'd fought the good fight but only had a few years to live, if even. Luke doubted the man could ward off any marauders, especially with the firepower they wielded.

The other thing he noticed was that Stanley's cattle, maybe fifty head, were scattered about in the fields at the rear of the property. They were easily visible from his perch atop his horse at the tree line. They couldn't necessarily be seen from the house.

He would have to dash across a clearing of nearly a thousand yards. It was a risky move; however, it was also before seven in the morning. Farm people were up and at 'em at that hour. Traveling refugees might not be.

Luke calmed his nerves by taking a deep breath. He readied his rifle. Grandpa Sam had taught him how to shoot while riding at full gallop, just like in the Western movies, he'd said. More importantly, Luke's mare had accompanied him on many hunting trips and was not spooked by the loud report of gunfire. If he had to shoot at the men, he could back them off with return fire. Also, he decided, he'd flee to the west, toward Harford, before he entered the woods again. This would throw the thugs off if they thought about pursuing him.

"Let's go, girl," he said as he dug his heels into the mare's sides and slapped her backside. She didn't hesitate to break out of her walking pace into a gallop.

Luke kept his rifle in his right hand, pointed in the direction of the smoldering barn. By design, he kept the gutted structure between his approach and the house. When he reached the barn, he exhaled for the first time and took in a deep breath of charred wood and burnt hay. Luke fought to stifle the cough that rose from his chest. He pulled his shirt over his mouth to mute the choking sound.

He dismounted and tied his mare to a water trough. A few mosquitos hovered about, so he shooed them away. He cupped the water to his nose and sniffed it. It didn't have a chemical smell or reek of rotten eggs, an indication of bacteria.

He rolled his head around his neck and began to walk around the barn. He knew the property and recalled there were only a couple of hundred feet between the barn, the smokehouse, which was the home's original kitchen, and the farmhouse. The smokehouse had been burned to its foundation. Only the chimney remained.

Luke had a plan that was risky and stupid. He knew there were at least four men in the party, and at least one of them possessed an AR-15. His hunting rifle was no match for the rapid-fire capability of the semiautomatic gun. If he encountered anyone inside, he'd have to move quickly to kill the men first.

He shuddered at the thought. He'd never shot at anyone, much less taken a life. He convinced himself he could do it to protect his mom and their farm. He justified it on the basis that these men had threatened them first. He cautioned himself not to freeze under pressure. If he did, it would cost him his life.

With another deep breath, Luke ran across the open lawn toward the kitchen door, which had been left open. He arrived at the door and pressed his back against the outside wall to gather his thoughts.

"Now or never," he whispered to himself. After a quick prayer asking God for safety, he swung his body into the door opening, where he immediately froze.

CHAPTER TWENTY-EIGHT

Monday
Stanley's Farm
Harford, Pennsylvania

Mr. Stanley's rotting corpse lay facedown in the kitchen. He'd been bludgeoned to death, probably with the bloodied rolling pin that lay near his crushed skull. The stench of death was overwhelmed by the smell of burnt rags and cereal on top of the stove. Apparently, someone had found a way to light the gas appliance without power and intended to burn the farmhouse with Stanley in it. They must not have waited to see if they were successful.

Luke reached a logical conclusion that the house was empty. However, he decided to search the clapboard-covered, two-story home, nonetheless. He shouldered his rifle and drew his pistol. He paused to listen for any discernible sound.

A snore. A cough. Someone speaking.

Nothing.

Walking heel to toe, as if he were stalking a deer, Luke eased his way from room to room. The house had been torn apart with no cabinet door left closed and no sofa cushion undisturbed. Out of spite, the vandals broke all the china in the dining room and smashed pictures wherever they hung on the wall. Their actions were spiteful and disrespectful although they paled in comparison to beating the elderly man to death.

After several minutes during which time Luke confirmed the house was empty, he returned to the kitchen with a bedspread. With due respect, he covered Stanley's body and said a prayer. He didn't bother to search the home for anything of value, as it had been cleaned out.

Besides, Mr. Stanley's most valuable assets were quietly grazing in the undiscovered pasture on the other side of the tree line. Luke planned on riding by there on the way home to get a head count and check on their condition. Fortunately, it was summertime, so the hay fields provided plenty of grasses to feed on. He considered the possibility he could lead them through the woods to the Cubbisons' farm.

He untied his horse and saddled up, ready to make his way west toward the next farm, which was barely a quarter of a mile away. The property had been purchased by a young Mennonite family just a year ago. It was small and would only yield enough crops to feed the Yoders. However, the two-story farmhouse was better suited for multiple families.

A four-wheeler path connected the two properties. In the early 1900s, the entire tract comprising the Stanley place and the Yoders' had been owned by the Roywell Miller family, one of the original nine founders of Harford Township. The large tract had been split and sold when Mr. Miller moved to head up a large railway system across the Midwest.

Luke's approach to the Yoders' property was more tenuous. Mr. Yoder ran a small company that built storage buildings, carports, animal shelters, and even gazebos. Large projects, like barns, would be built by a small army of Mennonite men who'd join together to construct the barn in just days.

Sadly, Luke was aware that the Mennonite religion frowned

upon the use of guns. They were known to be skilled crossbow hunters. Luke sighed. Crossbows were no match for an AR-15. As he exited the four-wheeler trail and gazed upon the Yoders' home, he found what he was looking for.

At just a mile away, they were way too close to home for comfort.

CHAPTER TWENTY-NINE

Monday
Cubbison's Farm
Harford, Pennsylvania

While Luke was on his scouting mission, Emma wanted to keep busy, not only because there was a lot to do but to take her mind off the safety of her family.

She began by taking the diesel fuel numbers Luke had provided her before he left and calculating how long it would last. She was correct on her original assumption of six months. The big question was whether she should conserve further or rely upon Sam's ability to make biodiesel.

Emma had researched the problem of long-term power outages years ago. Freezer food would remain safe for forty-eight hours if the doors were kept closed. Refrigerated food would only last four hours, hence the reason she'd set up the generator schedule the way she did. Emma focused on cooking the perishable foods that were likely to spoil first.

She picked from the gardens only as necessary for that particular meal. Every time she did, she regretted hosting the large gathering the night the power grid collapsed. She'd fed all of those people with enough food to spare. That food could've fed her family of six for many weeks. Not to mention the fact that she'd only received half payment prior to the event. The second check would never be forthcoming.

As she worked around the farm, she began to contemplate ways to protect their home and supplies. A three-rail wooden fence bordered the county road fronting the farm. A barbed-wire fence with steel gates was installed around the entire perimeter. The farm gates at the entrance to their driveway were always open. She closed them and ran heavy-duty chains through the steel bars to lock it. For good measure, she powered up the bulldozer and pulled a wagon full of hay bales behind the gates to block the entry. If anyone approached with a vehicle, she hoped this barricade would deter them from coming up their driveway and even deny them access.

The Cubbisons had never had a need for a security alarm system or cameras. They'd never had a burglary in Sam's lifetime and beyond. Not that it mattered, as such devices designed to detect an intruder didn't work without power. The best she could do to monitor their perimeter was study the surrounding fields and the roadway with binoculars or her rifle scope. Emma wished they had dogs. She'd tie one up at strategic points around their home, hoping they'd sound the alarm by barking at an intruder.

The upper doors to the hayloft in the barn were perfectly positioned to monitor someone coming from the road as well as the fields behind their home where Luke had led the cattle. Its height provided an unobstructed view. The other sides could be observed on foot, although they were more vulnerable from the sides. However, with the two of them being prepared for trouble, they could provide decent protection.

By noon, Emma was finished with her preparations and was checking on her garden and feeding the livestock. She kept a wary eye on the road with a secondary focus on the back of the farm. They were surrounded by the state's gaming lands, which did not contain any roadways. There were horse and four-wheeler trails, however. She had to focus her concentration on the most likely direction that an attack might come from. Like Luke, she felt she could trust their immediate neighbors. They'd all been casual acquaintances for years. It was the interlopers, the refugees spilling into the countryside after abandoning their inoperative vehicles, who concerned her most.

Emma took up a position in the hayloft, roaming back and forth between the two doors before settling in at the front overlooking the market and the driveway. She sat on the edge of the opening, allowing her legs to dangle freely over the ground. She'd set her rifle aside and used the twenty-year-old Bushnell binoculars to surveil the property. For nearly an hour, she didn't see another living being except for the occasional bird flying by. The world appeared almost lifeless.

Finally, out of the corner of her eye, she caught a glimpse of Luke emerging from the woods to the west. She stood and got a better look at him through her binoculars. He had two white milking goats in tow. She was anxious to hear the story behind them but was grateful for the addition to their livestock. Between the chickens and the goats, eggs, milk, and cheese could be made to supplement their vegetables. They could live off the frozen meat for several months before slaughtering any steers although the guys planned on hunting for deer first.

Emma, thrilled to see Luke safe, scrambled out of the hayloft and ran to meet him at the cross-fencing. He waved to her when she stood on the rails.

"How did it go?" she asked loudly.

Luke's grim face told the story. She was relieved that he was home alive. Relief turned to apprehension when he told her what he'd discovered. Their adversaries were sadistic killers without any standard of morals or decency. She and Luke had their hands full.

CHAPTER THIRTY

Monday
City Hall Park
Lower Manhattan
New York

"Geez, Dad. What the hell are we gonna do with this?" Matthew stood in amazement at the masses of humanity that pushed and shoved their way toward City Hall Park. If the goal of world leaders was to create absolute equality across all of mankind, there was nothing better than a catastrophic event of this magnitude to accomplish their purpose.

All races and nationalities were before them, shoulder to shoulder, sharing a singular purpose—enter City Hall Plaza to search for loved ones on the temporary bulletin boards. Initially, John had been told, there were notification boards set up nearby at the police commissioner's building a quarter mile to their east. According to others trying to enter the City Hall Plaza, the entry to One Police Plaza became so congested, the bulletin boards had been moved and were supplemented with larger ones from local schools.

Now they were lined up in front of city hall in Steve Flanders Square, protected by a police-guarded rope line. Those seeking to post pictures of lost family members, or wishing to view the messages posted by others, had to walk into the tree-lined square single file. It was a long, tedious process that had been backlogged for hours.

Yesterday, John had been told, a near-riot broke out as people began to collapse from heat exhaustion. With no water available and the cramped conditions stifling air flow, people began to pass out by the dozens. Sadly, their fellow man didn't always come to their aid, opting instead to step over them to keep their place in line.

John struck up a conversation with a man who, although disheveled, was dressed in a suit. "Do you have any idea how long it's taking to get through this line?"

The man shrugged. "I'm going on what others have said. Eight hours? Maybe longer. It moves slowly but steadily."

"Who are you looking for?" John asked.

"My girlfriend. I was in the city for a business meeting and brought her along. We were having dinner, and she went to the restroom. When the lights went out, we got separated, and I couldn't find her. She wasn't at the hotel, so I waited by our rental car in the parking garage for almost a day. Nothing." He grimaced as he shook his head in despair. Then he added, "I can't believe she'd try to walk back to Connecticut, but I guess it's possible. I thought I'd check here first."

John could relate to the man's plight. "We're searching for my dad and young daughter. We're from Pennsylvania." The concern in his voice was obvious.

The man nodded, indicating his understanding of John's emotional state. "From the people I've talked to, most of them are from outside the city. You know, tourists or people like me."

John inched forward as the group began to surge forward. "I'm not so sure they posted on these boards. I do have a lead, though."

"What is it?"

"Well, they were caught in the fire at Rockefeller Center. I found a nurse who was part of the medical staff treating the injured. They remembered my dad and Cat. The two of them were being assisted by a local man and his wife. Asher Doyle."

"That's something. Do you know where the guy lives?"

"No, which is the other reason we're here. I hoped to check the bulletin boards, but really, I wanted to find my way into the property appraiser's office or maybe even deed records. They told me this whole complex makes up city hall."

The man thought for a moment. "I might have a suggestion although I don't want to encourage you to get out of line. You know, in case you want to check the boards first."

"What is it?" asked John.

"The city's register's office is actually located farther down from City Hall Plaza. I'm a real estate agent helping a client look for office space."

John glanced at Matthew, who shrugged. "How do I get there?"

"You're gonna have to get out of this train wreck, for starters. I'd head west over to Church Street. Then south about eight blocks or so until you see St. Paul's Chapel. Take a left on Fulton, and that'll lead you over to Williams. Find Williams and John Street."

John repeated the directions back to the man from Connecticut, thanked him for his advice, and then forced his way out of the crowd with Matthew in tow. After being pushed, shoved, and cursed, they made their way to the uncrowded Church Street.

"Matthew, I hope this isn't a mistake," said John as he caught his breath. The sun's rays were beating down upon the concrete jungle, causing the heat index to soar.

"You know, Dad, if they had help from these local people, I doubt they came down here to post a notice. Even if they did, who knows if it's still up on the bulletin board. I never expected this kinda crowd."

John wanted to agree with his son. However, he silently admonished himself for breaking his *leave no stone unturned* rule. They began walking as instructed, searching for John Street. They were unaware that several of the east-west streets changed names when they crossed Broadway. Eventually, the vast, green space in front of historic St. Paul's Chapel came into view. The guys asked for directions and found people more accommodating. One man offered to lead them to the register's office in exchange for something to eat. With food scarce, John declined the offer.

Eventually, they made their way to the intersection of John and William Streets. They both turned in a circle, looking straight up at the high-rise buildings at the intersection. None of them were marked as being the city register's office.

"Did we miss it?" asked Matthew.

John responded with a question. "He did say the corner of John and William, right?"

"Yeah, I think so," replied Matthew, who began quizzing passersby. None of them had any idea.

"This is madness!" John exclaimed as he wandered several paces down William Street toward the New York Federal Reserve building. "Why would anybody want to live like this?"

Matthew walked away from his father and climbed through the steel scaffolding supports adjacent to the one building that didn't have a retail tenant on the bottom floor. A sliding door had been covered with opaque paper to prevent people from looking inside. The rest of the windows were blocked with a real estate company's lease signs.

Matthew thought for a moment, and then he said, "Screw it." Like his dad had done at the ice-cream museum, he smacked the plate glass with his gun until it cracked. With a mule kick, he knocked it inward through the thick paper covering it.

John heard the glass break and rushed to join his son. "You're right. We gotta start somewhere."

Minutes later, they'd wandered through an office space that was being readied for a new tenant. Deeper into the building, they located a bank of elevators that contained a directory. That was where they discovered the location of the register's office.

"Who would ever want to deal with all of this to come to the register's office?" asked John. "I bet Michelle doesn't get ten people a day to her office." He was referring to Michelle Estabrook, the Susquehanna County Recorder of Deeds, whom he'd grown up with. It would be fodder for a future debate regarding city life versus country living, fast pace versus slow.

They found the stairwell, where they began the arduous task of trudging up thirteen floors in the dark and stifling conditions. Out of breath and exhausted, they made their way into the hallway where the register's office was located. Because it had been after business hours when the grid collapsed, every entry into the offices was locked up.

Matthew sighed. "Now what?"

John walked down the length of the corridor, using the ambient light from the windows located at each end of the hallway to assess his options. The ceilings were smooth drywall, not drop ceilings as he'd hoped. Each of the doors was solid wood with lock guards on the strike plates to prevent tampering. The plexiglass divider separating public servants from the public was reinforced with roll-down steel grates. The place was a veritable fortress.

After staring out the window at the adjacent building, John collapsed in a heap onto the musty, carpeted floor. He buried his face in his hands and began to cry. His emotions poured out of him as he thought he'd reached another dead end. While he wallowed in his sorrow, Matthew took action.

He returned to the stairwell and retrieved the standpipe hose used in case of fire. He also smashed the glass of a wall-mounted case holding a large fire extinguisher. Using the heavy brass end of the hose, he began to beat the drywall separating the hallway from the offices.

"What are you doing?" asked John, who leapt to his feet.

"In the cop shows, they call it B&E," Matthew answered with a grin. "Wanna help?"

John picked up the heavy fire extinguisher and began pounding the wall. They located the soft spot between the steel studs. Once they breached the wall, they began tearing away at the drywall until it was large enough for them to slide through. After twenty minutes of pounding, they successfully cleared enough space to step between the studs into an administrator's office.

John and Matthew enthusiastically exchanged high fives. They found their way through the maze of offices until they located a large open space full of hardcover binders. Each binder held a computer-generated report of all the property owners in New York City.

"Asher Doyle. Right, Dad?"

"That's right, son," John replied as he walked through the tall bookcase-like shelves containing hundreds of binders. "I'm sure all of this is on computer, but hey, now it's old school like back in the Stone Age."

"Here are the *D*s!" exclaimed Matthew. "There's a bunch of them."

John joined his side. He ran his fingers down the spines of the binders until he came to several that read *Do-*. He pulled a couple of them down and laid them on a worktable nearby. Using his flashlight, he and Matthew flipped open the binders and began their search.

"Mine starts with Douglas," said Matthew, who quickly shoved it aside.

"I've got Doyle." John leaned closer to the book, his heart racing as he prayed to find the man's name listed. "There are so many," he mumbled as he ran his finger along the computer-generated pages. Then he slammed his fist hard against the book before flinging it off the table. It hit the waxed linoleum floor with a hard thud.

"No Asher Doyle?"

"Hell no. He must rent. Dammit, son!" John's eyes welled up in tears again.

Matthew tried to comfort his father by putting his arm around his shoulders. Then he thought for a moment. He looked toward the front of the offices.

"Maybe they have a white pages here? This is the government. They have useless stuff like that."

John regained his composure and took a deep breath. Then he grabbed his son's arm. "I'm sorry. It's just so frustrating. We're getting nowhere."

"I know, Dad. While we're here, let's try the white pages again. If that doesn't work out, let's search the offices for anything that might help us. Okay?"

John nodded and patted his son on the back. They spent the next hour rummaging through the register's office. They found the white pages, both current and past. However, none of them had a listing for Asher Doyle. The Doyles, like so many Americans nowadays, simply didn't have a traditional landline.

They were back to square one.

CHAPTER THIRTY-ONE

Monday
Cubbison's Farm
Harford, Pennsylvania

Luke slept hard for three hours. Accustomed to going to bed after eleven and waking long before dawn, three hours sufficed under the circumstances. He freshened up, donned his Realtree camo pants and an olive drab green tee shirt, and found his way to the kitchen, where his mom had laid out some biscuits she'd baked early that morning. Luke judiciously spread on some butter and squirted honey they'd purchased a week ago from a local farmer who was an accomplished beekeeper. The beekeeper had made a deal with Emma to trade jars of the delicacy in exchange for soups she'd preserved in Mason jars. The honey was a hit with her customers.

He was still munching on a biscuit as he grabbed his rifle and holstered his pistol. He grimaced and shook his head as he walked out the door in search of his mother. He was fully awake, not dreaming, and yes, he was walking out of his home prepared to shoot anyone who threatened his family.

"Mom!" he shouted, his eyes darting between the barn, the storage buildings, and the market.

"I'm in here!" she shouted back. Luke noticed the back door of the market was slightly ajar as he approached. The hot, stagnant air, coupled with the livestock being so close to the house, had drawn biting flies from around the farm. Luke was already concerned that the cattle would overgraze the undersized pens adjacent to the main house and the barn. He hadn't thought about how the dry weather of August would allow the mineral-rich cow pats to fester and therefore attract flies, which also fed on the cows' blood.

"Hey," he greeted her. "Tryin' to keep the flies out?"

"Vicious biters," she grumbled as she smacked at her thigh. Emma rarely wore jeans in the summertime as indicated by her tan, toned body. With the herd so close to the house, she might have to change her habits.

With a grunt, she lifted a wooden crate onto the checkout counter and turned the notepad toward her. She began to scribble some notes, which piqued Luke's curiosity.

"How's it goin'?"

"I've decided to kill 'em," she began, causing Luke's eyes to grow wide. Then she smiled as she finished her sentence. "With kindness."

"Oh, okay," he said hesitantly. He wasn't sure where his mother was going with this. He'd reconciled himself to the fact that they would have to kill them at some point. Hopefully, not today.

"Trust me, after last night, I'd rather shoot them. Especially after what you've told me. I can only imagine what happened to the Yoder family."

"Mom, I feel like I should've done something. You know, at least moved closer to get a better look. It was just, um, you're my priority."

Emma sighed and stopped writing the notes. She turned to Luke and grabbed him by his broad shoulders. She was proud of her son, who seemed to rationally think through his decisions. "Our family has to be our number one concern. Your dad and brother are searching a city of ten million people for Sam and Cat. Lord knows what they've encountered. Our job, as they say, is to hold down the fort. We need to minimize the drama and make sure they have a home to come back to."

Luke frowned and nodded. He diverted his attention to the crate and the notepad. "You seem to have a plan. Kill them with kindness?"

She smiled and hugged her son. "It probably won't work, but you never know." She led him to the counter and showed him the crate. It was full of jars and canned goods. Luke lifted it slightly.

"Jeez, that's heavy," he noted.

"I'm making four of these, one for each man. If they don't squander it, these crates will each feed a family of four for at least two days. I'm even writing out a note for each crate explaining how to prepare the food and a schedule so they don't run out."

"Do you think they can read?" asked Luke sarcastically.

Emma playfully pushed her son in the chest. "Surely one of them can manage. If they are staying at the Yoders' place, then this heavy load will wear them down by the time they walk the mile and a half. Those guys didn't strike me as being very athletic."

"Yeah, fat and lazy, from what I could see."

"Exactly. Now, I hate being extorted like this. However, my idea is to give them two days' worth, and hopefully our family will be back together by the time these jerks return for more."

"Then what?" asked Luke.

"Well, that'll be up to your dad and grandpa," she began in her reply. She took a deep breath. "Son, once we feed them, they'll keep coming back. Eventually, they'll decide our home is a better place to live than the Yoders' property. I have an opinion that goes against everything I believe in, but it may be necessary under the circumstances."

Luke glanced around the market to observe the shelves. They were thinner than normal because his mom had used a lot of their stored foods for the party. This week, she'd planned on replenishing their stock. Instead, they found themselves fighting off marauders.

"Just tell me, Mom. I'm not gonna be shocked at anything."

"Well." She paused to lean against the counter. With a grunt, as if to emphasize her idea, she moved the heavy crate over slightly. "These guys have a long walk back. By the time they reach the Stanley place, they'll be exhausted. They'll have to shoulder their rifles, and they'll let their guard down."

"I think I see where you're headed with this," interjected Luke.

"It's risky, but I think it would work," she continued. "If they come back for a second load, whether tomorrow or the next day, we need to put an end to this before they try to take it all. After we confirm they are headed back to the Yoders', you and I will take the horses and race to Stanley's. Just as they crest that hill near the driveway, we'll be waiting for them."

"Kill them?" Luke had to ask the question.

Emma lowered her head and nodded. "Especially if it's just the same four guys. That means they're leaving any women and children at the Yoders'. We take out the men who can threaten us the most. Secure their weapons, and to make it look like they were attacked by someone else, we'll retrieve our food."

Luke stepped forward and looked into the crate. "Are they all going to be this full?"

"Yes."

"Mom, this is a lot of food."

"I know. I wanted to make it last two days. When I felt how heavy it was, my mind wandered, so I came up with this plan."

Luke stood a little taller and turned to his mom. "We need this food for our family to survive. How would we feel if these four crates were the difference between our living a few more days and dying? Screw this. I think we should do it tonight."

"But—" Emma started to object, but Luke cut her off.

"Mom, you didn't see what they did to Mr. Stanley. It's one thing to hit an old man in the back of the head to knock him out. This was sadistic. They don't care about human life. Plus, there was no reason for them to burn everything down unless they're cold-blooded. I'm not gonna give them a second chance to do that to us."

"You wanna do this tonight?" she asked with a sudden feeling of dread.

Luke, however, was confident. "Absolutely."

CHAPTER THIRTY-TWO

Monday
Clifton, New Jersey

"They walk just like they drive." Cat's casual statement revealed the innocence that was still within her. As the group crested the rise atop the bridge spanning the Passaic River, the bedroom community of Clifton came into view. Abundant trees covered neighborhood homes. The eight-lane highway that carried a hundred forty thousand vehicles per day was littered with the broken-down remains of modern transportation. Interestingly, as Cat pointed out, those refugees moving west tended to stay in their own lanes. The eastbound lanes toward New York carried far fewer pedestrians.

As they continued to walk, Lauren and Cat made casual conversation. For the first time, Lauren noticed her clothes were soiled and hanging on her. She wondered whether it was possible to lose that much weight so quickly. Subconsciously, she tugged at the straps of the backpack they'd found on the highway. It reeked of motor oil for some reason.

She glanced back at Sam, who had soiled his pants. They'd found an empty suitcase on the highway and a pair of jeans that fit him. He was lucky.

A wave of sadness came over her as she realized all of her worldly possessions were gone. Her clothes. Her mementos. Their wedding photos. Childhood keepsakes. Everything had either been stolen by the carjackers or left behind at 455 Central Park West, where the other residents were probably picking through them.

Lauren noticed the abundance of retailers on both sides of the highway. She walked a little closer to Cat and lowered her voice as she spoke.

"Um, Cat." She hesitated to broach the subject. "I just realized I don't have any clothes except these."

Cat turned toward Lauren. Her eyes studied her from head to toe. The young girl would not consider herself a fashionista, but she certainly understood that a gal had to have more than one outfit.

"I'm sure my mom will let you wear hers, but she's bigger than you are. You know what I mean. Taller and heavier."

Lauren nodded. She had been afraid that her petite frame might be different from Emma's. She looked toward the stores again. She glanced back at her tall, lanky husband and managed a smile.

"What about your dad? Is he kinda similar in size to Asher?"

Cat turned to assess Asher's body type. "Shorter and heavier. Asher's more like my brothers. They are a little taller than Dad and thinner, too."

Lauren looked skyward and closed her eyes momentarily. *Great. It's just me who'll have to go through life in the same clothes.* She didn't want to risk the lives of the group over material items such as clothing. However, she suspected Harford didn't have the kind of options that surrounded them at the moment.

"I sense a conspiracy brewing up there," said Sam with a laugh. "What are you two plotting?"

"We need to go shopping to find Lauren some clothes," replied Cat without hesitation.

"Oh, I'll be okay," Lauren lied. "I'm sure there will be another place to look."

"Not really," said Sam. "I'm starting to recall the drive into the city. Once we reach the interstate, it's pretty much hilly countryside. Plus, I'm sure they've cleaned out the Dollar General in Harford already."

Asher walked ahead of the girls, studying both sides of the road to assess their options. Everyone was tired and hungry. There was still plenty of daylight to continue walking. However, searching for food and even fresh clothing might not be a bad idea.

"Okay, everyone. Compared to what we just came through, Clifton is not exactly a high-crime neighborhood. That said, everything has changed, so we have to be careful. If we're going to take a break, this looks like a good spot."

Lauren surveyed both sides of the highway. "Where do we start?"

"We need to think outside the box," began Asher. "For example, everybody ransacked the grocery stores and restaurants within hours of the power outage. We need alternative businesses that might have food products that others didn't think about."

"Like the movie theater?" asked Cat, pointing at the sixteen-screen AMC theater.

"Exactly," replied Asher, impressed with the young girl's instincts. "Look, we're not worried about nutrition at this point. We need calories for energy."

"Lots of calories in movie theater foods," Lauren said with a chuckle. She was already salivating over Haribo Goldbears and Twizzlers.

"Do you wanna start there?" asked Asher.

"Oh, yeah," replied Lauren as she led the way over the concrete barriers separating the east and westbound lanes. She'd put her clothing needs out of her mind for the moment. With a little luck, she could pig out on the real heavyweights of the candy world, Whoppers and Junior Mints, until she and Emma wore the same jeans size.

They walked through the parking lot, glancing toward the Barnes

& Noble bookstore. The window display showed a poster bearing the smiling face of a disaster thriller author hawking his book about nuclear winter.

"Look at that guy," said Asher sarcastically. "Big grin on his face. He's probably loving this crap."

"No doubt," Sam added as he shook his head side to side.

They made their way around the front of the massive building to enter through the front doors. The plate-glass windows were smashed, which dashed their hopes of finding anything to eat, Nonetheless, they entered hoping to discover anything edible that others had missed.

The southern exposure provided an abundance of light in the lobby. They stepped over the red velvet ropes that created a serpentine line toward the ticket window.

Sam suddenly stopped and pointed toward a display to the left of the booth. "Wait. Captain America is a woman?"

Lauren, who was not a frequent moviegoer, was the resident expert within the group regarding literary trends. "That happened years ago, Sam."

"Oh. Um, why?"

Lauren grimaced. "Well, do you remember when Disney purchased the Marvel franchise?"

"No."

Lauren stopped to study Sam's face to determine if he was pulling her leg. He appeared to be serious. "Anyway, Disney purchased Marvel and reimagined many of their characters."

"So they made Captain America a woman."

"Yes."

Sam jutted out his jaw and nodded. Then he bluntly explained, "I don't watch the news much anymore. I'll live longer for it."

Asher had already searched behind the food service counters of the theater. "Well, no surprise here. This has been cleaned out. Let's look for a storeroom."

"Asher, they have a dine-in theater here. I went to the one in

Scranton with Mom and Dad. I remember the kitchen was close to it."

Asher smiled and winked at Sam. Cat was impressing him with her fortitude and insight. She'd been forced to grow up fast and continued to contribute to their survival.

He stood still for a moment to focus his attention on the dark hallway leading into the right side of the theater complex. He glanced to his right at the ticket sales counter. The registers had been pried open and the money taken out. Underneath the counters, there were supplies such as brochures and rolls of receipt paper. He moved behind them to get a closer look because he had a thought.

Theater employees were required to enter the movies while in progress to make sure their customers were behaving. He dropped to his knees and started pulling items off the shelves.

"What are you looking for?" asked Lauren, who joined his side.

"It's a long shot," he mumbled as he crawled to the next ticket counter. He forced his head under the counter and reached for the back of the shelf. He felt around until he found a rectangular cardboard box. "Bingo!"

Thump!

Asher's head hit the underside of the countertop.

"Ow! Dammit!" Asher cursed his clumsiness.

"Watch your head," said Lauren, laughing at her husband.

"Shut up," he playfully fired back as he extricated himself from the counter and fell backwards against the wall.

He pulled out one of the squeeze flashlights bearing the AMC logo. He gave it a gentle squeeze. The three LED lights brightened the shelving under the counter.

"I sure wish we'd had these in the tunnel," commented Sam before adding, "Good work, Asher."

Asher used the light to scan the rest of the shelves and found another box of twelve flashlights. He tucked it under his arm and distributed the other box to the group.

Lauren examined the small device, which included a wristband. "What about batteries?"

"It's rechargeable," replied Asher. He began to turn the small crank located within the flashlight. He wasn't sure how long the charge would last, not that it mattered. It could be recharged quickly.

"I feel better about venturing in there," said Sam, pointing over his shoulder.

The group fanned out with Asher leading the way and Lauren bringing up the rear. They didn't go into the theaters in order to avoid anyone sleeping or hiding inside. Instead, they focused on storage doors and searching for the kitchen that serviced the dine-in theater.

"I see swinging doors," said Sam, using his flashlight to wash the wall. In the pitch darkness, the tiny LEDs were remarkably bright.

"Lauren, Cat, wait here, please. Sam, you're with me."

Asher's serious tone reflected his apprehension. Once Sam was by his side, he took a deep breath and slowly opened the kitchen doors.

CHAPTER THIRTY-THREE

Monday
Cubbison's Farm
Harford, Pennsylvania

While Luke prepared their horses for a quick trip to Stanley's farm to surveil the property and assess the possibility of driving his cattle to the Cubbisons', Emma finished preparing the crates of food. She'd changed her approach from her original plan of killing them with kindness, which had entailed balanced meals stored in glass Mason jars. She filled the crates with canned goods instead. They were just as heavy but less likely to break if dropped. If they were gonna go through with their planned ambush, she wanted to make sure they minimized the loss of food.

"I'm ready when you are," said Luke, who poked his head through the back door. Emma set the crates near the barn-door entrance to the market and stood over them for a moment with her hands on her hips. She'd written one additional note to the men, which basically said don't mistake her generosity for a sign of weakness.

She emerged from the market and immediately shielded her eyes from the bright sun. Luke tossed a John Deere mesh cap to her like it was a Frisbee. "Here. It's one of Dad's."

Emma pulled her hair into a ponytail and forced it through the plastic clasp in the back of the cap. After an adjustment, she gave Luke a thumbs-up and followed him toward the barn.

"I've put scabbards on our horses to carry our rifles and saddle-bags for extra ammo. Also, I rigged up a saddlebag and scabbard on a third horse, which we'll take with us as backup."

"Why?" she asked.

"Well, we haven't used this trail in a while, and there are some fallen limbs and low-slung branches. I thought I'd clean up the trail a little because after this is over, we're gonna need to get back home quickly. You know, just in case."

Emma hadn't thought about the *just in case* part of this planned ambush. If they failed to kill all the men or if there were more who might come looking for them, she and Luke would need to be prepared to defend the farm.

"Very smart, son. Also, when we get back, let's set up barriers in front of the market that we can hide behind. We'll make them look decorative, so they won't be so obvious. If these thugs decide to come down the driveway, they might think we're in the market instead of closer to the gate."

The two of them mounted up and slowly made their way across the fields toward the woods. It was midday, and they wouldn't be able to spend a lot of time conducting surveillance. As they approached the clearing near the side of the Stanley place, Luke tied off the extra horse and studied their surroundings with the binoculars. Comfort-able they were alone, he and his mom broke cover and rode at a steady gallop toward Mr. Stanley's driveway.

Mr. Stanley had adorned both sides of the driveway entrance with large clusters of quartz. Gathered from washes, streams, and abandoned mining operations, the quartz piled near his entrance not only glistened in the sunlight but would provide some protective cover for the Cubbisons as they awaited the men returning with the crates.

"I've got an idea," said Luke after he and his mom sat atop their horses for a few moments. He dismounted and wandered past the quartz into the middle of the road to study the other side. Then he continued, "We'll tie the horses behind the house when we return. You lie low behind this pile. I'll use those trees across the street to hide behind."

"A crossfire," said Emma, who rode her horse into the middle of the road. She urged her horse to take a few steps toward the crest of the hill. "Stanley put the entrance of his driveway here so he could see both ways when he pulled out. It's a long steady rise from the bottom to this point. They'll be exhausted by the time they reached this spot."

"Right," said Luke as he walked to a large oak tree that had grown with a V-shaped trunk. "I'll stay behind that tree. As soon as they hit this spot, we'll catch 'em in a crossfire. They won't have anywhere to turn for cover."

"They'll never know what hit 'em," said Emma. She eased off her horse and held her by the reins. She turned to Luke. "Honey, are you sure about this? We're planning on murdering these people."

The word *murder* sent shock waves through Luke's body. Somehow, he'd convinced himself that killing the men was the best course of action to protect his family and their farm. He looked up and down the road and gestured toward the Stanley home. He spoke as they walked. "Is it, Mom? Murder, I mean."

"Please, son. Don't get me wrong. I just don't know what else to call it."

Luke pointed toward the house as he retrieved the reins of his horse, which were tied off to the fence. "Would you like me to show you what they did to Mr. Stanley? That's murder."

"All right," she said. "I suppose you could call what we're planning some kind of retribution or even punishment. Heck, vigilante justice is more like it. But—" Her voice trailed off.

Luke had a better term that was probably not intended for what they were planning, but it fit nonetheless. "I prefer to look at it as a preemptive strike. It's us against them. Our army versus their army. Remember, they came to our home and threatened us first. If they show up tonight, and I expect they will, then that confirms their intentions. Our response is to stop them before they take their violence to the next level."

"It'll break the peace," added Emma. She sighed as she added, "However, I agree that it's necessary. I just wish you and I didn't have to go it alone."

"Mom, the next time they may not come at the appointed hour. I was scared all night that they had a sneak attack planned all along. Honestly, I'm surprised they didn't. I would've."

Emma nodded in agreement. Leading her into a false sense of security would've been the smart move. She glanced toward the open front door of the house. Part of her wanted to see what Luke had witnessed. The other part of her might be so repulsed that she'd opt to have a shoot-out with the men at her front gate. She suppressed her emotions. Their plan was solid, so they'd see it through.

Call it what you will.

CHAPTER THIRTY-FOUR

Monday
AMC Theaters
Clifton, New Jersey

Asher directed Sam using hand signals. It was deathly quiet inside the large commercial kitchen operation. Polished stainless-steel appliances and worktables covered most of the space. Their undershelves were full of pots and pans used in the preparation of the limited menu. The stench of rotted food, most of which was left exactly where the staff had been preparing it, found its way into Asher's nostrils, causing him to yank his shirt over his mouth and nose.

Sam was the first to announce any good news. "I've got shelving full of food products. Undisturbed, too."

Asher frantically shined his light around the kitchen. He spotted two walk-in doors, one for the freezer and the other for refrigerated foods. He dared not open either one of them for fear of choking to death.

"I've got condiments and drinks over here. Also, buns and loaves of bread." He walked closer to illuminate the racks of bread. He held up a pack of burger buns to inspect for signs of mold. His chin dropped to his chest when he saw the underside covered with the telltale white, powdery fungus covered with green mold. He rummaged through the rest of the packs. They were all ruined, not that he was surprised considering the dark, humid conditions within the space.

"Not much to go on here, but at least it's something," said Sam, who set a #10 can of salsa on the stainless table with a thud.

Dejected, Asher added, "It's a bust on my side."

He joined Sam and inspected the pantry shelves along the wall. He was starting to see the makings of a meal, albeit limited.

Sam hoisted another can onto the table. This label read Rico's Gourmet Nacho cheese sauce.

Asher added a large jar of jalapenos and began his search for the final ingredient. "Got it!" he exclaimed cheerily. He reached high overhead and pulled down a box of tortilla chips. They were in business.

With one hand toting the box and the other lighting the way, he carried the chips out to Lauren and Cat. They had to stifle their exuberance when he told them they were having nachos. Both were fans of the staple of Tex-Mex cuisine.

Sam found four medium-sized mixing bowls and some spatulas. He pushed the unfinished meals off the nearest table and took on the role of chef. After locating the counter-mounted can opener, he scooped out the ingredients into the bowls, trying his best to compartmentalize the salsa, cheese, and jalapenos separately.

He proudly presented the first two bowls to Asher to be delivered to their guests. "I call this the Ultimate Post-Apocalyptic Nachos!"

He and Asher got a hearty laugh, the first since the power grid collapsed. Each of the bowls had twenty ounces of cheese and salsa, together with at least a cup of jalapenos. As Asher made his way to the door with the first two bowls, he busted out laughing.

"We're gonna get the shits."

Half an hour later, they did.

CHAPTER THIRTY-FIVE

Monday
Cubbison's Farm
Harford, Pennsylvania

That afternoon as the shadows began to stretch across Cubbison's Farm, Emma and Luke scrambled to get ready. Each had their own duties to get prepared, so they worked separately until the time the men were expected to arrive. Without acknowledging it to one another, neither wanted to discuss the planned ambush for fear of changing their minds. They knew what had to be done. What they were uncertain of was whether they could pull the trigger to end another human being's life.

Luke remained behind in the woods to secure their third horse and provide it some hay to graze on. Emma rode back and immediately fired up the old bulldozer. She hadn't used it often because the Cubbison men were always there to run the machine. However, she was familiar with its operation, having watched John and Sam over the years.

First, she found a heavy-duty chain. She backed up to their useless pickups and SUVs, and she wrapped the hooks around the frame of the bulldozer. Next, after attaching the other end of the chains to the vehicles' frames, she towed them toward the driveway, where she parked them in a haphazard way between the gated entrance and the market.

She and Luke could take up positions near the gate so they could get a clean shot at their assailants before they came onto the farm. The men would have little cover at the gate and would have to rely upon their marksmanship to gain the upper hand. She hoped her close proximity to them, with ample cover, would deter them from taking that risk.

The goal, she kept telling herself, was to encourage them to pick up the crates and walk back toward the Yoders' place. She and Luke would observe them for as long as they had a line of sight through the binoculars. Once they were confirmed to be walking back, the two would ride as quickly as the trail would allow to get into position.

"It's almost time, Mom," said Luke. He handed her the rifle she was used to hunting with. "I've got the horses ready behind the market with two more rifles. If something happens at the road and we lose these, we'll have backups."

She took the gun and cradled it in her arms against her belly. She pulled the bill of John's cap over her eyes to help shield the setting sun. She'd grown accustomed to having her husband's John Deere hat on and wondered if she'd ever take it off. Maybe, she thought, when he was home in her arms.

"I took the crates and set them in the road. We'll settle in behind the trucks and wait."

She paused for a moment and allowed her chin to drop to her chest. After adjusting the cap, perhaps to secure it or to gain John's strength through the inanimate object, she added, "Are you sure about this? I mean, one hundred percent?"

"Mom, I am positive. If we don't face this threat now, we may not get to fight them on our own terms."

"What if they're bluffing? Maybe the guns are for show?"

"They didn't use guns to beat Mr. Stanley to death."

"But what if they didn't kill Mr. Stanley?"

Luke shrugged. "Who knows? All I do know is that they didn't ask us nicely last night. And don't forget, they demanded a cow, too."

Emma turned away and looked skyward. She'd forgotten about that. She turned to Luke with her head cocked to the side. "What if we give them one?"

"What? No way," responded Luke.

"No, hold on. Hear me out. We want them moving slow and tired out. Right? Distracted and outside of their comfort zone."

Luke nodded in agreement. "Yeah, that's right."

She explained, "You know how to lead a calf. It's not easy. Frustrating, too. They sure as hell won't know what to do."

Luke laughed. "It wouldn't surprise me if they let it go or tied it off to a tree somewhere."

"It's just one more way to throw them off their game."

Luke didn't hesitate. "I'm on it." He started jogging toward the barn to get a rope. He'd practiced putting a halter on a calf all of his life. He also knew their livestock well. He could easily identify one that would respond to him but be stubborn as a mule when led by an untrained person without patience.

Twenty minutes later, he led a five-hundred-fifty-pound steer up the driveway toward the gate. With his mom's assistance, he loosely tied the beast to the fence near the crates of food. After taking up positions behind the vehicles, they waited.

Using his rifle scope, he stared at the first available clearing that allowed him to get a look at the men as they approached. It seemed like it was taking forever when he finally caught his first glimpse.

Leading the way was the man holding his AR-15 in one hand and a bottle of water in the other. Alongside was another one of the men, the mouthy one who demanded the cow.

"Shit!" said Luke loud enough for his mother to hear.

"What is it?"

"Dammit, Mom," Luke began, his profanity revealing his consternation. "They've got two kids with them."

CHAPTER THIRTY-SIX

Monday
Cubbison's Farm
Harford, Pennsylvania

"Are you kidding me?" asked Emma as she broke cover. She also pointed her rifle toward the group approaching the gate to get a better look. The four men from the night before were also accompanied by two boys not quite ten years old. She studied them carefully to determine if they were armed. Although they didn't have rifles, it was possible they had handguns tucked into their jeans. She wasn't positive, however.

"What do we do?" asked Luke.

Emma's mind raced, full of uncertainty. This was a gamechanger. She'd been conflicted over whether this was the proper course of action. She'd finally reconciled with God that killing the men was necessary to protect her family and punish the men for what they'd done to others since the collapse. Kids, on the other hand, were innocents in all this. They didn't deserve to die. She wasn't even sure if they deserved to be orphaned.

Luke's voice reflected his apprehension. "Mom? They're getting closer."

In a sense, she was frozen. Her mind raced, but her body couldn't move. *I need time to think!* She touched the bill of John's cap, and his face flashed into her mind. Then Cat's, Matthew's and Grandpa Sam's. Her family.

She had very little to go on as she judged the men who were approaching their farm. Who were they? Were they evil or simply desperate to feed their family? Had they killed others? Would they kill her and Luke? She recalled the statements they'd made the night before.

She'd asked for ammunition in trade. Their response had been mockery.

Fat chance, lady.

I've got some ammo for ya!

They'd demanded food and a cow. They'd told her when they'd be back. They'd assured her, *this ain't over, lady!* That could only mean one thing in her mind.

She took a deep breath and finally responded to Luke. "Nothing changes. Trust the plan."

Both of them turned their attention back to the front gate, which was only a few hundred feet from their position. They eased their rifles into view and trained them on the first two men, who were ostensibly the leaders of the group. Luke had already made a mental note to kill the man with the AR-15 first.

The four men gathered around the crates of food. With a wary eye on the parked vehicles and the market, they reached down to pick up the handwritten notes. The two boys took turns petting the cow. After some quiet discussion that neither Emma nor Luke could hear, the man with the AR-15 walked toward the steer and then raised his rifle in the direction of Luke.

"All right, this is a good start. But you ain't dictatin' the terms of our arrangement. We're not waitin' until no Thursday to come back. We'll be back tomorrow. We want double the food and another cow.

I've seen what you got back behind the barn. You can spare another."

"And another!" hollered the mouthy gunman. "Plus, we're thinkin' a horse or two might be a good idea. You got that!"

The men were shouting in the direction of Emma and Luke although they couldn't see their exact position.

Luke wanted to answer them with a barrage of expletives. However, he'd promised his mom she could do the talking. He glanced over at her, anxious to hear her response.

"When is this gonna end?" she shouted her question.

"When we say it does!" the mouthy gunman responded.

Then the oldest of the bunch, who raised his AR-15 menacingly in Emma's direction, spoke to her. "We told you yesterday, we've got mouths to feed."

Emma took a risk, perhaps to clear her conscious about what would be happening next. "Why did you kill Mr. Stanley?"

"He had it comin'," the mouthy one said loudly before he was cut off.

"We don't know nothin' about that," their leader lied before he quietly rebuked his partner. "Um ..." His voice went silent as he became unsure of what to say.

Emma made it easy for him. "Okay. You gotta deal. As long as you stay on that side of the gate, we'll help you out. Tomorrow, more food, another cow, but only one horse. Deal?"

The men spoke amongst themselves for half a minute before the leader shouted his response. "Deal. Same time tomorrow!"

Luke and Emma held their positions, nervously pointing their rifles in the direction of the group as they wrestled with the young steer, which wanted nothing to do with them. Foolishly, the men used the buttstock of the rifle to urge the steer to move along. While steers are more docile to handle than bulls, their instincts still react to abuse.

Luke could hear him snort from a hundred yards away. He mumbled under his breath, "Here it comes."

The steer kicked forward and then kicked backwards, catching mouthy in the thigh, sending the fool spinning to the ground. He groaned and complained until he was finally helped to his feet by his fellow marauders. It was an odd sight seeing the two kids each holding a side of the basket while the man limped along behind them. They pulled and tugged at the bull until they finally got him moving.

Emma stood from behind the pickup truck bed and moseyed toward the gate. A slight gust of hot wind picked up and blew her notes down the pavement toward the east. She followed the papers with her eyes. She knew what had to be done. She patted Luke on the shoulder once he'd joined her side.

"They signed their own death warrants. Let's roll."

CHAPTER THIRTY-SEVEN

Monday
Midtown Manhattan
New York

Despite the stuffiness of the register's office, it was still cooler than outside. John and Matthew gave one another pep talks. While they'd reached the end of their leads in New York, John was convinced that Sam and Cat would make their way home. Admittedly, he said he might regret not checking the bulletin boards at City Hall Plaza. However, he was willing to take the risk. His gut told him it was time to get back to the farm.

During their search for the white pages, the guys grabbed anything of value that they could carry. They scored a couple of backpacks and a duffel bag. Personal hygiene items were abundant. Office supplies included letter openers and battery-operated reading lights. The field assessors had compasses.

Then they broke into the vending machines to diversify their snacks with protein bars and energy foods. The five-gallon water coolers throughout the offices yielded fresh drinking water they used to fill the numerous sport bottles found on employees' desks. Neither Cubbison was worried about whether the employees might pass on their germs during the drinking process. A few other personal items like caps, sunblock, and sunglasses were a bonus.

With a map in hand, the two set out refreshed and ready to travel. They were approximately five miles from the entrances to the Lincoln Tunnel. They decided to take a different route into New Jersey this time just in case they could learn something about Cat and Sam.

They made their way west toward the Hudson River, stopping to pray at the North Tower Pool, the memorial to the heinous attacks by Islamic terrorists on 9/11. The long walk along West Street overlooking the river was far different from what they'd observed along Broadway and Fifth Avenue.

Evidence of looting was there; however, the bulk of activity related to people traveling up and down the major thoroughfare, attempting to get out of the city. Some opted for the Holland Tunnel and Interstate 78 to the south. Others, albeit fewer, headed north toward the Lincoln Tunnel.

Several times along the way, John and Matthew recalled the route they took into the city, vowing to avoid the neighborhood where they had been attacked. They also discussed whether they should walk through the populous townships on the New Jersey side of the river at night. They expected their journey to become more dangerous as the days went on.

The shadows grew long as they entered the Lincoln Tunnel. They were surprised to find the cars had been pushed to the sides of the narrow tunnel, allowing ample walking space for the pedestrians. They made good time in the tunnel, avoiding those who begged for food and water. John had a difficult time saying no to them, so he simply avoided eye contact.

Toward the bottom of the tunnel, they came across an abandoned Humvee. For fun, Matthew sat behind the wheel, pretending to drive. Much to his surprise, the keys lay on the floorboard near the gas pedal. He even started it up, the big diesel engine roaring to life and startling the other refugees in the tunnel. However, the rest of the tunnel was blocked, so he simply shut off the engine and didn't give it another thought.

By the time they emerged from the other side of the tunnel, it was pitch black outside and likely approaching ten at night. Exhausted, the guys searched for a place to rest and catch some sleep. Their goal was to wake up in the early morning hours, around four, when they'd continue their journey home. In John's mind, even the worst of humanity would be finding a place to sleep at that time of night.

They made their way onto State Road 495 in New Jersey, a major thoroughfare they'd avoided while on their bicycles. The heavily traveled road leading to Interstate 95 was filled with people all traveling in one direction—away from New York City.

That night, they slept in the truck bed of a New Jersey toll plaza utility vehicle. Using their backpacks as pillows, the guys lay prone in the back, staring at the aurora that continued to paint the skies over America. They marveled at its beauty and then reminded one another of the sun's destructive power.

They talked about home and how much they missed it. John speculated about how long it might take for the power to be restored. Matthew suggested maybe it wouldn't be such a bad thing if the utility company took their time about it. They ran down a checklist of their daily activities to consider whether they could survive if the world never righted itself. John made valid points regarding their shortcomings. Surprisingly, Matthew had several good suggestions on how to overcome their deficiencies.

They wondered how Emma and Luke were doing tending to the farm chores alone. They tried to imagine Cat talking her grandfather's ears off as they walked along the highway somewhere nearby. They even imagined coming upon them in the truck and asking, "Do you guys need a lift?"

The father and son who'd rarely had the opportunity to bond

with one another suddenly found themselves best friends. Some-times, catastrophes can bring a family closer together.

CHAPTER THIRTY-EIGHT

Monday
Clifton, New Jersey

Medical professionals refer to it as *early dumping syndrome*. Symptoms develop when one's small intestine isn't able to absorb nutrients from poorly digested food. Lauren was the first to be afflicted with the symptoms. Before they left the theaters, she could feel the bloat coming on as fluids rushed into her intestines to counteract the sudden influx of food. The telltale *rumbly-in-the-tumbly* feeling began to enter her consciousness. She knew what was coming. And she barely made it into the already stinky bathroom before her body spewed out the contents of her meal.

One by one, the entire group was hit by diarrhea. Lauren had the worst episode. Cat tolerated the nachos the best. All begged for the episode to pass and swore off food until they reached the farm.

The unexpected bout of diarrhea forced them to gulp down their water sooner than planned in order to avoid dehydration. The extended stop at the theater put them behind schedule, making it seemingly impossible to reach the interstate before dark. Their bodies were weakened by the shock to their systems. However, they unanimously agreed to continue on.

Before returning to the highway to join the exodus of refugees from the populated areas, they tried a couple of retailers that carried clothing. Target, Kohl's and Burlington had been ransacked. Looters even took the coats from the Burlington store despite the hundred-degree heat index. The group had given up and began the trek through the parking lot toward the road when Sam noticed a Goodwill drop-off location.

"Hey, let's check that out," he said as he pointed at the three dumpster-looking drop boxes located near a mattress store.

"They'll be locked, Sam," said Asher. "I've seen these before."

They walked closer, rounding the block walls of the strip center. A large, white trailer bearing the Goodwill logo on the side was attached to a pickup truck. Apparently, it had been time to gather the day's donations when the process had been interrupted by the solar flare.

Lauren had never been to a Goodwill store, so she had no idea what to expect. Her days of shopping at Talbots and Ann Taylor were over. She no longer required business dress attire in order to make a good impression on clients and coworkers. Somehow, at Cubbison's, she imagined anything would be just fine.

"Hey, Asher, look in the back of the pickup for a toolbox. I could use a crowbar, of course, but a hammer and heavy-duty screwdriver would do."

Asher, still in a good mood despite their bout of diarrhea, returned with both options. "Sam, you and I are getting good at this burglary stuff."

"We all have our talents, young man," he said jokingly as he took the tools from Asher. "Let me give it a go."

While Asher studied passersby to make sure none of them took more than a casual interest in Sam opening up the trailer, he suggested Lauren and Cat be ready to enter quickly in the event a crowd showed up.

"Let's just look for clothes," instructed Lauren. "I was thinking we'd just drag them out into the parking lot and pick through them after. The guys can guard the pile until we empty the trailer."

With the plan set, Sam popped the lock and opened the dual gates. Warm air that smelled of cardboard greeted them. Fortunately, the Goodwill driver was well organized. Any household items were stacked near the front of the trailer closest to the tongue, while the clothing was piled in heavy-duty boxes by the gate. It only took them a couple of minutes to pull everything out.

So far, they'd not been bothered by anyone, so Lauren was able to take her time. Even the guys got into the act as Asher began to look for pants and shirts that fit him. They were being selective in their choices. By the time they were finished, they all had newer backpacks, and the Doyles had two pieces of rolling luggage.

Lauren and Asher were able to find their sizes in jeans, shirts, and outerwear. They marveled at the quality of apparel, including brand names, that had been donated. One man's trash was another man's treasure.

Sam found camping supplies. A small pup tent. Cookware. A kerosene lantern. A sleeping bag. He opined that a teenager had owned the things but had outgrown their interest in camping.

Asher also found more burglary tools and a couple of weapons in the form of hunting knives. There was even a remarkably realistic pellet gun that looked just like the sidearms carried by the detectives on *Blue Bloods*. Although the weapon wasn't real, there might be a need to bluff their way through a situation in the future.

In good spirits, the group walked briskly up the ramp to merge into the pedestrian traffic. They were slowed somewhat by pulling the luggage; however, their pace was quicker than earlier as they exited the densely populated areas around Secaucus.

Asher struck up a conversation with a couple walking nearby who lived in Lincoln Park, a small town just past the interstate near the Great Piece Meadows Preserve. They told him I-80 was about ten miles ahead. Once again, Asher's brain performed the calculations. Three to four hours. After dark, but not so late as to be concerned about being assaulted.

He hoped.

CHAPTER THIRTY-NINE

Monday
Stanley's Farm
Harford, Pennsylvania

Luke led the way through the woods, relying upon instinct and familiarity to escort his mom safely along the treacherous trail that was growing darker by the minute. He slowed them as he reached the clearing overlooking what was left of Stanley's farm. The bright, setting sun temporarily blinded him, forcing his eyes shut to adjust.

As they rode, Emma contemplated what was about to happen. Throwing the two boys into the equation complicated matters. However, in her mind, it didn't change what had to be done. Her analysis kept coming back to protecting Luke, their farm, and the rest of her family upon their return. The men they planned on killing had established the rules of the game. It was a matter of time before their threats escalated to action.

The two quickly moved into position as previously planned. They waited for an inordinate amount of time. At one point, Luke moved from behind the tree and ran across the road to speak to Emma.

"Are you sure we didn't miss them?" he asked.

"I don't know how unless they had a truck or car hidden between here and our place."

"Horses, maybe?" asked Luke.

"I guess that's possible," she replied. "But what did they do with the—?"

She stopped mid-sentence as Luke raised his hand in the air and then placed his index finger over his lips to indicate they should be quiet. Emma began to nod her head rapidly as she shooed him away.

Luke raced across the street in a low crouch. His heart was pounding from adrenaline by the time he reached the tree. He stuck his head around the side to get a better look. Through the shadows, he could make out the group slowly lumbering up the hill. Their voices carried as they approached. Mouthy continued to moan in pain as he walked stiff-legged at the rear. The two boys complained about the heavy crate. The other two men cursed the steer, which barely kept up. The leader of the group, the man who'd be Luke's first target, seemed to keep his focus on the road ahead.

Luke glanced to the west, once again blinded by the sun. He shut his eyes until the purple and bright orange spheres disappeared. That was when he realized the advantage the setting sun gave them. By agreement, he would take the first shot. Their order of targets was the leader first, followed by the two uninjured men, with the mouthy gimp last. What Luke had in mind was a risk, but one worth taking.

The group was bunched together as they approached the crest of the hill. The man toting the AR-15 casually strolled ahead of the others, periodically turning to admonish them for one thing or another. He'd just entered the kill zone. However, Luke waited another moment.

His mom took her eyes off her target and looked toward Luke. She was unsure if he'd decided to back off, or perhaps he was frozen in a panicked state at the possibility of shooting someone. She wasn't sure if she should take the first shot. Unlike Luke, who was well hidden behind the large trunk of the oak tree, she had minimal coverage behind the quartz pile. She would be easily seen as soon as the group neared the driveway.

Her eyes darted back and forth between the group and Luke's position. Then, unexpectedly, he finally fired.

The report of his powerful hunting rifle echoed across the countryside. The leader fell backwards until he landed on the pavement in a heap. Caught off guard by Luke's inaction and then startled by the sudden firing of his weapon, Emma struggled to find her target. She fired wildly toward the group, missing her target but obliterating the crate the man had dropped to the pavement in response to Luke's shot.

Luke fired again, this time catching one of the gunmen in the shoulder. The boys shrieked out of fear. One of the other gunmen fired back at Luke, his shot ripping the bark off the oak tree before embedding in the trunk.

Emma fired again, shooting the already wounded man in the chest, killing him instantly.

Luke's next shot found the mark, hitting the other gunman, who fired at him simultaneously. The gunman's bullet whizzed over Luke's head, forcing him to drop to the ground.

Emma stood and searched for the man who'd been injured by the steer's kick. He was no longer on the road. The boys dropped to their knees on the pavement, wailing in anguish as they begged for their lives. The two looked around, eyes wide with fright, hands covered in the blood of the men, who might have been their fathers.

Luke walked from behind the tree with his rifle pointing at one of the boys, then the other. He bellowed at them as he spoke. "Where's the other guy?"

One of the boys' bowels released into his pants, too frightened to respond. The other made a near-fatal mistake. He lunged for the leader's AR-15.

However, Luke rushed toward him with the rifle barrel of his rifle pointed at his head. "Don't touch that gun! Don't make me kill you!"

Suddenly, several shots rang out. Bullets flew all around Luke, ricocheting off the asphalt, with one embedding in the body of the group's leader.

Emma responded. She stood and fired toward the woods where she thought the gunfire came from. Her shots hit the trees but missed their target. The man fired toward her; however, his shots dug into the ground yards in front of her.

Luke kept his cool and eased forward, searching for movement through is rifle's sight. His mind remained focused on the shooter and blocked off the sound of the boys running down the road away from the massacre.

There! The man revealed himself. Ever so slightly, in an effort to take a shot at Luke, his body moved from behind a tree. Luke didn't hesitate to send a single round into the man's heart.

Hyped up, Luke moved from gunman to gunman, kicking their legs, with his rifle pointed at their heads. He even kicked their wounds to see if they reacted to the painful stimuli. Nothing. They were dead.

Emma stood in the middle of the road, watching the two boys run for their lives although she had no intention of shooting them.

Luke jogged up next to her. "Should I go after them?"

"No," she replied softly.

"Mom, I've got a lot of questions for them. I need to know if this is over."

Emma dropped to her knees and vomited in the middle of the road. She set her rifle to the side and threw up repeatedly until she had the dry heaves. Luke knelt down next to her, helping his mom keep her hair out of her face.

After she stopped vomiting, she began to cry. In between sobs, she asked God for forgiveness. "Please, Lord, don't punish me by harming my family. I made the decision to do this, not them."

She began crying again. Luke tried to comfort her while looking in all directions. Somehow, he sensed this wasn't over. At least for now, it was.

PART 3

———

Tuesday
If you are afraid of confrontation,
you're doomed to failure.

CHAPTER FORTY

Tuesday
Near Wayne, New Jersey

Exhausted and sore, the foursome made their way to the shopping area around Willowbrook Mall located just south of Interstate 80. It was a milestone in their one-hundred-forty-mile journey to the Cubbisons' farm. Asher and Sam grew concerned about the large concentration of people who'd gathered in the area to rest for the night. Refugees from the city merged with travelers along the busy Christopher Columbus Highway to find a suitable place to sleep.

Lauren and Asher were both concerned that being around so many desperate created a potentially volatile scenario. None of them were enthusiastic about sleeping with one eye open.

Instead, they continued on, urging their weary bodies to make it another mile. Walking parallel to the interstate, they came across a Kids Empire location, an establishment much like a Chuck E. Cheese restaurant without the food other than light snacks. It was one of those places Asher had talked about earlier in the day. Looters weren't interested in floor-to-ceiling climbing walls and the expected drop-in ball pits. They wanted valuables or items to help them survive.

Well, the Kids Empire unexpectedly checked a lot of boxes. Despite being open at the time the grid went down, the store had not been subjected to looters or those who simply wanted to ransack the place.

Its doors were still locked, which provided Sam the opportunity to use his newfound burglary tools. In this case, a swing of the hammer did the trick. Once inside, they confirmed the business was empty. Confident in its safety, they moved several tables against the plate-glass windows and doors and turned them on their sides. The makeshift barrier wouldn't keep out the most determined intruders; however, it would certainly slow their entry. The group identified the emergency exit through the stockroom as the rally point in case they were surprised during the night.

Because they were a little gun-shy about eating, they forced themselves to consume the healthiest of the limited snack options. There was an abundance of bags of chips and boxes of candy. Non-refrigerated snack packs, which included Fig Newtons, apple sauce and chocolate pudding, were a hit. Drinks included Capri Sun packs and bottled water.

This was a rare, welcome find compared to what they'd observed during their first day on the road. The group spent some time going through their backpacks and luggage to discard some items in favor of food and drinks. Lauren and Asher sacrificed the most in order to fill the rolling luggage with nourishment.

Sam estimated they had at least a hundred miles to travel through mostly desolate back roads. While there were towns along the way, he imagined the retail businesses had been picked over already. The food they carried from Kids Empire might be the extent of their meals for the next several days.

After winding down and a last look at their surroundings to confirm their rapid exit plan in the event they were surprised during the night, the four found sleep easily. Huddled near one another inside a bouncy house at the back of the large play area, they slept hard for nearly seven hours. Only the sun peeking above the tipped-over tables caused Asher and Sam to stir at nearly the same time.

Sam crawled out of the play structure and made his way onto the artificial carpet delineating the indoor soccer field. He pushed off one knee until he stood upright, creaking and cracking as he rose.

"I heard all of that," whispered Asher as he joined Sam. "You doin' okay?"

"Yeah, actually. Considering I've never walked that far in a day, I'm kinda proud of myself."

"How about the muscles and joints?" asked Asher as the two men walked together toward the restrooms.

"Muscle soreness is expected. The joints being pissed off have become the norm. You'll see when you get to my age."

Using their squeeze flashlights, the two men relieved themselves in the urinals, which were low to the floor to accommodate the young boys who frequented Kids Empire. Asher, out of habit, tried to flush before rolling his eyes at himself for forgetting the apocalypse was still upon them.

"Should we let them sleep?" asked Sam.

Asher sighed. Everyone was tired. He knew it would be best for the group to get an early start to take advantage of the cooler morning temperatures.

"Can you recall how long you drove on the interstate before you reached the Willowbrook exit?" asked Asher.

"Maybe twenty minutes, if even."

Asher muttered, "Twenty miles." His brain calculated a seven-to-eight-hour walk to the back roads, as Sam called them.

"That sounds like a full day," said Sam.

"Yeah. Let's get them started. At least we can take some of the excess bottled water to clean up. A little breakfast might be good before we get too far away from the restrooms."

Sam laughed and patted his new friend on the back. "I see you remember yesterday's after-meal extravaganza."

"I'll never forget it. Then again, there's a lot of things about the last several days that I'll never forget."

The guys exited the restroom after rinsing their hands. They found Cat and Lauren making their way out of the bouncy house, wiping sleep from their eyes and complaining that it was too early to get their day started.

Asher and Sam set up breakfast for everyone. They chatted about life on the farm and the beautiful scenery they'd enjoy as they trekked across the mountains toward Harford. Lauren commented how much she looked forward to walking along the roads without bumping into others. Sam said the only congested area would be when they traveled through Milford. Interstate 84 ran through the town toward Scranton. It wouldn't be as congested as what they'd experienced, but they'd need to be careful, nonetheless.

With their minds and bodies refreshed, they exited through the rear of the building and made their way onto the highway. The stretch along the nature preserve was quiet with a minimal amount of stalled traffic. Most of the vehicles were occupied by sleeping refugees, while only a few people had ventured out as early as their group had.

Rejuvenated, they made good time as they approached the twin cities of Parsippany-Troy Hills. It wasn't until they walked off the interstate later that day that the journey became interesting once again.

CHAPTER FORTY-ONE

Tuesday
Lake Wallenpaupack
Wayne County, Pennsylvania

Years prior, in 2021, Afghanistan exploded into chaos as the United States government suddenly pulled its military forces out of the country. The void left by the elimination of the security presence of the U.S. was quickly filled by the Taliban, who established a new government, and ISIS-K, the Afghan affiliate of the Islamic State in Iraq and Syria.

With the security forces gone, the Afghans who'd remained loyal to the U.S. and who worked closely with the American military were left to fend for themselves. In order to protect the most Afghans in the face of the Taliban and ISIS threat, Washington began an evacuation program that resulted in one hundred thousand Afghan refugees rushing into America, mostly unvetted. One year later, almost half of these refugees, who'd been resettled across the nation, were unaccounted for.

Further, after they'd already arrived in the States, hundreds had been reclassified and identified as security concerns by the administration. These potentially dangerous refugees had been flagged in the National Counter-Terrorism Center database as missing. At the time the perfect storm hit, those unvetted Afghans had been narrowed down to fifty who had reached the highest threat categories on the Terrorism Watch List.

Although the American intelligence apparatus could not locate these fifty most dangerous Afghan men with deep terrorism ties, the men were able to find one another. Officially, many of them had been resettled in the northeastern states. Over the years, they'd quietly disappeared and found their way into remote towns in Northeastern Pennsylvania and Upstate New York.

Between the very beginning of dawn and sunrise, a large contingent of Afghan men gathered for Fajr prayer, one of the five mandatory Islamic prayers to be performed in a given day. As an Islamic day starts at sunset, Fajr, the Arabic word for dawn, was technically the third prayer of the day.

After prayer, as the sun began to make its appearance in the east, the men followed their undisputed leader, Abdul Rahimi, down to the western shores of Lake Wallenpaupack in remote Wayne County located in Northeastern Pennsylvania. The clear lake water was as smooth as glass that morning, no longer disturbed by early-morning fishermen.

Abdul was a fierce warrior for the Taliban, leading many insurgent operations into Kabul during his tenure. With most of his family alongside, he'd pushed and shoved his way onto the aircraft that managed to leave the Kabul airport before it was closed down.

Initially, he was settled in Rochester, New York. When he was reclassified by the Department of Defense as a Category 3 terror threat, he fled Rochester with his family across state lines into Pennsylvania.

From the beginning, Abdul knew what his duty was. He and his family never accepted the visas, green cards, and especially the offer of naturalized American citizenship. He surmised all the free benefits being offered to him were designed to track his whereabouts and to cause him to disavow his home. As a result, he took advantage of the incompetence and inattention shown by the refugee contractors who accepted billions of dollars to assimilate him into American society. He disappeared and found his way to Wayne County to reunite with his top lieutenants.

Abdul and his comrades were patient people. They believed in being prepared to strike against the U.S. in the name of their god. They were able to patiently bide their time until the perfect opportunity presented itself. They game-planned various scenarios that could possibly play out. What they never imagined was the mighty hand of Allah clubbing the infidels in America for them.

Abdul stood at the edge of the water and quietly motioned for the men to sit on the banks of the lake. His lieutenants sat closest to the front with rolled-up maps near their side. The army of operatives had prepared for this moment. However, their first operation was just the beginning of many more to come.

"After evening prayer, my brothers, with the will of Allah, we will begin the next phase following years of planning on the infidels' soil together with many more years of battles fought by our fathers and their fathers before them. It is our time to make the Great Satan feel our wrath for that which they have inflicted upon us. As we fight our battle, we will joyfully dance on their dead bodies, giving praise to Allah!"

"*Allahu Akbar!*"

"*Allahu Akbar!*"

Hassan continued. "Tonight, we will go our separate ways and follow the routes that have been assigned to you. We will arm ourselves and our brothers with the tools necessary to bring the Great Satan to its knees. Praise Allah, and peace be with you, brothers."

The men shared embraces and broke off into groups led by Abdul's lieutenants. These men were loyal and every bit as ruthless as their leader. Like Abdul, they'd been reclassified to the highest categories of terrorism threat after they'd arrived in the U.S.

Abdul motioned for his most trusted friend and confidant, Jamal Khan, to join him. Khan stood respectfully in front of his mentor without speaking.

"We are ready," started Abdul. "We have prayed for strength and guidance. We will not fail Islam or Allah."

"This I know, my brother. Tonight, you and I will bring weaponry to our brothers that surpasses anything currently in our possession. The well-armed children of Allah will fight in his name and be given a great reward."

"As will we all."

"*Allahu Akbar!*" exclaimed Khan.

"*Allahu Akbar!*" Abdul responded in kind and then placed his hand on his number one lieutenant's shoulder. He spoke in a hushed tone of voice. "Is there news of your daughter?"

Khan visibly slumped as his chin dropped to his chest. "She has shamed our family and Allah. We have not found her, but I assure you, my brother, we will."

"She became an impetuous teenager as she embraced the ways of the infidel Americans," said Abdul.

Khan became nervous. His daughter's running away from home was considered a betrayal to his family as well as the entire community of Afghans living in Wayne and Pike Counties.

Abdul continued. "Is it your belief that she fled to New York? Have you sent someone to Rochester?"

Initially, over eleven hundred Afghans had been resettled in New York, the vast majority in cities like Buffalo, Syracuse, and Rochester. Over time, thousands more were released into the same locales.

"I did. She was not there."

Abdul frowned. He clasped his hands behind his back and walked along the lake's edge. Khan dutifully followed, struggling to keep the maps rolled up under his arm.

"My brother, are you troubled by her disappearance?" asked Abdul.

"She has brought shame to our family. She has dishonored our people. She has angered Allah."

Abdul turned to Khan. "Are you distracted by this? Can you fight?"

"I am with you, my brother. I will fight by your side to my death if Allah wishes it. There will be time to find the girl another time."

Abdul studied Khan for a moment and then nodded slightly. He patted him on the back and said, "Let's go over our plan again."

CHAPTER FORTY-TWO

Tuesday
Cubbison's Farm
Harford, Pennsylvania

After the ambush on the armed men, Emma's emotional breakdown continued until she returned to the farm. Initially, she was too distraught to rest. She paced the floor of their living room, even taking a shot of Quarter Horse Reserve bourbon given to John by a high school classmate, Jon Stiles. Stiles had moved to Kentucky to form a very successful retail store outside Cincinnati on the Kentucky side of the river, specializing in adult beverages and party supplies. In the past, the bourbon, made by one of the oldest distilleries in Kentucky, helped calm her nerves. Not on this night, however.

Luke was exhausted. Emma insisted Luke join her to keep watch over the front gate from the safety of the market's front porch. Earlier, while his mom was trying to regain her composure, Luke had scrambled around to move the dead bodies to the side of the road to avoid them getting run over by a seemingly rare occurrence—an operating vehicle. He also rushed into the Stanley place and retrieved some sheets and bedding to protect the corpses from critters. He'd not stopped since the last man fell.

After Emma recovered enough to function, they retrieved the horses and loaded them with the supplies that had survived the gunfight or that weren't blood-soaked. The men's weapons and ammunition were a bonus. It was close to midnight when the two of them led the loaded-down horses and the steer back to Cubbison's Farm. Despite the late hour, Emma insisted upon watching the front entrance. She'd convinced herself that the families of the dead would be arriving at any moment.

Finally, they stopped pacing in front of the gate and made their way to the rockers on the market's porch. With their rifles laid across their laps, they both eventually nodded off until sunrise.

The warmth found Emma's cheeks and slowly woke her up. The sun blinded her temporarily until she could adjust her eyesight. That was when she saw the silhouettes at their gate. She closed her eyes and then blinked rapidly, trying to confirm she was not dreaming. She cupped her hands over her eyes to limit the sunlight that invaded her pupils.

At first, the silhouettes registered as an apparition, ghostly figures coming to haunt her. A woman with two young children holding her outstretched hands stared directly at Emma. She managed to find the strength to stand, clasping her rifle with both hands.

She raised the weapon and used the scope to confirm they were human and not ghosts. It was a woman in a simple dress together with two young girls under the age of eight. Her hair was mussed, and the children appeared unkempt.

Emma slowly slid sideways until she reached Luke's rocking chair. She gently touched his shoulder to avoid startling him.

"Luke, wake up. There's a woman and two children at the front gate."

Luke shot up out of his rocker and nearly lunged off the porch into the landscaping. He caught his balance and immediately raised his rifle. "Are they armed?"

"Not that I can see."

He studied them through his scope. "Man, they look worn out."

"That's one way of putting it. We need to see what they want."

Luke wasn't so sure. "Mom, are you sure about this? It could be some kind of trap."

Emma ignored his concerns and stepped off the porch and began walking toward them with her rifle cradled in her arms. Without debating the point, Luke rushed down the stairs to join her. He walked several feet to her right, leaving some distance between them in case they had to dive for cover behind the vehicles they'd towed into the driveway.

With Emma focused on the newcomers, Luke kept his rifle ready, scanning in all directions for an unexpected attack of some kind.

"May I help you?" asked Emma from a distance of forty feet. The sun no longer affected her vision, and she didn't want to get too close.

"I, um, my name's Jenna, and this here's my daughters, Kay and Jewel. Um, we wanted to thank you," the woman said in an emotional tone of voice. "We're free now."

Puzzled, Emma asked, "What do you mean by that?"

"My boyfriend was one of the men, um, you know, from last night."

Emma raised her rifle a little more but did not point it at them. She was on guard now but was curious as to why the woman was thanking her.

"We're sorry it came to that. We truly are. Those men left us no choice."

"I know. Actually, we know. All of us, my girls included, have been abused by them. We've been trapped, you know, financially. That's how they keep ahold of us."

Emma and Luke exchanged glances. Emma lowered her rifle; however, Luke was still keenly aware of his surroundings.

The woman continued her explanation. "My husband, the father to these two young'uns, died. I took up with that man because he

PERFECT STORM 2

promised to take care of us. I was weak, lonely, and broke. The EBT debit cards ain't enough, you know?"

Emma took a few steps forward. "Which one was your boyfriend?"

The woman described the mouthy guy to a T. Once again, Emma and Luke exchanged glances. Then she added, "He was an angry drunk. He'd take it out on all of us until I taught the girls to hide from him when he was in a mood. I took the beatin' for them. When we all figured out what had happened, we were relieved. I told them I was gonna come here to thank you."

"Why didn't they come with you?" asked Luke as his head nervously remained on a swivel.

"They're scared."

"Are there more men?" asked Luke.

"No. Just me, my sister with two kids, and another woman and her boys. Her boyfriend was the man with the beard, who came up with this idea to begin with. We met up with them on the interstate."

"Are you sure?" asked Emma, uncertain about the woman's veracity.

"No, I swear."

"Guns?" asked Luke. He stepped forward slightly to get a better look at her face in order to gauge her honesty.

"No. Just bullets. We don't have anything, you know, after we ate them other people's food."

Emma sighed. She stepped closer to them, and Luke matched her progress. When they were only a dozen feet away, she asked the question that she didn't want to hear the answer to.

"What about the Yoders? They're the people who live in the house where you're stayin'."

The woman closed her eyes, and she shook her head slowly from side to side. She was slow to respond as she fought back tears. "They're gone, if you know what I mean," she replied as she looked down at her daughters, neither of whom had attempted to speak.

Luke stepped closer. He had one more question. "Jenna, how can I believe you? How do I know you're being sincere?"

She wiped the tears off her face. "I'll send the others and let them tell you their stories. The young'uns may not understand what you've done for 'em, but we sure do."

Luke walked over to his mother and whispered, "Whadya think?"

"I wanna believe her. Do you?"

Luke shrugged. "I guess so. There's only one way to find out."

Emma studied the woman as she spoke. "Should we have them come back one by one to be questioned?"

Luke took a deep breath and exhaled. "Let me go see them. I'll return with these three and take them some food."

"It's not safe," argued Emma.

"I don't know, Mom. Somehow, I think it will be. Either way, we have to know if they're gonna seek revenge. It'll catch them off guard if I return with Jenna and her kids, if that's what their real names are."

"What were they?" asked Emma, who'd been focused on the mom and missed the girls' names.

"Kay and Jewel."

"Wait a minute. Like the jewelry store, Kay Jewelers?" asked Emma. She gripped her rifle, and her face began to turn red with anger. "This is bullshit."

"Hang on, Mom, Maybe so. But we have to know. This will give me a chance to talk with her and quiz her some more to see if she keeps her story straight."

Emma scowled. "I don't like it."

"I'll be okay. Besides, I'm gonna take that guy's AR-15. I seriously doubt they have another one. Why would they leave it behind if they knew they might be in for a fight, right?"

Emma sighed and nodded. "I still don't like it, but it's a good plan." She turned toward the mother and her daughters. "Wait here. I'm gonna put together some food for you. My son's gonna get his horse and will accompany you back."

"Really? Some food? How much? I mean, thank you. We'll take anything. Thank you both so much."

Luke turned to wink at his mother. He left for the barn first, jogging along the gravel drive while occasionally glancing over his shoulder.

Emma slowly walked backwards toward the market to put together a couple of bags of staples they could eat without cooking them.

She still didn't like what Luke was potentially walking into.

CHAPTER FORTY-THREE

Tuesday
Secaucus, New Jersey

John and Matthew slept uninterrupted until seven that morning. After checking on his son, he eased out of the utility truck bed and found a private place to relieve his bladder. The sun was rising over New York City, causing the plate glass of the skyscrapers to shimmer as they reflected the rays differently. Coupled with the fires that raged in several buildings on the horizon, the daytime light show that morning rivaled its aurora counterpart during the evening.

The quiet was unsettling. To be sure, John was used to waking up to pleasant silence around the farm. However, the fact he was surrounded by a concrete jungle filled with millions of people who could barely be heard unnerved him.

He allowed Matthew to sleep so he could gather his thoughts. He walked through the parking lot of the toll plaza, stopping to look inside the vehicles that had been abandoned when they ceased functioning. In that moment, John adopted a different mindset.

While he still had hopes of coming across Sam and Cat, he reconciled himself to the belief they'd have to manage to survive on their own. Perhaps with the help of this man named Asher Doyle and his wife.

He verbalized his thoughts. "But why would they risk their lives for strangers? They are New Yorkers, after all."

John hadn't realized he spoke out loud until he noticed Matthew stirring. Then he chastised himself for stereotyping people from the city. He'd always been a small-town guy living in what the media and politicians call flyover country. You know, the vast majority of America that urban dwellers fly over without stopping as they criss-cross the country from coast to coast.

John chuckled when he recalled the old book named *Men are from Mars, Women are from Venus*. It was a self-help-style book to assist men and women to understand their differences. Well, John thought they should write a book called *City Folk Don't Know Squat-Diddly About America's Heartland, and We Don't Understand Them Either*.

"No. Too long," he muttered to himself, referring to the book title, not its contents. "We're all different." Maybe the Doyles were different.

"Dad?" asked a still-sleepy Matthew. His head slowly popped up over the side of the truck bed.

"Yeah, son. I was stretching my legs while I let you sleep."

"Were you talking to somebody?" asked Matthew as he crawled out of the truck bed.

"Oh, nah. Just mumblin'. That's all. How'd you sleep?"

As Matthew relieved himself, he rolled his neck around his shoulders. "All right, I guess. What's the plan?"

John hadn't really thought about the details of what their day looked like. His experience taught him you never know what's put before you during the apocalypse. He laughed to himself. That word —*apocalypse*. He'd always associated it with zombies like in *The Walking Dead* or space aliens extinguishing all human life on the planet. You know, the stuff of science fiction.

This apocalypse was anything but fiction. It was very real and more like a slow death. It was gonna be the worst kind of torture for people who didn't know how to survive off the land. Sure, they could loot and steal until at some point, they'd run out of options. Then what?

He wanted to believe the best of mankind would rise to the surface. People helping people. Banding together to survive. In the end, he feared, the human instincts of survival and self-preservation would become pervasive.

This had been on his mind often as they'd traveled to New York to find the rest of his family. Of course, he was compassionate and sharing. However, there were no givens in life. Without power, he was unable to irrigate the vast gardening operation Emma had created. Would they have to limit their harvest because water was scarce? If so, how could he justify feeding his neighbors or refugees when he had his own family to feed.

The same applied to his livestock. Livestock required maintenance. Hay in the winter. Medical care throughout the year. Breeding to replenish what they slaughtered. He'd tried to calculate whether they had sufficient hay stored to feed their cattle through the winter.

Ordinarily, they cut their hay around this time of year when the weather was dry. He always planned for a window of at least three days of dry hot weather. That was now, not that it mattered. His hay baler was inoperative.

These were all variables he and his family understood. Those who'd never planted crops or raised livestock wouldn't appreciate the challenges. To them, it was all available at Wegmans, or it came from a farm nearby that had plenty to spare.

Wrong.

"Dad? Are we gonna head out now?"

Matthew was growing impatient, rightfully so. *There'll be more time to contemplate life later, John Cubbison*, he thought to himself.

"Okay, here's the plan," John replied. "Before, we kinda avoided the main roads with our bikes. This time, I vote we take the most direct route back to the truck. There'll be more people, but if we keep our eyes open, we can avoid trouble."

Matthew scowled. His voice turned somewhat whiny. "Are we gonna look for more bikes? That's a long way to walk."

"It is, but you're a healthy young man. Imagine what Cat and Grandpa Sam are facing. A hundred forty miles is a long way. At least we have the truck."

"Hopefully," mumbled Matthew as he began gathering his things.

John was puzzled by his son's change in demeanor. He'd been supportive and energetic in the city as they searched for his sister and grandfather. His moodiness suggested he was over the search. John decided to let him wake up more before addressing the issue.

The guys retrieved some water and snack bars from their backpacks as they began their trek home. For the first couple of miles, they spoke very little, taking in their surroundings while studying the faces of their fellow travelers. It had only been a few days since the collapse of the grid; however, it had taken its toll on the people they passed. Their faces were forlorn. Devastated. Most were exhausted, barely moving one foot in front of the other.

John and Matthew, on the other hand, strode with a purpose. Perhaps the difference between them and the refugees streaming away from New York was they had a place to go.

CHAPTER FORTY-FOUR

Tuesday
Cubbison's Farm
Hartford, Pennsylvania

Emma was more generous than she intended to be. She provided each of the young girls two bags full of bread with apple butter. The mother was given two bags of nutritious snacks that Emma sold in the market. Luke stuffed four plastic bottles of apple juice in his saddlebags.

By agreement, Luke instructed the mom and daughters to walk several paces in front of his horse so he could keep an eye on them and the wooded areas they passed through. He made for an easy target atop his horse. When he felt most exposed, he dropped to the ground and led her by the reins, keeping the beloved animal between him and any potential ambush locations.

As they talked, he deftly struck up conversations with all three of them to have them confirm their backgrounds and provide information on the others. As it turns out, the daughters were in fact named after Kay Jewelers. When Jenna and her first husband were married, they didn't have a lot of money. Kay Jewelers at their local mall was running a promotion to give away a bridal set to the lucky couple whose name was pulled out of the drawing. Jenna and her betrothed won, so they promised to name their first two kids Kay and Jewel if they were girls.

Luke was beginning to feel better about his decision to help Jenna and her young family. The more he talked with her, however, the more he realized they might be taking on all the mouths that their lousy men had been trying to feed. They were either gonna have to teach them to fend for themselves or send them away. Then he thought they'd simply be replaced by more refugees who happened to notice his mom's massive billboard. He intended to talk with his parents about cutting the thing down or at least spray-painting over it.

Eventually, the Yoders' home came into view. Luke mounted his horse so he could break away quickly in case of trouble. He wondered if he could shoot a woman. He decided a killer was a killer. If they tried to shoot at him, he'd return the favor.

As they got closer, the kids in the front yard, who were playing soccer, noticed they were coming. At first, they froze and turned to look for their mothers. Then when Kay and Jewel hollered at them, they all came running. Even the two boys who'd accompanied their fathers and witnessed their deaths.

By the time they reached the front lawn, there was a sizable welcoming committee consisting of three adult women, four young girls, and two boys—the same youngsters who'd approached the Cubbison's gate with the armed men that fateful night.

Jenna spoke first. "Everyone, this is, well, um, sir, I don't know your name."

"Luke. Luke Cubbison."

"Hey, mister. Can we take a ride on your horse?" said one of Jenna's nieces.

"No!" Her mother issued a stern rebuke.

"Sis, Luke's a nice man. He's brought us some food."

"And apple juice," said Luke. He pulled the plastic bottles out of the saddlebags and handed them down to the boys, whom he'd met the night before. They looked up at him sheepishly and swallowed hard. One of them, who'd reached for the AR-15, probably recalled Luke's promise to shoot him.

They all gathered around Jenna and looked in the bags. Luke understood their difficulty. *So many mouths to feed.*

"Thank you, mister," said one of the young girls.

"Yes, thank you, Luke," added Jenna.

Luke was not concerned about Jenna as a threat or any of the children. The two women were still an unknown. As they handed out the snacks, Luke glanced up at the Yoders' house. He saw a curtain move in one of the forward-facing windows.

His back immediately stiffened as he turned the barrel of the rifle toward the house. He looked around at the tops of the trees. The lack of wind failed to account for why the curtains would be disturbed from the outside.

Then they moved again. This time, he was certain he saw a shadow walk past. Incensed, he began shouting at the women. "Who's inside? You lied to me! You said this was everybody!"

Luke was agitated and began swinging his rifle from window to window in the house.

Jenna ran toward the house and then nervously turned back to Luke. "Okay. Okay. I'm sorry I lied. She's not dangerous. I swear. It's just, well, she's very scared of her family. She just showed up early this morning. We had to help her the best we could."

"Get her out here!" demanded Luke. Jenna and the others had lost his trust. Now he was on alert again. His horse became fidgety as he waited, drawing from his nervous energy. He tried to calm her down while being completely aware of his surroundings.

Jenna ran inside. Luke could hear her imploring the other woman to come outside. She insisted that Luke was not dangerous and certainly wasn't looking for her. After Jenna begged her again, she emerged through the front door with the woman.

At first, Luke was stunned by her beauty. His mouth fell open, and he lowered his rifle. In Italy, the women would've said that Luke had been hit by the thunderbolt—a powerful form of love at first sight that overwhelms a man.

She was wearing jeans and a short-sleeved shirt. She also wore a lightweight hijab, the long headscarf traditionally worn by Muslim women around the world, used to cover their head and hair. Her face was unemotional as her eyes darted about in search of someone or something that might harm her. Luke had seen that look in a kitten born in the barn that had been separated from its mother.

He scanned her jeans to confirm she didn't have a weapon tucked away. Then he looked toward the windows again to confirm nobody was ready to shoot at him. Satisfied she wasn't a threat, he dismounted. He simply had to get a closer look at the exotic young woman.

He cradled the AR-15 in his arms and quickly tried to spruce up his hair. He shyly smiled at her, and her facial expression seemed to soften.

"I'm Luke Cubbison. Um, we have a place down the road."

"Yes. I've heard about you and your mother."

She was standoffish. Luke wasn't giving up. "What happened was unfortunate. I'm truly sorry, but none of that was our idea."

"Okay."

"What's your name?" asked Luke.

"Vida."

Luke nodded. "Okay, Vida. Are you in some kind of trouble? Maybe we can help?"

The other three adults and their kids had become spectators at this point, as the world seemed to revolve around Luke and the Afghan woman who'd suddenly appeared on the doorstep of the Yoders' home.

Luke continued to quiz Vida, who was only marginally cooperative. Eventually, Jenna stepped into the conversation and invited Luke inside so he could see how they were living. She wanted to assure him that nobody else was there and they were unarmed.

He let his guard down and accepted her offer. This time, he didn't pay a price for his casual approach to strangers. He was too smitten with the intriguing beauty he'd just met.

CHAPTER FORTY-FIVE

Tuesday
Clifton, New Jersey

John and Matthew had made good time, keeping a steady, untaxing pace. As John had explained, his goal was to reach the truck before dark. He preferred to make the two-and-a-half-hour drive home in the dark anyway. After Matthew's prodding, John committed to having them home by midnight, barring unforeseen circumstances.

They slowed their pace as they passed through the retail shopping district located on both sides of the highway. The guys debated whether they should look for anything of value. After considering the additional burden of carrying more than their backpacks, they agreed to revisit the issue once they retrieved their truck. While in the metropolitan areas, there were too many opportunities to acquire needed supplies for them to pass up.

As they approached the Garden State Parkway intersection with NJ 3, Matthew grabbed his father's arm and pulled him to a stop. "Did you hear that?"

John held his breath for a moment to focus his hearing on their surroundings. He shook his head side to side.

Matthew walked ahead and leaned over a steel guardrail to inspect the road below them. The street was flanked by a mini storage facility on one side and a Stop & Shop on the other. People were periodically exiting the grocery store although they were mostly empty-handed.

The woman screamed louder this time and then managed to shout, "Help me!"

Matthew broke away from John and raced to the other side of the highway, hurdling the concrete divider and then dodging refugees, who appeared disinterested in the pleas for help.

John, too, wanted to be disinterested. His son had almost shot somebody in the dark as he seemingly attempted to rescue a woman from attackers. He'd turned out to be mistaken about what was happening.

However, John heard the woman holler for help, and it certainly didn't sound playful. He chased after his son, slowly crossing the barrier, as he had no expectation that he could jump over it like his son.

He called after Matthew in a loud whisper, "Son! Wait for me!"

The woman screeched this time. Then he heard the telltale sound of a palm slapping a face. She was sobbing, which caused anger to rise inside him. His blood boiled when he noticed the pedestrians were continuing to walk away, uncaring as to the woman's plight.

Matthew jumped the steel guardrail and began thrashing through the underbrush in search of the woman.

"Hold still, dammit!" A man's voice, husky and coarse, was demanding her compliance.

"Puhleese don't do this," she begged in between sobs.

Matthew had disappeared from John's view. He could see the tops of saplings being pushed back and forth, which was the only way he could follow.

"You wanted food. Now you gotta pay me!"

"Nooo, please leave me—!"

Boom!

The gunshot sounded like a cannon in the near quiet surroundings. John had no way of knowing if it was Matthew who fired the shot or the attacker.

Pop! Pop! Pop!

Shit! John shouted in his mind. Two different guns. Matthew had fired first. He was sure of it.

Pop! Pop!

Two more shots were fired. However, they were too high, and they splintered the treetops above John's head. He could hear people shouting from the roadway. Suddenly, the disinterested couldn't turn away from the drama unfolding in the woods.

"Leave her alone!" Matthew shouted.

Boom! Boom!

Pop!

"Arrrgggghhh!"

One of them had been shot. Panicked, he dropped his backpack and pressed forward with both of his pistols drawn. The underbrush began to thin, and then he saw a heavyset man with a hole in his chest slumped over a young girl. She was too distraught to respond to Matthew's questions as he tried to roll the heavy man off her.

He finally succeeded as John appeared in the clearing. Then Matthew, out of adrenaline-fueled anger, shot the man in the head.

"Jesus, Matthew!" John shouted as his son swung around with his pistol leading the way. "He's dead already. Now put the gun away."

Matthew fell back so that his butt rested on his heels. The woman was no longer screaming. Rather, she was gasping for air as she tried to wipe the man's blood off her bare chest. Both of them were stunned by the sudden turn of events.

John quickly glanced around to make sure there wasn't another threat. His eyes washed over his son's body to confirm he hadn't been shot. Then he turned his attention to the distraught woman.

Nervous, John asked, "Was he alone? Was he the only one?"

She nodded rapidly. Her eyes darted around as she covered her chest. Her shirt had been torn off her and her pants partially removed.

John pulled his tee shirt off and handed it to her. "You can have this," he said in a softer tone of voice.

The woman quickly pulled it over her head and then yanked up her pants. She mouthed the words *thank you.*

John glanced at Matthew and then looked around the clearing. Thus far, none of the onlookers from the highway had ventured into the underbrush. He returned to the young woman. He retrieved a sport bottle filled with water out of Matthew's backpack and handed it to her. She quickly gulped it through the straw before her gag reflex caused her to cough violently.

"That's okay. Drink slowly."

"I just wanted something to eat," she muttered before the tears began to flow again.

"What's your name?"

"Melody."

"Melody, um, did he, you know, hurt you?"

She slowly shook her head and whispered while looking at Matthew, "No. He stopped him first."

John closed his eyes. *Thank you, God, for not making this young woman suffer.*

"Dad, people are coming." It was the first words Matthew had spoken.

John turned around toward the street. He didn't want to get any more involved than they already were. New Jersey wasn't exactly a gun-friendly state, regardless of present circumstances. He saw a trail leading deeper into the woods that likely came out in the residential areas he'd observed on both sides of the highway.

"Are you gonna be okay?" he asked the woman.

She nodded and turned to Matthew. "Thank you."

Matthew was shaking. He leaned forward and awkwardly

extended his hand to shake hers. She leaned forward and hugged him, ignoring the man's blood that was now seeping into John's white tee shirt.

"Matthew, we need to go."

"But what about her?"

"I'll be fine. I understand, too." She turned toward the woods where the underbrush was rustling. She gestured toward the Cubbison men. "Go. Hurry!"

John stood and wrapped his arm around Matthew. He pointed up the hill toward the trail, and they darted off together, not looking back at yet another body they'd left behind.

CHAPTER FORTY-SIX

Tuesday
Clifton, New Jersey

John picked up the pace, practically dragging Matthew along as they extricated themselves from the situation. He remembered that he'd dropped his backpack to fight his way through the brush to help his son. Now he was shirtless with both of his weapons revealed in the waistband of his pants.

As soon as they rushed out of the trail, they found themselves facing several privacy fences along the backyards of the residences. John directed Matthew away from the trail entrance until they could make their way toward the street. They immediately drew the attention of the locals.

Ironically, they were in the middle of Holster Street, which reminded Matthew to put away his handgun. People were gawking and pointing at the guys. Suddenly, John felt naked.

"I need a shirt," he said to Matthew. He turned his son sideways so he could reach into his backpack. He fumbled around and pulled out the first shirt he could find. It was a black tee featuring the heavy metal band Metallica and their hit song "Enter Sandman."

John pulled it over his head and tried to hide the handguns on each hip. The shirt was tight; however, it served its purpose. He was covered and so were his guns.

He turned to Matthew, who'd barely uttered a word since they'd left the girl in the woods. "Son, we need to go. Are you okay to move along until we can find a place to talk?"

Matthew shrugged. "There's nothing to talk about. It's over."

John looked around to get his bearings. It was still early afternoon, so the sun was mostly overhead. Because more people were emerging into their yards, he decided to just go regardless of whether it was in the right direction. He wished he had his backpack and the compass he'd found.

They walked briskly through the neighborhood, making several turns to ensure none of the residents or the people who were coming through the woods were pursuing them. They finally found their way onto a major street, and John noticed several condominium complexes to their right. He presumed they were close to the highway, and he was correct.

When a man in gym shorts and a tank top went jogging past him, striking John as odd, he shouted at him, "Is that Highway 3 up ahead?"

The man waved and gave John a thumbs-up.

"Dad, was he seriously exercising?"

John chuckled. "Yeah, it appears so. He's not gonna let a little thing like the collapse get in the way of his health."

Matthew laughed. "Pretty ballsy. I wouldn't draw attention to myself like that."

John agreed and then smiled. It appeared his son was slowly recovering from the shooting incident. He glanced behind them one more time before suggesting they drink some water before they started walking again.

He worried about his son. They'd never had a chance to dig deep into his feelings after he'd killed the young man who'd attacked them and taken John's gun. There was no doubt the outcome of that encounter would've been much different if Matthew hadn't responded so decisively.

This time was different. The attacker had taken a shot at Matthew. Several, in fact. During the bicycle theft, the attacker had barely started to raise John's gun before Matthew killed him with a single shot. This had been a gun battle during which Matthew went from protecting a woman being attacked, to defending himself to prevent being killed.

John recalled watching news reports following a mass shooting that took place during a presidential political rally years ago. Psychologists were interviewed to discuss what the survivors of the shooting were going through.

Initially, their anxieties associated with the near-death experience were masked by their outward denial that they were ever in danger. Matthew and the attacker were firing at one another at close range. It was a kill-or-be-killed scenario. Matthew, like many shooting survivors, seemed to be denying there was ever a threat. John knew better.

Over the next several hours, days and weeks, John would have to monitor his son for increased anxiety or depression. Lack of sleep, outward fear, and increased anger were all indicators of a larger problem.

The worst case, one that John had no idea how he'd address, was if Matthew developed PTSD. Post-traumatic stress disorder can change a person permanently, or at least for several years. The worst part was that there were no hospitals or doctors available, much less mental health professionals.

The two sat in silence on the overpass, watching the refugees continue to stream toward the west. They each finished a sport bottle full of water to rehydrate themselves following the flurry of activity. John had hoped their water and snacks would last until they reached the truck. From there, they could do without for the few hours it took to return to the farm.

Finally, John broached the subject. "You wanna talk about it now?"

Matthew shrugged. "Seriously, Dad. There's nothing to talk about. I'm fine. Promise."

John rested his elbows on his knees and clasped his hands together. He stared at the pavement and noticed a penny. It hadn't been worth much before. Now it was worthless copper-colored aluminum.

"Son, I'm here for you if you wanna talk."

Matthew abruptly stood and adjusted his backpack. "Fine. But can we do it while we're walking? I'm ready to get home."

John stood and hugged his son. Matthew returned the hug, but just barely. In that moment, he knew that it would be a challenge as Matthew slipped in and out of his doldrums.

They continued traveling westbound, at a faster pace now, thanks to Matthew's long strides. He was walking with purpose, wholly opposite to his gait at the start of the day. John surmised that his son was *over it*, as they say.

He didn't bring up the shooting again and tried to avoid small talk. He wanted to give Matthew some space to allow him to process what had happened. The best John could hope for was that his son didn't shut him out completely. As a result, he didn't press the issue to avoid angering the young man. When Matthew was ready, he'd find someone to talk to about the shooting incidents.

It was late in the afternoon when they arrived at the major retail area anchored by Willowbrook Mall. While reaching the landmark lifted their spirits, they still had a considerable distance to walk.

When they'd arrived on Sunday, John had searched for a suitable place to hide their 1956 GMC pickup so it wouldn't be discovered. As he'd noticed on their long walk from New York City, there were no other operating vehicles on the roadways. Now, that wasn't to say they weren't around somewhere, he thought to himself. They were being well hidden. Soon, he'd learn if he'd kept Old Jimmy suitably out of sight.

An hour later, they'd walked halfway around the seven-thousand-acre Great Piece Meadows Preserve. He found the gravel driveway that led past the gun club toward the landscape supply. The club's steel-grate doors, which resembled jail cell bars, guarding the front entry had been ripped off their hinges and lay on the gravel sidewalk. The doors were open, and the inside appeared to have been ransacked. Both of the guys stared continuously as they briskly walked past. They weren't interested in another shoot-out.

On the other hand, the landscape supply store appeared to be untouched. The doors were still locked up, and the bags of mulch, seed, and fertilizer in front remained neatly stacked. John eyed the fertilizer as he walked past. He tried to remember how much garden fertilizer they had stored in the barn. It gave him an idea.

"Matthew, listen to me for a moment."

"Sure."

John pulled him into the trees across the gravel drive from the landscape supply. "I'm pretty sure your mom could use several bags of that Miracle-Gro fertilizer. There are possibly other things we could use inside."

"Like what?" asked Matthew.

"You know, I'm not sure. Gas cans, for one. I just need to look around."

Matthew stepped away without breaking their cover. "Dad, it looks deserted, but there's a reason nobody has broken in there."

"Maybe they don't want plant food?" John asked facetiously.

"I'll check it out with you. I just wanna be careful, you know?"

John immediately felt guilty. He was angry with himself for putting Matthew in this position, considering what had happened earlier in the day.

"You know what. Let's not do this. It's not worth—"

"Dad," Matthew began emphatically, "I'm fine. You don't have to baby me. Of all the stores we've seen walking down the highway, this is the one that can help us the most. You know nobody has been inside there."

John nodded. "Okay. Here's the plan. These people might live nearby. This driveway leads into the preserve somewhere. The four-wheeler trail where we parked is a quarter mile away or so.

"First, we need to circle the building and look for anyone guarding the place as well as a way to get inside. Then let's gather what we want and hide it behind that pallet of Miracle-Gro.

"When we're finished, we'll fetch the truck. Its engine is not exactly quiet. It might draw attention, so we're gonna have to move quickly. You know, swoop in, load up, and then haul ass."

"Sounds like a solid plan. You know, Dad, you're getting pretty good at this."

Great, John thought. *Now that I'm a criminal, my son looks up to me.*

CHAPTER FORTY-SEVEN

Tuesday
Pine Brook Landscape Supply
Fairfield, New Jersey

John grew concerned. Not because there were obvious measures being taken to prevent someone from breaking into the landscape supply store. Rather, because there weren't. None of it made sense in the scheme of things. Barely a football field's distance away, a gun club had been ransacked. Virtually every office or retail location they'd passed had been broken into. Inexplicably, here was this out-of-the-way landscape store that remained untouched. He began to wonder if there was some old guy holding a shotgun, seated in a rocking chair inside, waiting for the first fool, like John, to break in.

They looked in every window, and thus far, nobody had shot their heads off. John even tried the old-fashioned approach of knocking and asking for directions. It was a laughable excuse, but he managed to make it seem sincere. He got no response.

So they found a side entrance and gently pried the old wooden door open with a shovel that had been left near a pile of sand. Apprehensive, the guys split up with their weapons drawn. They resembled a couple of gunslingers from an old Western searching for the bank vault. A minute later, they'd made their way to the other side of the building and found it uninhabited.

John opened the bolt lock on the front doors and slowly opened one of them. He left it cracked so it could be easily pushed if someone approached from the back. He turned to Matthew.

"Stay by my side and watch every entrance, especially the front. We'll start at the rear and work our way forward. As I hand you things, run them outside and set the items behind that pallet of Miracle-Gro I pointed out."

"It's starting to get dark," Matthew observed.

"Good. Burglaries are more successful in the dark. I think."

John took a deep breath and inwardly questioned his sanity. Was this really a risk worth taking? He thought about the fact the feed stores and Tractor Supply in Susquehanna County had probably been looted the morning after the perfect storm hit. Nobody in this densely populated bedroom community was interested in landscape supplies.

"I'm ready," said Matthew as he stood at John's back.

Systematically, John walked through the entire store, picking out tools, heirloom seeds and chicken feed. Matthew made trips back and forth as instructed. By the time he returned, John was prepared to load him up for another run outside.

John even handed Matthew several twenty-pound bags of Lyric Delite bird seed.

Matthew studied the packaging. "Bird seed?"

"Well, it's a special treat for your mom's bird feeders. Not to mention the stuff tastes good. I made trail mix with it once. Add some Chex cereal and you're good to go."

"You're weird, Dad," said Matthew dryly. He immediately turned and delivered the bird food outside.

After they completed their *shopping*, nobody would've noticed they'd been there except for the pried-open side door. He was proud of the fact that they didn't tear the place apart, as it appeared looters enjoyed doing. He was a shopper, not a looter.

They locked the doors again and exited through the side. John tried to obscure the fact that he'd broken in but gave up when the door kept falling sideways. The guys ran swiftly across the gravel drive until they were in the woods. They moved through the tree canopy for fifty yards toward where the four-wheeler trail was located. Once they were well away from the landscape supply, they nonchalantly emerged from the wooded nature preserve and began walking toward Old Jimmy's hiding place.

Initially, John was relieved to see that there was no sign the trail had been disturbed. He had used a fallen tree limb to scrape the dirt tracks to obliterate the tire tracks. There were no new tracks or footprints that he could see.

Matthew noticed as well. "Dad, I think we're good. Nobody found it."

John breathed a sigh of relief. While it had only been forty-eight hours or so, the potential for the truck being discovered was high.

The guys moved quickly to remove their minimal camouflage using fallen tree limbs. Before starting the truck, he reminded Matthew to move quickly once they stopped in front of the store. John said he'd load up the fertilizer if Matthew could get the rest.

Because they talked the plan through in advance and discussed potential contingencies, they were extremely efficient once he wheeled the truck in front of the store. In less than a minute, the pickup was teeming with useful supplies for their farm.

Feeling confident, they made their way to the interstate, and they headed home.

CHAPTER FORTY-EIGHT

Tuesday
Near Wharton, New Jersey

"Not much longer," said Sam encouragingly.

"Hey, look!" exclaimed Cat. She pointed toward the south side of the interstate. "There's another AMC theater. Anybody up for some nachos."

The moans, groans, and hell nos came in rapid succession.

Cat burst out laughing, clearly enjoying her opportunity to tease the adults. They'd suffered the agony wrought by Grandpa Sam's nachos far worse than she had.

Asher, who'd been leading the group out of the city, was ready to turn the guidance over to Sam. While they were still just under a hundred miles from the farm, the hills and forests of Eastern Pennsylvania were familiar to Sam. Asher would trust his judgment as they made their way toward the northwest.

"It's getting dark fast," said Sam as he pointed toward the hilly terrain ahead. "We may still have a few hours of daylight, but the shadows will decrease our visibility rapidly. I suggest we start looking for a place to rest for the night."

"Check it out," said Lauren. She pointed at an off-ramp sign. She read it aloud. "Picatinny Arsenal. What's that all about?"

"There's another sign up ahead," said Cat. She pulled away from the group and walked through the gravel along the guardrail to get a closer look. "It's an Army base. I don't remember this from before, do you, Grandpa Sam?"

"No, not really," he replied. "I was probably staring at Google Maps to make sure I turned the right way at the interstate."

Lauren read the monument sign. "Welcome to Picatinny Arsenal. Joint center of excellence for lethality."

"Catchy byline," said Asher sarcastically. "I suppose, in the Army, if you're going to be lethal, you'd better be excellent at it. Right?"

"Better than the alternative, I suppose," added Sam. They studied the emblems on the signage for a moment and then moved on.

They walked another half mile and stopped to consider a New Jersey Department of Transportation building. However, they decided to keep looking. Cat and Lauren doubted there was anything comfortable to sleep on in the corrugated steel building.

"They must really mean business in there," speculated Sam as they walked along the chain-link fence topped with barbed wire. Every third panel had a sign that read *Warning, Restricted Area. Keep out.*

"I'd love to see what they do in there," said Cat. "Do you think they have bombs and stuff?"

Sam shrugged. "Maybe? My guess, they're shut down like everything else."

They continued on for another mile until they reached a turn lane serving as a utility entrance into Picatinny Arsenal. All commented on the size of the facility. However, it was Sam who found a possible resting place for the night.

"I know the sign reads arsenal traffic only, but it looks like that Winnie coasted to a stop down the road. Let's check it out."

Sam led the way with Asher close by his side. Anytime they approached an abandoned vehicle, their level of awareness ticked up several notches. The large, newer model Winnebago could be occupied by someone with a gun. They didn't need that kind of trouble.

Asher asked Sam to ease up toward the driver's window while he checked the door. Asher arrived at the door before Sam reached the window. He took a deep breath and pulled at the door latch. It opened with a loud click. Asher took a chance.

"Hello! Is anybody here? We wanted to make sure nobody was in need of help."

He paused and listened for a response or sound that indicated somebody was inside.

"Asher!" said Sam in a loud whisper. "I don't have any movement over here."

Asher took the risk. He stepped into the Winnebago and called out again, "Hello? Is everybody okay in here?"

As he took another step inside, the motor home listed slightly to the right from his weight. It startled him, as he presumed somebody else had moved inside. He called out one more time. "Hello?"

When no one answered, he illuminated two of the squeeze flashlights and shined them inside. He breathed a sigh of relief when he realized the motor home had been abandoned.

"I think we're good." Asher continued inside and checked the forty-foot-long behemoth that must've been a handful to drive, he thought to himself. "Wow. It's no wonder it coasted so far down the military access road. Even with a slight downhill slope, it would be impossible to stop until it was good and ready."

The motor home was as functional as it was luxurious. Apparently, the electromagnetic pulse associated with the perfect storm had destroyed the electronics required to operate the slide-outs. The queen beds and the bunkbeds were not fully accessible. Still, there were enough cushions and pillows to provide some creature comforts until the next morning.

After he made his way to the back, he turned around and found the rest of the group examining the inside. Lauren and Cat were sliding open windows to provide some cross ventilation into the motor home. Perhaps it was wishful thinking, but all of them believed the temperatures were cooler than what they'd experienced in the urban areas around New York. Plus, the fresh air was a welcome relief after the city's aroma.

"Home sweet home. Whadya think?" asked Sam. Everyone chimed in with their thoughts.

"Sure," said Cat. "There's no food."

"It has a toilet," added Lauren.

"We're off the beaten path, so we should be safe," said Asher.

Sam dropped his backpack onto the kitchen table and slid onto the seat. Cat flopped on the couch, where she was joined by Lauren.

Asher walked from one end of the motor home to the other, looking through the windows to gauge their surroundings. He made his way to the driver's seat and sat down behind the wheel. He tried to imagine himself cruising around the country in a Winnebago. He chuckled as he thought about the process of parking the beast. No wonder the driver coasted down this access road and gave up.

He was about to return to the others when, in the disappearing daylight, he noticed the chain-link fence came to an end at a double gate. Just beyond, a guard gate stood in the middle of the road with two large barricade arms standing upright. They had most likely been stuck in position when the power went out. Then something about the chain-link gates struck him as odd.

"I'll be right back," he announced although nobody seemed concerned about where he was going.

Asher walked a hundred yards down the freshly paved access road until he reached the open gates. The security chains locking the two gates together had been cut. There were steel shavings and particles on the asphalt pavement between the two gates. He took another look around and jogged back to the motor home.

Sam greeted him just outside the door. "What's going on?"

"I don't know. Maybe nothing. Can you see the gate and the two chains dangling in the middle?"

Sam squinted his eyes in an effort to focus. "Nah, I'm on the verge of being nearsighted. Well, I mean, I am. I just stubbornly refuse to get glasses."

Asher stood with his hands on his hips and looked around. "The chain locking the gates together was cut. Sam, they had to use a heavy-duty grinder to get through the links."

"Whadya think it means?"

"Here's what we don't know. Did somebody cut the chain to get in, or get out? And when?"

The men stood there for a moment and contemplated what to do.

Lauren broke the silence by hollering for them. "Dinner is served. We're having Doritos!"

CHAPTER FORTY-NINE

Tuesday
Undisclosed Location
New Jersey

Abdul, his trusted allies, and dozens of sleeper cells throughout the Northeast and Mid-Atlantic states sprang into action that night after prayer. They'd been called to action by Abdul and others of equal stature. The flag of Allah and jihad had been raised.

It was purely by happenstance Abdul had access to multiple vehicles that survived the electromagnetic pulse generated by the perfect storm. The Afghan refugees did not have access to the financial resources once at their disposal in their native homeland. The U.S. banking system was watchful of unusual transfers of monies from nations loyal to the Taliban government in Kabul.

The families were loyal to one another and especially to the close-knit communities they'd established across America. They pooled their resources, shared their financial gains, and were prepared to make the sacrifices necessary when called upon by their leaders.

There weren't fancy new cars in the refugee communities. It was not unusual for several families to share a vehicle. Cars and trucks were purchased with cash. Oftentimes, wrecks in need of repairs were obtained for pennies on the dollar. The enterprising Afghans often shared information across their communities to obtain the parts required to make the vehicles operable.

They praised Allah when they learned several of their old vehicles had not been subjected to the power of the sun's blast. This mobility served them well as they prepared for this night.

As did Abdul's guidance on arming his soldiers of Allah. The Americans' Bureau of Alcohol, Tobacco, and Firearms had a tight grip on the sale of guns in stores. Forms required identification, and information was catalogued in a vast database.

Abdul sent his lieutenants to gun shows, garage sales, and even swap events advertised on gun enthusiast websites. They were able to amass an arsenal for his fighters while gradually purchasing ammunition over the years. None of the Afghan communities in Northeastern Pennsylvania had fallen under the scrutiny of the FBI.

The day before, Abdul had ordered a dry run of their approach to their target. His lieutenants reported back to him. They said the attack on the facility would not be nearly as difficult as driving their vehicles on the roads. The local residents had attempted multiple times to stop them. Their concern was that some might dare to use force.

He advised Khan, who would assist him on their mission that night, to take a route different from the day before. They would find a third way to return to their home to ensure they were not followed. The car would lead the way while the three pickup trucks with armed fighters would follow. Their instructions were simple. Kill anyone who gets in the way of Allah's will.

After they reached their destination, Abdul and his men moved swiftly and decisively with the quiet knowledge of knowing one's fate and being prepared to face it with honor. Abdul remained with the vehicles, allowing Khan to lead the assault on the U.S. Army weapons facility. The weak points of the perimeter security had been identified long before the power grid had collapsed. The inability of the base guards to communicate with one another made them especially vulnerable.

Abdul had identified the Picatinny Arsenal early on as a target when the opportunity presented itself. The personnel at Picatinny were the Army's leaders in research, development, and testing of advanced conventional weapon systems and ammunition.

For almost a year, Abdul's men, via Picatinny internet postings, had marveled at the new designs in mortars, howitzers, and small-arms weapon systems. The gunner protection armor being tested intrigued Abdul. He envisioned marching into battle with Allah by his side but the new armor protecting his body.

As midnight approached, the men advanced toward the perimeter of Picatinny. They were well armed with semiautomatic rifles, two handguns, and fighting knives for close-quarter combat. The real prizes, the advanced small-arms systems with the latest in ammunition, together with shoulder-launched missiles, would supplement their existing arsenal.

Abdul gave his men plenty of time to get into position. They'd have time to observe their point of entry and any security personnel to be targeted. He waited, studying his Rolex watch, which had been stolen for him as a gift. He'd never worn it until he realized it was immune to the EMP.

It was almost time.

CHAPTER FIFTY

Tuesday
Interstate 80 Eastbound Lane
Parsippany-Troy Hills, New Jersey

Before they drove up the entrance ramp to Interstate 80, John had a thought based upon his observations leaving New York. The farther they traveled away from the more densely populated areas, the more the stalled traffic seemed to spread out. When they'd crossed the interstate to retrieve Old Jimmy, he'd noticed the westbound traffic was heavier than the eastbound. Also, for some odd reason, pedestrians were more likely to be in the westbound lanes. Then again, as he thought about it, he and Matthew had walked in the westbound lanes along NJ 3.

He laughed at himself and muttered, "Who else would think like this?"

"What, Dad?" asked Matthew, who'd been deep in thought.

"Nothing, son. Just running scenarios. So, since we're seeing how many laws we can break today, whadya think about driving down the wrong side of the interstate?"

"Sure, why not?" Matthew replied with a laugh. "What are they gonna do? Write you a ticket?"

"Exactly. Let's go."

Darkness had set in, so John traveled slowly along the roadway to avoid hitting a group of stubborn pedestrians who were slow to yield. They'd barely driven a mile when he wished it was broad daylight. Their headlights betrayed their approach to the refugees heading west toward Stroudsburg, Pennsylvania, and beyond. Old Jimmy was probably the first operating vehicle they'd seen since Friday night. It didn't take long for people to jump the medium and rush toward the truck, begging for a ride.

"Dad! They're trying to climb in the back. One guy grabbed a bag of the bird seed!"

John began to search in all directions for a way off the highway. He steered toward the shoulder and eventually onto the grass that separated the interstate and the access road. For a half mile he was able to speed forward, leaving dozens of people in the rearview mirror chasing after them, waving their arms in an attempt to get his attention.

"There's an exit ramp up ahead," said Matthew, pointing to his left. "I see cars but not very many people."

John accelerated as some of the people pursuing the truck threatened to catch up to them. He drove up the ramp and turned right onto the overpass overlooking the interstate. When he didn't see anyone around them, he stopped the truck and took a deep breath.

"That sucked," he said finally.

"Yeah, it did," added Matthew, who was looking around again. "There's another road up ahead. We could try it."

John wasn't sure that was a good idea. He planned on turning off the interstate in about eight miles. They could drive the back roads to Milford and directly home. With the populated areas of Parsippany and Rockaway coming up, he came up with a plan.

"Let's do that again," he said without explanation.

"Very funny," said Matthew.

"No, I'm serious. There's probably an exit every mile or so until we turn north. Let's drive on the eastbound lanes, dodge cars and people. When it gets to be too many around us, we'll dart up the exit ramp to get away from them. Just like now."

"That'll take forever," Matthew said.

"Well, sure. Definitely longer," said John, who looked ahead to a major four-lane street with gas stations on two of the corners and drugstores on the other two. There were dozens of people wandering aimlessly through the parking lots.

He continued. "At least the interstate is wide open, giving us room to maneuver. We could get stuck on these side streets and lose everything to a flash mob."

"What about everyone trying to jump into the bed?" asked Matthew.

"If they get too close, we may have to fire a warning shot into the air to back 'em off."

Matthew thought for a moment and then nodded. "Okay. Let's give it a try. Worst case is that we look for another way at the next exit or the one after that." Then he asked, "How far to the exit you want?"

"Seven or eight miles."

"I'm in," said Matthew. He drew one of his pistols and laid it in his lap before pulling his hair out of his face. He dropped his right arm out of the window to slap the side of the door. He confidently pointed west. Having forgotten about the shooting, he was now on a mission.

PART 4

Wednesday
"… coming down the home stretch!"

CHAPTER FIFTY-ONE

Wednesday
Picatinny Arsenal
New Jersey

Precisely at midnight, Abdul gave a long blast on his air horn. He closed his eyes and said a brief prayer. At this moment, Allah's soldiers were hitting their targets hard and fast in multiple sections along Picatinny's perimeter. They entered with reckless abandon, using the strength of Allah to kill every soldier they encountered.

As gunshots reverberated through the heavily wooded area surrounding the arsenal, he thought of his brothers who'd perished at the hands of the infidels in the past. Their lives would be avenged, and the infidels would suffer.

At this moment, others like him were descending upon their targets, taking advantage of the power outage and downed communications to surprise the security patrols. They'd planned, rehearsed, prayed, and steeled their nerves. They'd all accepted the inevitable outcome of their action.

Around the perimeter, his fighters were now engaging soldiers who were easily surprised and overwhelmed. He could hear the loud, exuberant voices of his men yelling instructions to one another in Arabic. *Allahu Akbar* was included as they joyously attacked the infidels.

The return fire from the Americans was sporadic, indicating their momentary confusion. This was expected, but Abdul knew the advantage would be short-lived. He had to move quickly now. His men had opened the gates to the northern service road shortly after their arrival. They were shocked to find the guardhouse unmanned. The Army had opted to rely upon the gates, barriers and threatening signs to prevent access by intruders. Abdul laughed at their incompetence and naiveté.

The four vehicles raced toward the center of the facility with one man driving and a single man standing in the back of the three pickup trucks, prepared to open fire. Abdul brought up the rear. They found the street leading toward the armory. As they'd planned, Khan would meet him there and lead the assault to obtain the weapons.

The headlights of his car illuminated the crouching figure near the edge of the woods. Khan quickly stood and raised an arm.

"Very good, brother," said Abdul through the window as he skidded to a stop. Abdul slid into the passenger seat of the 1969 Pontiac GTO. He quickly took the wheel and raced past the pickup trucks to lead the assault.

"Praise Allah!" he responded breathlessly. Despite the disappearance of his daughter, Khan was singularly focused on the mission.

In the next ten minutes, Khan proved why he was Abdul's most valuable asset. He'd stealthily gained access to Picatinny Arsenal in the last several days, enabling him to accurately identify the facility's layout and security strength.

By the time they arrived at the armory building, the Army's security detail was being engaged in a firefight by Khan's men.

Many of the arsenal's personnel had left to take care of their families. It was a problem experienced around the country as governors tried to deploy their National Guardsmen to protect government facilities or to keep the peace. The soldiers, however, chose to protect their families first. Those few who'd remained behind at Picatinny were either single or too far away from their hometown to travel on foot. While the military was in possession of some hardened vehicles, meaning they were protected from the devastating effects of an EMP, secondary and tertiary facilities like Picatinny Arsenal had not been assigned that luxury.

Khan and his men were fierce fighters, having been trained in the mountains and deserts of their homeland. They were disciplined soldiers as well. Unlike the U.S. military, which had a seemingly endless supply of resources, the Afghan fighters were accustomed to making every shot count. The same was true as the men fought in America. Their focus and determination were paying off as they began to fight through the last few soldiers defending the armory.

Using blowtorches and pry bars, they gained access to the building. There were no Army personnel inside at that hour, so the men were able to concentrate on obtaining the weapons and matching the ammunition. Under Abdul's direction, they quickly began to empty the armory into the pickup trucks. At one point, his men began to take on fire. Fearing being trapped in the isolated building, Abdul declared the raid to be a success and ordered everyone to leave.

Exuberant with his success, he slapped the dashboard of the vintage muscle car several times and cheered Allah at the top of his lungs. They raced across the base onto Phipps Road. Within minutes, they roared past the unmanned gate. Internally, Abdul patted himself on the back. His patience and planning had brought them a great victory. The first of many, he was sure.

However, Abdul failed to expect the unexpected.

CHAPTER FIFTY-TWO

Wednesday
Near Wharton, New Jersey

John executed the plan. With each mile, they moved as quickly as possible until they had to begin dodging people. Matthew only had to fire his weapon once, a well-intentioned decision that only served to draw more attention to their truck. Now they were greeted on the road with people who'd heard the gunshot.

"There are fewer people now, but they all seem to be interested in what we're doing," Matthew observed. Then he suddenly pointed ahead. "Hey, look!"

It was minutes before midnight when Matthew spotted the exit sign for State Road 15 leading north toward Milford. John slowed the truck and snaked his way through a gap in the concrete barriers under an overpass. A New Jersey highway patrol officer had been running his radar gun in search of speeders when the solar flare hit. His stalled patrol car was partially blocking access to the other lanes. The vehicle had taken a beating. It had even been tagged with spray paint as if it was somehow law enforcement's fault for the predicament everyone was in.

Once they exited the interstate and slowly headed north, they were able to relax for the first time since the shooting. They passed a monument sign directing Army personnel and visitors to the Picatinny Arsenal. John exhaled as he loosened his grip on the steering wheel. He wiggled his fingers to relieve the tension in his hands.

"Son, how 'bout some water?"

"How about I pee first?"

John laughed. "Fair enough. I'll find a rest area."

Matthew shook his head and smiled. "Gimme a break. I'll whip it out in the middle of the road. How's that?"

John, who was truly enjoying the company of the twin son who rarely showed an interest in anything his dad was doing, decided to accept his son's challenge. It took him back to his high school days when he was a bit of a rebel, like Matthew.

He rolled to a stop across the median from a New Jersey Department of Transportation facility and shut off the engine. Both of them looked in all directions before they unzipped their jeans to urinate on the pavement.

"It's a different world, right, son?"

"You know, Dad, once we get everyone together again, I think I could get used to it."

John sighed. He furrowed his brow as he wondered if life on the farm would be simpler after the power grid collapsed. Certainly, they'd be working to feed themselves. However, the modern tools once available to them were no longer an option.

He was deep in thought when the flow of urine was abruptly cut off. Shouting and gunfire had broken the silence and scared the guys into ducking behind their truck.

CHAPTER FIFTY-THREE

Wednesday
Picatinny Arsenal
Wharton, New Jersey

After an upbeat meal that only a teenager could dream of, Asher and Lauren made themselves a bed at the rear of the Winnebago while Sam and Cat assembled beds from the seat cushions. All of them were fast asleep within minutes of their heads hitting the pillows. It was Lauren who stirred awake around midnight.

She looked around the Winnebago, thinking that Sam and Cat were having a late-night conversation. However, Sam was blissfully snoring, and Cat was curled up on top of a quilted blanket.

There it was again, she thought to herself. She was fully awake now. She crawled up onto her knees and peeked over the edge of the slide window kept open to provide ventilation in the motor home. Her eyes roved the woods near the motor home, searching for any signs of movement.

The men spoke again. Louder this time. Their accent and language were unmistakable. She had to wake Asher.

She gently nudged him and whispered into his ear, "Asher, wake up. Somebody's outside."

"Guns?" he mumbled as he tried to kick the sheet away from his feet. Being unarmed was Asher's biggest concern.

"Hold on," said Lauren. She walked to the other side of the bedroom space and looked outside. Shadows loomed on the edge of the woods and then disappeared. Asher had recovered from his deep sleep to join her.

"What did they say?" he asked.

"I don't know, but I'm certain they were speaking in Arabic. Their accents were heavy." In Lauren's position, she'd dealt with authors and their agents from many nationalities. From time to time, she'd had the pleasure of meeting authors of Middle Eastern descent. Their dialect was unmistakable.

"We need to get ready," said Asher as he searched for his sneakers on the floor. He sat on the side of a bench seat and fumbled in the dark to lace them up. "Wake up Sam and Cat."

Lauren had placed her shoes next to the toilet door so she could find them easily. She picked them up as she moved through the motor home. She woke Sam first.

"Sam, it's Lauren. Wake up."

"What?" Sam came out of his slumber too loudly under the circumstances. Lauren gently placed her hand over his grizzly, unshaven face.

"Shhh!" She urged him to be quiet before explaining, "I heard men's voices and saw shadows moving along the edge of the woods before disappearing."

"They're not coming after the Winnie?" he asked in a muted tone of voice.

"I don't know. We have to be ready just in case."

Asher joined them, walking through the motor home in a low crouch to lower his silhouette to anyone outside searching for movement. He seriously doubted the walls of the Winnebago would stop a barrage of bullets.

Lauren continued while Asher brought Cat up to speed after she'd awakened on her own. "Sam, I'm certain they were speaking in Arabic. It's hard for me to tell you any more than that other than the fact their tone of voice was, um, urgent."

Sam took a deep breath and sat upright. "Asher, what if they are attacking this place? You know, the armory or whatever it is."

Asher stayed low and joined them. "Or they're refugees who are making their way home. They might be just as afraid of us as we are of them."

Lauren was skeptical. "Arabic-speaking refugees? Out here? That doesn't make sense."

"Actually, it does," Sam responded before explaining, "Thousands of Afghan refugees were resettled in the tri-state area in late 2021. You know, after we pulled out. It would make sense they'd be traveling up this highway toward Milford."

"But, Sam, they were sneaking into the woods and headed toward the military base."

Cat joined the conversation. "What should we do, Grandpa Sam?"

Before he could answer, all hell broke loose.

CHAPTER FIFTY-FOUR

Wednesday
Picatinny Arsenal
Wharton, New Jersey

With the sound of gunfire erupting in the woods, it was near impossible for Asher to determine what direction it was coming from. He did know, however, that the bullets weren't directed at them. If they were, the shooters were horribly bad with their aim. It would've been impossible to miss the broad side of this barn on wheels.

The question Cat posed was not only pertinent to what the men were undertaking. The choices they made next meant life and death. Should they stay hidden under the limited cover afforded by the motor home? Or should they make a break for it, racing through the woods or down the street until they found their way back onto the highway? Asher was truly unsure of the correct approach.

"Asher? Whadya think?" Sam's calm demeanor helped ease the tension rising inside Asher.

"I don't like being trapped in here," he replied. "However, we're in no position to make assumptions about their intentions. I do know they're not shooting at us."

"It sounds like its farther away," added Cat.

"We could make a run for it," suggested Lauren. "You know, cut through the woods onto the highway."

"My guess is that the fencing with barbed wire on top extends beyond this service road on one side," began Sam before relaying what he'd seen when he'd relieved himself before going to sleep. "On the other side, there is a deep ravine full of briars and underbrush. Our only option is to go back the way we came. You know, toward that DOT utility yard."

Asher walked up and down the length of the motor home, looking out every window as he passed.

Just as he rejoined them, Cat made an observation. "The shooting stopped."

Sam knelt on the cushions next to her. He closed his eyes to concentrate all of his senses on what was happening outside. For a moment, his mind played tricks on him, as he thought he heard a car engine off in the distance. Oddly, it was familiar.

"Sam, that means they'll be coming back this way if they've finished their business," Lauren suggested. "Guys, we have to make a decision."

Asher finally gave his opinion. "Let's go for it. If they're killers and their work is done, they could turn their attention to other opportunities."

"Like us," Sam said, finishing Asher's thought. "Let's go."

"What about our backpacks?" asked Cat. She glanced at the rolling luggage. "And the suitcases?"

Asher looked to Lauren and shrugged. "We'll find more. Backpacks only unless they slow you down. Then drop them if necessary."

The weary group, amped up under the threat of gunmen in their midst, piled out of the Winnebago and began walking briskly along Phipps Road toward the highway.

Sam continued to look over his shoulder until he sounded the warning to the others. "Cars coming. Fast. More than one."

The roar of the GTO's exhaust reverberating off the tree-lined access road caught everyone's attention.

"Come on! Run!" Asher encouraged everyone to move faster.

"We'll never make it!" Sam shouted. "We've got to cut through the woods."

"I see the pavement change up ahead," said Lauren as she took the lead in the race to safety. "We're almost there!"

However, it was too late. The lead car's headlights washed over the Winnebago as it approached at a high rate of speed, followed by the older trucks struggling to keep up. Within seconds, all four of them were illuminated in the road as they ran away.

Just as the group reached a Y in the service road, another set of headlights turned on, catching them in the crosshairs. They were trapped.

CHAPTER FIFTY-FIVE

Wednesday
Outside Picatinny Arsenal
Wharton, New Jersey

"Kill them!" Abdul shouted at Khan, who was navigating past the Winnebago without crashing the GTO into the ravine to his right. Once he'd cleared the motor home, he pulled his AK-47 off his lap, awkwardly forcing it through the driver's window. He tugged on the trigger and fired several shots wildly in the direction of the people running away from them.

He cursed in Arabic and gripped the wheel to center the car in the middle of Phipps Road. He held the powerful rifle in his left hand and fired again toward the runners. Khan was so intent on shooting them that he temporarily lost control of the car. The two left wheels rolled off the asphalt onto the shoulder that lay several inches below the street. The steering wheel lurched to the left, causing him to fight for control. Then the front end leapt up slightly when the tire hit a pothole.

Khan narrowly missed a power pole although he dislodged the

guide wire stabilizing it to the ground. The barrel of his rifle was yanked backwards, dislodging his weapon from his grip until it flew against the chain-link fence.

With Khan cursing the turn of events and Abdul cursing Khan's failure, the remaining trucks in the entourage sped up behind them, nearly crashing into their rear bumper. Despite the near collision, Khan had closed on the runners, enabling Abdul to get a clear shot with his handgun.

The nine-millimeter pistol exploded in the night, sending several rounds toward the four people evading death. One of them struck a woman in the back, her body flying forward. Abdul was mesmerized by how the body reacted to being struck by the force of the bullet. As the woman fell forward, her ponytail flew upwards and seemingly remained there in a state of suspended animation until her body hit the pavement hard.

"Just go!" he shouted at Khan, abandoning any effort to eliminate the witnesses, not that it mattered. His concern was that they might identify his fighters as being of Middle Eastern descent, which would immediately point the FBI toward local Afghan refugee settlements. He hoped that the death of the female infidel would be sufficient to make the others cower to the will of Allah.

As they drove past the group, who'd stopped to help the woman, he and Khan stared out of the driver's side window at them. Abdul could've shot again but chose to leave with his new weaponry.

In the split second they turned their attention, they were blinded by the headlights of a vehicle stopped in the road in front of them.

CHAPTER FIFTY-SIX

Wednesday
Outside Picatinny Arsenal
Wharton, New Jersey

"Dad, should we turn around?" Matthew's head was hanging out of Old Jimmy's window, searching for the source of the gunfire. It was impossible to discern if it was coming from the woods or the highway up ahead.

John chose to pull onto a service road rather than drive directly into an ambush. This enabled them to use the trees separating the road from the highway. The Y in the road also gave him options to escape.

For the moment, the gunfire appeared to have stopped. That didn't make him any more comfortable. It could've meant that the gunmen were lying in wait for their next victim.

Then he heard shouting, followed by the roar of a powerful engine approaching. The exhausts reminded him of the muscle cars from the sixties and seventies that he'd coveted as a teen. They weren't running now. Or were they?

His mind quickly processed the possibilities. Depending on how old the car was, it didn't have the computerized electronics that seemed to have been destroyed by the solar flare.

"I see headlights!" exclaimed Matthew, pointing in the direction of the service road.

"Dammit!" John exclaimed as four people running toward them were fired upon. He started to put the pickup in reverse to back out onto the highway, but Matthew asked him to stop.

"Dad, they'll be killed. We have to help them!"

"It's not our fight, son!"

"We have to! It's bad karma. What if we needed help? Like the girl today and these people. We'd need somebody to help us, right?"

They heard tires squealing as the headlights of the car came into view and immediately began to swerve wildly back and forth. Then the driver seemed to steer back into the center of the road just as more headlights barreled up behind them.

"Oh, my god! Oh, my god!" shouted Matthew. "They shot one of them!"

He impulsively jumped out of the truck and drew both of his weapons. He raced around the truck in front of the headlights.

"Get back in here! Matthew! Please!"

John slammed the steering wheel and then slapped the pull-out knob that turned off the headlights. He slid onto the pavement and quickly circled the open door with his pistols drawn. The car continued to barrel toward them with multiple pickups behind it.

Matthew opened fire first. He shot one gun after the other at the lead car. The bullets ricocheted off the shiny steel bumper and fenders.

As the car continued toward them, John fired as well. He missed at first until several of his bullets embedded in the front fender.

The driver abruptly jerked the car to the right to avoid colliding with Old Jimmy and the Cubbisons. John jumped to the left to avoid the collision, but Matthew held his ground and fired several rounds at the driver.

In the dark, he couldn't confirm that he hit his target, but the reaction of the vehicle indicated he was damn close. It bounced through a grassy median, wiped out two road signs, and then crashed hard into a concrete curb near the highway. The explosion from the right front tire blowing out sounded like a cannon being fired in the still night.

"Look out!" shouted John, who rose to his knees.

The pickups barreled toward them with a hail of gunfire accompanying them. Bullets flew all around John and Matthew, skipping off the asphalt and peppering their truck. None of them hit flesh.

A man called out to the drivers of the trucks in Arabic. The trucks followed the taillights of the crashed car, shooting wildly as the drivers took the corners too fast, almost throwing the shooters out. They reached the wreck, stopped momentarily to pick up the passenger in the car, and then sped off into the night, leaving the carnage behind them.

John and Matthew had rolled across the pavement to avoid getting shot until they were behind Old Jimmy's truck bed. Their hearts were beating out of their chests after they came so close to being riddled with bullets.

Then, spontaneously, John began to nervously laugh. He made an attempt at humor to ease the tension. "So, on a scale of one to ten, how exciting was that compared to your video games?"

At first, Matthew looked at his father as if he'd lost his mind. Then he too chuckled. "Those game developers couldn't have imagined a better shoot-out. But, hey, let's not do it again."

"This was your idea," John pointed out. "You bailed out of the truck first."

Matthew was about to justify his actions when they heard the voice of an older man scream out.

"Help us!"

CHAPTER FIFTY-SEVEN

Wednesday
Outside Picatinny Arsenal
Wharton, New Jersey

Frantic to get help, Sam shouted again, "Please! Anybody? Please help us!"

Lauren lay face down on the pavement after being struck in the back by two bullets. The rounds had hit the center of her backpack and propelled her forward until she face-planted on the pavement. Her head had hit the asphalt several times as her body rolled over and over.

Asher knelt over her unconscious body. He gently tried to revive her after removing the backpack that saved her life. The two bullets had struck the bulkiest part of the contents. Fortunately for her, only one of them had found its way through the thickly packed clothing. It had pierced her shirt and hit her in the back. Although it had embedded in the fleshy side of her back, it easily fell out during Asher's examination of the wound.

Now his concern was that her head had been beaten against the asphalt, resulting in her being knocked unconscious. He tried to revive her; however, she remained unresponsive.

Asher looked up as he heard heavy footsteps running in their direction. He instinctively cradled his wife in his arms to protect her from the killers.

"Please don't shoot us!" begged Cat. "Our friend is hurt."

The men suddenly slowed their approach.

"Cat? Is that you?"

"Daddeeee!" Cat leapt up from her crouch and ran wildly down the road. She flung off her backpack as she raced toward her father.

"Cat! You're okay!" Matthew shouted, who rushed side by side with his father to embrace the brave young girl.

Seconds later, Sam joined them, exchanging hugs with his son and grandson. They were crying uncontrollably when Sam pulled away from the guys.

"John, this woman needs your help. She's a dear friend. Please."

"Yes, Dad," replied John. He turned to Matthew. "Son, fetch the blankets and first aid kit from behind the seats. Hurry."

"Okay."

John ran toward Lauren, who was being cradled in her husband's arms. John fell to his knees and looked into Asher's face. "You must be Asher Doyle."

Dumbfounded, Asher simply stared at John for a moment without responding. He finally regained his composure and replied, "Um, yes. How would you know that?"

"Long story, young man. Thank you for protecting my family. Now, let's see about her. Your wife?"

"Yes. She was shot in the back. The backpack stopped one bullet, but the other made it through and broke the flesh. She's bleeding." Asher removed his hand from her back and showed John the blood.

John said, "We've got to get that bullet out of her. There aren't any operating—"

Asher interrupted him. "It wasn't deep. It fell out easily." He showed John his hand again, this time opening the palm flat. The bullet that almost killed Lauren was still in his hand.

Matthew returned with the blankets and the first aid kit. John leaned into him and whispered, instructing him to make sure the driver of the car was dead. Matthew understood and rushed toward the stalled Pontiac.

John turned his attention back to the others and continued to issue instructions. "Dad, we have water in the truck. Get it, please. Cat, I need to moisten these shop towels with the water, but not too much. Asher, use this flashlight and shine it on, um, what's her name?"

"Lauren," replied Asher.

John spread out the blankets and assisted Asher in gently lowering Lauren to the ground. He slowly tilted her head backward and listened to her breathing.

"That's good," he mumbled as he poured water over his fingers and checked her airway. Then he leaned his face over Lauren's to feel her breath on his cheek. He nodded his approval and turned to Asher. "Would you unbutton her shirt so we can watch her breathing?"

"Yes, sir," Asher replied.

"John."

"Okay, John."

"Now, we have to keep her head tilted back and monitor her breathing. If your wife starts to throw up, we want it to drain out rather than allowing it to choke off her airway."

"What else can I do?" asked Asher.

"Talk to her. Calmly and quietly. Reassure her even though she appears to be in a deep sleep. She can hear you."

"Okay," said Asher.

"Dad, help me keep her covered with the blankets," instructed John. "We don't want her going into shock."

Sam knelt next to Lauren, the woman who'd saved his life. He wanted to return the favor.

John hugged his daughter again and whispered to her, "Wait here. Asher seems to be a good man, and he needs us right now."

She hugged him tight until the tears began to flow for both of them. "He saved me, Daddy. From some very bad men. Can they come live with us? They are the reason we're still here."

John hugged her tighter. "You betcha, honey. Just like they're family."

CHAPTER FIFTY-EIGHT

Wednesday
Outside Picatinny Arsenal
Wharton, New Jersey

Although he was concerned about Lauren, John was wary of the men who'd just sped off into the night. If their mission was to steal weapons from the armory, it wouldn't surprise him if they regrouped up the highway in order to return to finish what they started on the service road. If they were going to take advantage of the aftermath, they needed to do so quickly. The Pontiac GTO that rested quietly on the grassy shoulder of the merge lane was the type of asset they'd rarely come across.

Matthew dragged the body out of the car and pushed it into the tall grasses near the guardrail. The GTO's steel bumper had only received a few scratches from the street signs it had plowed over. The windshield and driver's window, however, had been completely destroyed.

"He's Middle Eastern, Dad," said Matthew once his dad arrived. "Do you think he's one of those people from Afghanistan?"

John shrugged. "Honestly, son, I couldn't tell you. I doubt he's carrying identification."

Matthew handed his father four magazines to an AK-47. John studied the curved shape. They were different from the straight magazines he'd examined at the gun store when he'd considered buying an AR-15 for the family's collection of weapons.

He'd decided against it at Emma's request because she didn't think they needed the high-powered rifle in the house. John had tried to explain to her that the AR-15 caliber was benign compared to some of their hunting rifles. However, she'd stood firm. Now John regretted not being more persistent.

He stuck his head into the car and looked around. There were broken pieces of glass on the seats and blood all over the passenger side. The door had been flung open.

Matthew explained what he'd found. "So, I couldn't find the rifle that goes with the magazines. He may have dropped it somewhere, or the other guy took it when he bailed out."

"Other guy?" asked John.

"Yeah, I'm sure of it. The passenger door was open when I got here. This guy certainly didn't open it." Matthew pointed at the dead driver, whose face had been imploded by one of their bullets.

"Makes sense," mumbled John.

Matthew looked past his father and then leaned in to whisper, "Dad, with everything happening so fast, I didn't think about the other guy who got away. What if he saw the logo on our truck?"

John glanced back toward Old Jimmy. He rolled his head around his shoulders and then grimaced. "It's possible, I suppose. I think it was probably too dark."

"Okay. I just wanted to mention it." Matthew stood out of the way to allow his father to inspect the wrecked car.

"What about the damage to the car?" asked John as he began to wander in front of the Pontiac. "I see a busted right front tire. Anything else?"

"Nope," replied Matthew. He dangled the keys in his left hand. "I was about to check for a spare."

They walked around to the rear, and Sam joined them. "Is it drivable?"

"We're about to find out," said John as Matthew unlocked the trunk.

The spare tire was nestled in the trunk, but they were unable to locate the tire-changing tools or the jack. Sam pointed out the New Jersey DOT facility might have the tools they needed.

"That's gonna take some time," said John, who was still concerned the men might come back.

"Matthew and I will find what we need," suggested Sam. "You tend to Lauren. She's a special woman, John. I wouldn't be standing here without her."

His son smiled and reached over to pinch his dad's shoulder. The two men shared an embrace and smacked each other on the back.

"Dad, um, we tried to find you. I never gave up on you."

Sam laughed. "You did find me. Just in time, obviously."

John hugged his dad again and encouraged them to make it snappy. He went back to check on Lauren, who was beginning to come to. She complained of a massive headache and then asked if the men had run over her. He wasn't sure if she was joking or not. However, the good news was that Lauren remembered what had happened. With some rest, she'd be okay.

"Cat, you wanna help me grab their things? We need to prepare to travel."

She glanced over at Asher, who nodded, indicating he'd be fine alone with Lauren. The two needed some quiet time alone to process how close to death she'd come.

As they walked to the Winnebago, John noticed the AK-47 lying at the base of the fence. He patted his rear pocket to feel the shape of the magazine and realized they belonged to this rifle. He carried it cradled in his right arm and then put his left arm around Cat.

"They're good people, it seems," he said.

"Yes, Daddy. Great people. They helped me and Grandpa Sam from the beginning when the lights went out. They took us to their home, and when their neighbors tried to throw us out, Asher and Lauren chose us instead of their own place."

"Well, they're welcome to join us at the farm. Without question."

"Daddy? Asher said you knew his name. How?"

He patted the top of her head and hugged her tight against his body. "Matthew and I have been searching for you guys. We tried all the places we knew of, which included Rockefeller Center. Luckily, we came across a nurse who remembered you. You made quite an impression, young lady. I gather you and Dad went through a rough time."

"The building was on fire. We barely got out alive."

"Wow. Well, that's what they told me. You are very brave, Cat. I love you."

"I love you, too, Daddy. Listen. Um, maybe we shouldn't tell Mom about some of this stuff. She might not let me go back to New York to see the museums again."

John burst out laughing and looked at the sky to determine if God had heard the innocence in his little girl. "We'll see, missy. Your mom is not easily shocked, not to mention I doubt anybody is going back to New York anytime soon."

Cat shrugged. "I'm just sayin'."

The two of them retrieved the rolling suitcases and made their way back to John and Lauren. She was standing now and stretching in an attempt to alleviate the pain her entire body felt.

Ten minutes later, the men had jacked up the Pontiac and worked together to change the front tire. Then it was Sam who began laughing as he questioned their sanity for not confirming the car still ran first.

He was given the honor to fire up the powerful GTO since he was the only one alive when it was introduced in '69. As the engine roared to life and the rumble in the exhaust calmed down slightly, he declared the car to be his.

The sun was beginning to rise on another day as they began the final hundred-mile leg of their adventure. Asher and Lauren were excited about seeing Cubbison's Farm, their new home. Matthew looked forward to giving his brother a blow-by-vicious-blow recap of what he'd been through.

And John couldn't wait to see the look on his loving wife's face when he delivered their daughter in one piece.

CHAPTER FIFTY-NINE

Wednesday
Cubbison's Farm
Harford, Pennsylvania

Normalcy. Just five days ago, the world as she knew it had come to an end. Her precious daughter had been lost in New York City, a frightening thought that continuously consumed Emma's mind. Her husband and one of her sons had raced to rescue Cat with very little to go on and against all odds. Just days ago, armed men had arrived at their farm, demanding to be fed. By the end of the next day, she'd become a murderer. Yep. It was the new normal, and Emma Cubbison wasn't totally on board with it.

Yet, there she was, just before sunrise, standing in her kitchen. She brewed a pot of coffee, just like always. She made biscuits and sawmill gravy, a family favorite. She'd already poached eggs from the henhouse and thanked her chickens for their efforts. Bacon was frying in the skillet on a stove powered by a generator that could only run a few hours a day. It was the new normal, with a twist.

However, instead of a sleepy-eyed Luke descending the stairs in search of breakfast, which had been the norm prior to the perfect storm, her nineteen-year-old warrior emerged through the kitchen's side door armed to the hilt. He set the newly acquired AR-15 against the wall and removed his pistol from its holster, gently setting it on the kitchen counter next to a useless telephone.

"Everything good?" she asked before greeting him with the customary good morning. In this new world in which man's laws were ignored and the laws of the jungle prevailed, their way of life would always be threatened. The first thing on her mind was their safety. If all was good, then she would declare it to be a *good morning*.

"I heard a coyote off in the distance. Toward the north, I think. Other than that, it was very quiet. Kinda liked it, to be honest."

Emma walked over and presented her son with a mug of black coffee. She planted a kiss on his cheek and said, "Good morning."

"Good mornin', Mom."

Luke slumped in a chair and sipped the hot brew. Like his father and Grandpa Sam, he'd acquired a taste for drinking his coffee black and strong. He allowed the warmth to coat his parched throat.

"I got bad news for you boys about your coffee," began Emma. "We only have a couple of bags left."

"Seriously, Mom? We can't run out of coffee. Grandpa Sam can't survive without it."

"We won't be able to survive Grandpa Sam without it either. He'll be insufferably grumpy."

Luke took another gulp and glanced over at the pot. He felt guilty for drinking more than this single mug.

"I was thinking. I'm gonna sleep a couple of hours, then head over to the Stanley place. With that coyote lurkin' about, I'd feel better about moving his herd to safety, especially his calves. Well, they'd at least be better off than left alone on the back of his property."

Emma furrowed her brow as she studied her son. "Is it the coyotes you're worried about or something else?"

Luke didn't want to go there. "Mom, there will be more men.

They may not come from the direction of the highway. They might head this way from Gibson. They might come through the state lands behind us. But I have no doubt they'll be comin' at some point."

Emma grimaced and nodded. She drank some of her coffee, sweetened with a tablespoon of sugar. "Is that all that's on your mind?"

Luke could never hide anything from his mother's gaze, which seemed to reach deep into his soul. "Mom, those women and kids are just as vulnerable as Mr. Stanley's calves. They have no protection. They don't even keep an eye out. For Pete's sakes, their kids were running around in the front yard playing when I rode up on them yesterday."

"I understand. You know, there are women, children, and vulnerable people all over the country at risk from predators—four-legged and two-legged."

She presented Luke his breakfast, which he immediately began to hungrily gobble down.

With his mouth full of biscuits and gravy, he continued. "Do you think there's a way we can help them while benefitting us at the same time?"

"Whadya have in mind?"

"They're gonna starve to death," he replied matter-of-factly. "I mean, they have absolutely nothing in that house to eat. They also have no idea where to start. Mom, I don't even think they're capable of looting, to be honest."

"Again, Luke, this same story is being told all over the nation."

Luke swallowed hard as he relayed his thoughts. "So, here's what I see happening. They're gonna wind up in the very same abusive situation that they thanked us for rescuing them from. A bunch of guys swoop in, promise to take care of them, and then do Lord knows what in exchange."

"Maybe," added Emma.

"What if we gave them jobs in exchange for food. By that I mean meaningful work that can truly help us."

"Like what?"

"Security, for one. Let's use them to help patrol our perimeter at night. Not just the gate leading to our front door. I'm talking around the back forty as well."

Emma raised her eyebrows. "Are you suggesting we put a gun in their hands? I don't think so." *Asked and answered*, as the lawyers say in court.

"No, not at first. Down the road, maybe. Think about this. Even the kids can help. Our gardens need to be expanded, not shrunken. To do that, we need to maintain what we have by keeping weeds out, etcetera. We'll eventually run out of Preen and have to do it old school. We'll just need to teach them the difference between a weed and a tomato plant."

Luke won her over with his sense of humor. Emma laughed and patted her son on the back. "I like your thinking, son. Let me consider this, and we'll discuss it with your dad once he returns. It's a big decision that we shouldn't make on our own."

Luke smiled and finished his breakfast. He appreciated his mom's support; however, he wondered if the women and kids would still be alive when his dad came home.

CHAPTER SIXTY

Wednesday
Cubbison's Farm
Harford, Pennsylvania

Luke took the once overgrown trail through the state recreation lands toward the Stanley farm. With each pass, he'd cleared a little more until it was nearly wide enough for the four-wheeler to pass through. After today, if he was successful, the bulk of the herd would tromp down the foliage, leaving a fairly wide, mile-long trail he could pull a wagon through.

Luke stopped by the field where they were grazing and partaking of the slowly disappearing pond to counteract the excessive heat. Stanley had separated the steers from the calves and cows, which made Luke's job a little easier. He'd leave the steers for later when he had some help.

His challenge was made more difficult because he was unfamiliar with the herd. He'd prepared himself for the challenge of moving the fifty-head herd through the trail, albeit a few at a time. Whether you're moving three hundred head or just fifty, it helps to know the cattle.

He'd learned to read his own during their duration on the farm. He had no idea how these would react to the drive. Cattle were prey animals, and a fight-or-flight mechanism was ingrained in them. That was why he decided to move a few at a time. During the unpredictable drive, a few might prefer to run toward Cubbison's Farm, while others might prefer to say, "All right, bring it on." It all depended on how they were wired.

After a moment, he opted to satisfy his desire to check on the women at the Yoders' place. Especially Vida. He couldn't take his mind off her last night. Truth be told, he needed more sleep than the few hours he'd gotten that morning. Luke wanted to look for an excuse to come back in this direction. The cattle needed to be moved, and he needed to see Vida.

"Later, guys," he shouted to the indifferent cattle. He turned his horse and took off at a gentle gallop across the back fields of the Stanley place, studying the condition of the home as he rode along. The house had been spared the arson attempt by the men he'd killed. The charred remains of the outbuilding reeked of burnt lumber. However, it could be cleaned up, and the larger Stanley home might be more suitable for the women and children who'd taken up residency in the Yoder place. Plus, they'd be closer to Cubbison's Farm.

Not unexpectedly, Luke rode up on the Yoder home without being noticed by any of its occupants. He slowly rounded the side of the house and made his way toward the front door, when two of the children raced out onto the porch. They were playing some kind of chase game as they bounded down the stairs into the front yard. They barely gave Luke a second glance as he sat atop his horse.

He took a deep breath and exhaled. He looked up and down the road running in front of the property. It was just as deserted as it had been the day before. Maybe he was overreacting, he thought to himself. Maybe, with each passing day, the number of people wandering from one place to another would subside. Or were people starting to die already? So soon? He shuddered at the thought.

"Hi, Luke." Jenna's greeting startled him, causing him to react abruptly. She stepped back slightly and asked, "Is everything all right?"

"Oh, yeah. Fine. I was just thinking about something."

"About us?" she asked.

He broached the subject of their security. "Jenna, do you guys have any kind of system of keeping watch? You know, in case someone tries to sneak up on the house."

She shrugged and looked around the front yard. "No, not really. I mean, what're we gonna do about it? We don't have a gun, so I'm not gonna try to bring a kitchen knife to a gunfight."

"Okay. But do you have a plan to escape if bad people show up?"

"To where?"

Luke didn't want to belabor the point. He could only help someone who wanted to help themselves. "I'm just saying, if you wanna avoid running into the kind of trouble you just got out of, maybe you should consider setting up a watch patrol of some kind coupled with an escape plan. Even if it means running into the woods behind the house."

"To where? Your place?" She folded her arms as she spoke.

"At least closer. Like the Stanley place, which is the next farm over."

Jenna's sister stepped outside to join the conversation. "They said they burned it down."

"Not the house," said Jenna.

Luke explained, "They tried and failed. It would need some repair, but it is bigger than this one. All I'm saying is that you need a plan in case of an emergency." He glanced toward the house and noticed Vida watching him through the window. He smiled and nodded at her. He wasn't sure, but he was certain she smiled back.

"Can you guys spare any more food?" Jenna's sister asked. "We've gone through what you brought yesterday."

Luke bristled. His mom had packed enough to last them through today. He was beginning to question his own suggestion of incorporating these people into the Cubbison operation. Not only were they argumentative when it came to protecting themselves, which made him wonder why they would help protect his farm, rather than following his instructions on food allocation, they seemingly devoured it, expecting more to come due to his generosity. On top of that, he didn't like the sister's attitude.

"We'll see. I just wanted to stop by and check on you. Be safe."

He was too frustrated to ask about Vida. At that point, he simply wanted to get back to moving cattle and question the willful nonchalance of his fellow man. He turned his horse and slowly made his way to the back of the house, where Vida was waiting for him.

"Hey, Luke," she said in a soft voice. She stood shyly in the shadows of the house, leaning against the wall.

Luke looked behind him to see if the women had followed. Satisfied they were alone, he slipped off his horse and held the reins as they spoke.

Vida continued. Her near-perfect English was delivered in her native accent. "I heard your conversation with them. They have no idea how dangerous it is right now."

"I'm simply trying to help," said Luke as he shook his head in dismay.

"Yes, I understand that. You should know they will try to manipulate you into feeding them."

Luke wiped the sweat coupled with nervous perspiration off his face with his forearm. "I'm starting to see that."

"They have no desire to protect themselves, either. For that reason, I'm leaving."

Her words hit Luke like a ton of bricks. He nervously asked, "Leaving? Already? Why? Crap, I know why, sort of. To where?"

He'd raised his voice slightly, causing Vida concern their conversation would be overheard. "May I walk along with you? Um, if it's okay. I won't follow you to your farm."

Luke's heart leapt in his chest. He still had a shot.

CHAPTER SIXTY-ONE

Wednesday
Stanley's Farm
Harford, Pennsylvania

Luke and Vida walked his horse across the field leading toward the woods. They made small talk at first until she explained why she needed to move on.

"Luke, my culture is different from America's. In Afghanistan, women are treated poorly. They say ninety percent of us have experienced some form of domestic violence. I say the other ten percent are lying.

"My mother has been physically beaten by my father and raped by my uncle. My father and uncle beat me from time to time. I am one of the fortunate few who hasn't been raped, yet."

Luke couldn't decide if he wanted to cry or to grab up all his guns and start hunting down Afghan men to administer punishment.

"They are disgusting cowards," mumbled Luke. "And I'm sorry for saying that about your father. It's just the way I feel."

She nodded and studied his face. In the few years she'd been in

America, she'd met many boys her age, or slightly older, like Luke. Most avoided her. She appreciated his honesty.

"I'd hoped they would change after coming to your country," she continued. "I wanted desperately for them to adopt American culture and see there was no place for violence against women anymore. They have not changed."

"I can understand why you ran away," added Luke. He suddenly stopped and turned toward her. "But do you have any kind of plan?"

She nodded. "Yes. I have cousins in New York near Rochester. Their families have adapted better. I talked with them on WeChat. I'm pretty sure they'd take me in."

"Wait, pretty sure?" asked Luke. "When did you make this decision?"

"Before the power went out."

Luke's uncertainty was evident in his voice. "Vida, that's a long way from here. Not to mention you might not be welcome. It sounds like the Afghan men stick together."

"Yes, that is true. My uncle in Rochester is my mother's brother. My cousins told me he was very angry when my mother was raped by my other uncle—my father's brother."

"Wait. Did your father know about this?"

She dropped her head in shame. "Yes."

Luke continued walking until they reached the trail connecting the Yoder place to Stanley's farm. He looked back toward the farmhouse.

"Vida, you barely know me, so I will respect you if you don't follow my advice. Here's the thing. The only reason those women and children down there aren't being subjected to the same poor treatment that Afghan women are used to is the fact that my mom and I killed their boyfriends. If you had arrived here a day sooner, there's no telling what they would've done to you."

She studied Luke's face as she spoke. "They told me the stories. I believe you're right."

"You heard me talking to them. Warning them. There will be

more jerks coming along who will promise them safety in exchange for, you know ..." His voice trailed off because he couldn't bring himself to describe the obvious.

"Yes. You are correct, Luke," she added. "My father and uncle will come looking for me. He is a very important part of our community. He will look at what I've done as an insult to him and our family. Without doubt, the men will rally behind him and search for me."

"All the more reason we need to find a safe place for you," said Luke. "I'm sure they will consider that you went to your cousins' home in Rochester. It's a logical place for you to hide."

Vida nodded in agreement. She looked him in the eyes and asked, "What do you think I should do?"

"You can be safe with us, and I'd like nothing more to take you to the farm right now. Unfortunately, we have our own family drama going on that I can't talk about."

Her eyes grew wide. "I do not want any more trouble. I will just leave for Rochester."

Luke realized she was equating the Cubbison-family drama with abusive men. "No, no, no. It's nothing like that. My family is very loving, caring, and generous. It's just that we were separated when the power grid went down, and we're working to bring everyone together."

Luke gulped. He'd said way too much, but he was desperately trying to gain her trust.

She allowed herself a slight smile. "Okay. I believe you."

"Anyway, let me show you Mr. Stanley's farmhouse. You can be safe there. Safer than trying to walk all the way to Rochester."

"I don't know," she interjected.

"Vida, please believe me on this. I can help protect you. I can bring you food and teach you how to defend yourself. And when the time is right, I can see if you can join us at the farm."

"When would I do this?" she asked.

Luke became excited. He'd kept her from leaving. "Right now. I mean, well, after you gather your things. I just need to ask a favor."

"Okay."

"Please, you cannot tell the others what you are doing. When you leave, walk in the opposite direction. Once out of sight, circle back along the edge of the woods, just deep enough to remain hidden but close enough to find your way back to this trail."

"I can do that. I don't have much to carry."

Luke took a deep breath and exhaled. He tried to control his exuberance. "Okay. Great! Listen, I'm supposed to be moving cattle from the fields at the back of Stanley's farm. My mom's probably worried about where I am, so I've gotta go."

"I will wait a couple of hours so it isn't obvious that I might be meeting you. Is that okay?"

Luke grinned from ear to ear. "Absolutely. I'll see you later."

Before he could turn to mount his horse, Vida leaned in and kissed him on the cheek. She whispered, "Thank you."

Luke's face was on fire as he blushed. It was the second kiss on his cheek that day, although this one had a far different effect on him than his mother's.

CHAPTER SIXTY-TWO

Wednesday
Stanley's Farm
Harford, Pennsylvania

When moving their own livestock from one field to another, Luke worked with his dad and grandfather. Grandpa Sam would take the lead while Luke brought up the rear as what was known as the drag rider. John, whose horsemanship was unparalleled, was capable of performing the task of flank rider, managing both sides of the herd without spooking them.

As Luke led two calves and their mothers through the trail, he recalled a conversation the three of them had had sitting by the creek one day. His dad was bragging about how he could move the herd on his own if he had a couple of well-trained border collies. Naturally, Luke asked why he didn't have any of the herding breed of dog. John laughed and replied, "Because I've got sons. Unfortunately, only one took a liking to farming and ranching." So Luke had forced himself to pick up the slack for his disinterested brother. Over the years, he'd picked up his father's skills and love for ranch life.

On his first trip back with three cows, his mom had quizzed him about his delay. He'd made up excuses about preparing the herd and the trail. He didn't like lying to his mother. However, these were unusual times, and he didn't want her to think he was taking care of every stray traveler, albeit a pretty one.

The heat was crushing him, even in the shade, despite being before noon. He made frequent stops to allow the cattle a respite. He filled up his canteen twice in an effort to remain hydrated. All the while, he waited for Vida to emerge from the woods to join him. He was anxious to get her settled into the Stanley place before he had to return home.

Despite Emma's request that he stop for the day, Luke hadn't seen Vida yet. He promised his mom that he'd make just one more trip, focusing on driving back the last set of calves and their mothers. He rode quickly through the trail that was now soft from the cattle digging into layers of decayed leaves, twigs, and pine needles. All of the activity in the field that morning had caused the livestock to become agitated. The cows and their young he planned on moving last had wandered toward a small barn at the far side of the field. They were straining to eat the stacks of rolled hay bales Mr. Stanley had stored near it. Luke had studied the bales earlier and noticed they were rotting from trapped moisture in the middle. The cows were stretching their necks through the barbed wire, intent on getting a nibble of the rotted hay.

Luke tried to shoo them away, but they stubbornly refused. Using his reins, he twirled his rope around and around, trying to move the stubborn beasts away from the fencing. Eventually, one of them had had enough of his incessant prodding. The protective mother unexpectedly turned on Luke, startling his horse.

The series of events that happened next occurred in a flash. One last run to move a handful of cattle coupled with the hope of helping a girl he barely knew resulted in Luke being knocked unconscious. Lying flat on his back, he was on the precipice of meeting his maker.

CHAPTER SIXTY-THREE

Wednesday
Northeastern Pennsylvania

The hundred-mile trip home took the group much longer than expected despite having the luxury of the two vehicles to ride in. The stalled vehicles along the way certainly presented obstacles at times, as did the groups of people walking along the back roads of Eastern Pennsylvania. However, the biggest challenge was getting through the towns they encountered.

In Milford, a small town located on the west bank of the Delaware River, the police had worked with town leaders to effectively close off U.S. Highway 6 to pedestrian traffic. The townspeople had complained of break-ins as well as encounters with refugees flooding into town off nearby Interstate 84. It had been effective at reducing the crime, so they barricaded all the roadways leading into town.

Sam, who was driving the GTO, led the way and purposefully scowled when he encountered anyone on the road. Between the broken windows and the bullet-riddled exterior of the vintage car, he gave the impression to all that he shouldn't be trifled with. That, however, didn't impress the Milford police officers manning the barricades preventing traffic from entering the town. Sam and John, who was driving Old Jimmy, were forced to turn around. They ended up driving twenty miles out of the way before they could resume their trip home.

Also, along the way, they were challenged on multiple occasions by groups of men who tried to take their car away. Gunfire was exchanged on the northeastern edge of Lake Wallenpaupack, where they were just forty miles from their destination. John critically wounded one of the men, a death sentence when there were no doctors or hospitals available.

The most frightening part of the trip was at the end. They'd just passed through the small town of Gibson, a one-red-light community that boasted a bed and breakfast as well as a post office. As soon as they passed the rock yard, Sam drove around the curve and almost ran into a tractor driving five miles an hour in the center of the highway.

He slammed on the brakes and laid on the horn. Then he noticed the bluish-white smoke billowing into the sky off in the distance.

"Matthew, that smoke's coming from the direction of the farm!"

Sam blared the horn at the tractor. He was unfamiliar with the man who was driving it, which surprised him because he thought he knew everyone in that part of the county.

John pulled up behind the Pontiac.

Matthew stuck his head out the window and began pointing toward the farm. He yelled at the top of his lungs, "Fire!"

Sam whipped the GTO around the tractor and raced at nearly ninety miles an hour, leaving John well behind. He wheeled around a couple of stalled cars and sped closer to the entrance of the farm.

In the backseat, Lauren buried her head in Asher's chest as they both slumped as low as possible. As the wind whipped through the broken windshield, bits of glass they'd failed to remove took flight, peppering the couple in the backseat.

"Grandpa Sam! I think you can slow down. I see the house!"

"Where's the fire?" he asked.

Matthew replied, "It looks like it's miles away. The woods, maybe?"

Sam took a deep breath and exhaled. He looked in the rearview mirror to see where John was. The Cubbison's Market pickup was closing in. Then he apologized to Lauren and Asher. "I'm sorry. It looked like, um, well, I thought there was a fire at our place."

"There's not?" Asher asked.

"No, I don't think so. It looks to be off in the distance."

They slowed to a stop at the gate, which was still barricaded. John honked the old horn on the pickup. Sam did the same to let Emma know they were home.

Cat bailed out of the front seat of the pickup and hopped the fence before racing down the gravel driveway.

Seconds later, a concerned Emma emerged from behind the market. She was carrying her rifle and looking through the scope as she walked. Then she dropped it in the gravel and began running to meet Cat halfway.

Mother and daughter crashed into one another as their emotions poured out. Neither was coherent as they tried to speak in between sobs. Emma would push Cat away at arm's length in order to examine her for injuries before immediately pulling her back into a bear hug. The two only stopped their joyous reunion when John led Matthew and Sam down the driveway.

They laughed. They cried. They expressed their love for one another as Lauren and Asher respectfully stood near the cars before John waved them over. After they gained control over their emotions, he looked around for Luke.

His face was washed with worry. "Honey, where's Luke? Is he, um, okay?"

She stretched her arm out to reach for his hand. "He's fine. He's been over at the Stanley place all day, moving his livestock in with ours. It's a long story but no longer than yours, I suspect."

John nodded and looked past his wife. He cupped his hands over his eyes and studied the riderless horse that was slowly making its way toward the barn.

Sam saw it, too. "Isn't that Luke's horse?"

"She's draggin' her reins," noticed John.

The family embrace broke apart as John and Sam began jogging toward the barn. John kept glancing at the smoke billowing into the air and then turned to Emma. "Where did you say he was? Moving cattle?"

Emma quickly replied, "Yes. Old man Stanley died. Luke wanted to bring his herd over to—is that fire? I've been inside and didn't ..." Her voice trailed off as she cupped her hand over her mouth. Her eyes grew wide as she stared at the smoke.

John put his hands on his hips and began to slowly walk in the direction of the fire. He looked toward the left in the direction of the Stanley home.

Emma provided him additional information. Her voice quivered as she spoke. "He's been bringing a handful of cows and their calves all day. When he went to check on the Stanley property, he noticed they were pushed back into the far back side of his pasture."

John swung around and looked at Emma, then at Luke's horse, which was drinking furiously from the water trough.

"Shit!" A rare utterance of a curse word flew out of John's mouth. "Sam, Emma, we need to saddle up. Hurry!"

"John, I didn't know!" Emma was beside herself.

He ignored her and yelled to Matthew, "Grab the rifles and get them settled. Let's go. Now!"

"I can help," said Asher.

"Help guard the house and take care of your wife."

Minutes later, John was speeding along the muddy trail on his stallion, lowering his head to make his body more aerodynamic. Sam and Emma raced well behind him, their horses struggling to keep up with the high-spirited stallion.

As John approached the opening, the heat of the fire began to sear into his face. "Please, God. Don't take my son," he begged as he urged his horse toward the flames.

CHAPTER SIXTY-FOUR

Wednesday
Stanley's Farm
Harford, Pennsylvania

Spontaneous combustion was mysterious. Some attributed it to devilish intervention. Others in the scientific community cautioned against the misuse of chemicals and other flammable materials. Firefighters recognized many fires had been blamed on spontaneous combustion that were not, while others were not properly attributed to the misunderstood phenomenon.

Science had proven that the right combination of materials could undergo a reaction to external stimuli, like heat, resulting in a runaway rise in temperature within a combustible material. The spontaneous combustion of a flammable material could result when air or water, coupled with heat, caused a reaction that exploded with fire.

Such was the case with the hay bales located at the back of Stanley's farm. The large, round bales were extremely dry on the outer layers thanks to the sun beating down on them day after day.

However, because they were unwrapped and stacked on top of each other, moisture was trapped inside them. The moist heat was festering and continued to build day after day. As the cows ate into the side of the bales on the bottom of the stack, the air acted to ignite the superheated moist hay.

The result was spontaneous combustion. Once ignited, the fire sought oxygen and fuel. It shot out of the hole created by the hungry cows and sparked the dryer layers as well as the surrounding grasses. Within seconds, the mostly dry bales were fully engulfed, sending smoke and flames high into the air.

Spooked, the cattle began to run in all directions in an attempt to avoid the fire. Eventually, franticly attempting to flee, they burst through a weakened part of the fencing near the gate and burst into the woods. They stampeded in all directions, trampling foliage and crashing into trees. The cattle ran for a quarter mile in all directions before finally sensing safety.

They weren't the only animals seeking a way out of the pen. Luke's horse, which had been startled by the charging cow, reared up on her hind legs and bolted forward as if the gates had just opened at the Kentucky Derby. She effortlessly hurdled the downed barbed-wire fence to escape.

At first, she raced into the field behind Mr. Stanley's house and inexplicably calmed herself by stopping to graze. Then she moseyed toward the trail leading to Cubbison's Farm and disappeared.

There was only one remaining living being in the field that was now surrounded by flames on all sides.

Luke Cubbison.

THANK YOU FOR READING PERFECT STORM 2!

If you enjoyed this installment in the Perfect Storm series, I'd be grateful if you'd take a moment to write a short review (just a few words are needed) and post it on Amazon. Amazon uses complicated algorithms to determine what books are recommended to readers. Sales are, of course, a factor, but so are the quantities of reviews my books get. By taking a few seconds to leave a review, you help me out and also help new readers learn about my work.

VISIT my website to subscribe to my email list to learn about upcoming titles, deals, contests, appearances, and more!

Sign up at BobbyAkart.com

**PERFECT STORM 3, the next installment in this epic survival thriller series.
Available for preorder on Amazon by clicking here.**

Imagine the unimaginable.

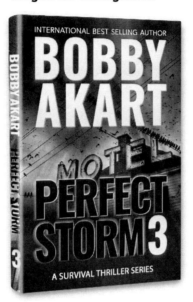

A powerless world. Food is scarce. Water is contaminated. Medical care is unavailable. A lawless society filled with an unrestrained criminal element.

Who can you trust? Anyone?

AVAILABLE ON AMAZON

OTHER WORKS BY AMAZON CHARTS TOP 25 AUTHOR BOBBY AKART

The Perfect Storm Series
Perfect Storm 1
Perfect Storm 2
Perfect Storm 3
Perfect Storm 4
Perfect Storm 5

Black Gold (a standalone terrorism thriller)

Nuclear Winter
First Strike
Armageddon
Whiteout
Devil Storm
Desolation

New Madrid (a standalone, disaster thriller)

Odessa (a Gunner Fox trilogy)

Odessa Reborn
Odessa Rising
Odessa Strikes

The Virus Hunters

Virus Hunters I
Virus Hunters II
Virus Hunters III

The Geostorm Series

The Shift
The Pulse
The Collapse
The Flood
The Tempest
The Pioneers

The Asteroid Series (A Gunner Fox trilogy)

Discovery
Diversion
Destruction

The Doomsday Series

Apocalypse
Haven
Anarchy
Minutemen
Civil War

The Yellowstone Series

Hellfire
Inferno

Fallout
Survival

The Lone Star Series
Axis of Evil
Beyond Borders
Lines in the Sand
Texas Strong
Fifth Column
Suicide Six

The Pandemic Series
Beginnings
The Innocents
Level 6
Quietus

The Blackout Series
36 Hours
Zero Hour
Turning Point
Shiloh Ranch
Hornet's Nest
Devil's Homecoming

The Boston Brahmin Series
The Loyal Nine
Cyber Attack
Martial Law
False Flag
The Mechanics
Choose Freedom
Patriot's Farewell (standalone novel)

Black Friday (standalone novel)
Seeds of Liberty (Companion Guide)

The Prepping for Tomorrow Series
Cyber Warfare
EMP: Electromagnetic Pulse
Economic Collapse

Made in United States
North Haven, CT
24 November 2023